BLUE STRING

BOOK FOUR, BLUE MOUNTAIN SERIES

TESS THOMPSON

The School Mistress of Emerson Pass:
"Sometimes we all need to step away from our lives and sink into a safe, happy place where family and love are the main ingredients for surviving. You'll find that and more in The School Mistress of Emerson Pass. I delighted in every turn of the story and when away from it found myself eager to return to Emerson Pass. I can't wait for the next book." - *Kay Bratt, Bestselling author of Wish Me Home and True to Me.*
"I frequently found myself getting lost in the characters and forgetting that I was reading a book." - *Camille Di Maio, Bestselling author of The Memory of Us.*
"Highly recommended." - *Christine Nolfi, Award winning author of The Sweet Lake Series.*
"I loved this book!" - *Karen McQuestion, Bestselling author of Hello Love and Good Man, Dalton.*

Traded: Brody and Kara:
"I loved the sweetness of Tess Thompson's writing - the camaraderie and long-lasting friendships make you want to move to Cliffside and become one of the gang! Rated Hallmark for romance!" - *Stephanie Little BookPage*

"This story was well written. You felt what the characters were going through. It's one of those "I got to know what happens next" books. So intriguing you won't want to put it down." - *Lena Loves Books*

"This story has so much going on, but it intertwines within itself. You get second chance, lost loves, and new love. I could not put this book down! I am excited to start this series and have love for this little Bayside town that I am now fond off!" - *Crystal's Book World*

"This is a small town romance story at its best and I look forward to the next book in the series." - *Gillek2, Vine Voice*

"This is one of those books that make you love to be a reader and fan of the author." -*Pamela Lunder, Vine Voice*

Blue Midnight:
"This is a beautiful book with an unexpected twist that takes the story from romance to mystery and back again. I've already started the 2nd book in the series!" - *Mama O*

"This beautiful book captured my attention and never let it go. I did not want it to end and so very much look forward to reading the next book." - *Pris Shartle*

"I enjoyed this new book cover to cover. I read it on my long flight home from Ireland and it helped the time fly by, I wish it had been longer so my whole flight could have been lost to this lovely novel about second chances and finding the truth. Written with wisdom and humor this novel shares the raw emotions a new divorce can leave behind." - *J. Sorenson*

"Tess Thompson is definitely one of my auto-buy authors! I love her writing style. Her characters are so real to life that you just can't put the book down once you start! Blue Midnight makes you believe in second chances. It makes you believe that everyone deserves an HEA. I loved the twists and turns in this book, the mystery and suspense, the family dynamics and the restoration of trust and security." - *Angela MacIntyre*

"Tess writes books with real characters in them, characters with flaws and baggage and gives them a second chance. (Real people, some remind me of myself and my girlfriends.) Then she cleverly and thoroughly develops those characters and makes you feel deeply for them. Characters are complex and multi-faceted, and the plot seems to unfold naturally, and never feels contrived." - *K. Lescinsky*

Caramel and Magnolias:

"Nobody writes characters like Tess Thompson. It's like she looks into our lives and creates her characters based on our best friends, our lovers, and our neighbors. Caramel and Magnolias, and the authors debut novel Riversong, have some of the best characters I've ever had a chance to fall in love with. I don't like leaving spoilers in reviews so just trust me, Nicholas Sparks has nothing on Tess Thompson, her writing flows so smoothly you can't help but to want to read on!" - *T. M. Frazier*

"I love Tess Thompson's books because I love good writing. Her prose is clean and tight, which are increasingly rare qualities, and manages to evoke a full range of emotions with both subtlety and power. Her fiction goes well beyond art imitating life. Thompson's characters are alive and fully-realized, the action is believable, and the story unfolds with the right balance of tension and exuberance. CARAMEL AND MAGNOLIAS is a pleasure to read." - *Tsuruoka*

"The author has an incredible way of painting an image with her words. Her storytelling is beautiful, and leaves you wanting more! I love that the story is about friendship (2 best friends) and love. The characters are richly drawn and I found myself rooting for them from the very beginning. I think you will, too!"
- *Fogvision*

after we'd had room service waffles. In the picture, her copper hair was wild and her green eyes soft and dreamy. She sat cross-legged on the bed, wearing one of my pajama tops. No prettier woman had ever graced God's green earth. I sat upright so fast that black dots danced before my eyes. Taking in a deep breath, I read the words I'd longed to hear for months.

Just checking on you. I saw on the news that you canceled the rest of your tour. Are you okay?

Teagan. The woman I loved. The only woman I'd ever loved. The woman who thought of me as nothing more than a reckless fling. We'd enjoyed a month of hot sex and a ton of laughs after meeting about a movie project. I'd been given a part in the movie playing a down-on-his-luck country singer. She was the costume designer. Teagan picked just the right cowboy hat to cover my fat head and the perfect faded jeans to convey a man who still thought of himself as a country boy even though he lived in a mansion in Nashville. Then, before the movie started shooting, she disappeared without so much as a goodbye note.

The girl I'd wanted to call the night it all went down. My pride had not allowed for that. No, not Wyatt Black, big shot. I couldn't bring myself to call her and beg to see her. I mean, truly, what would I have said to the woman who clearly didn't want anything to do with me?

I wrote back to her with trembling fingers.

Where the heck did you go? Where in the name of all that's holy have you been?

There were crickets for a few minutes before a reply came through.

None of your damn business.

I smiled into the phone. Teagan was as feisty as her red hair. She was the only woman I'd ever met who had no time for my antics. From the beginning, she'd made the rules. No strings. No contact with her six-year-old son.

Another text came through.

3

Answer my question. Are you okay?

I sent a reply back.

I'm fine. Thanks for asking.

No, you're not. You love to tour. What you went through must have been awful. I can't imagine.

It was rough, yeah. I hesitated for a moment, unsure if I should continue. Finally, I decided what the heck? I had nothing to lose. She'd already made it clear she had no use for me. *I thought I'd hear from you afterward. But why should I have expected that since you bailed on me without so much as a Dear John note?*

A few minutes later, another text came through.

I'm no good with goodbyes. You know that. I'm sorry I didn't reach out after the shooting. I wasn't sure what to say. However, when I saw the news this morning about your tour, I started to worry about you.

I stared into the phone. Damn if tears hadn't gathered at the corners of my eyes. I punched in a response.

Let me put it to you this way. I haven't left my couch in two weeks.

Wyatt, you should see someone. Get some therapy.

Does that sound like something I would do? Music's my therapy.

Then why did you cancel the tour?

I sighed, knowing there was no point in arguing. Anyway, communicating with her was futile. She didn't care about me. Not really. Not enough to call me after the shooting. Suddenly, I was seized with a desire to make her tell me where the hell she went after leaving me.

Where are you?

A few minutes went by with no answer. I was about to toss the phone aside and start drinking when my phone pinged again.

I went home to Idaho. I built a house on the family property in Peregrine.

The Lanigan family owned property outside the little town of Peregrine, Idaho. Teagan had talked about it a few times. Her three brothers had built houses there after their dad's death.

4

She'd mentioned her desire to do the same at some point. After she got the movie business out of her system was how she'd phrased it. Now, hearing that she'd gone home surprised me. I'd figured she'd returned to LA.

Another text came through before I could ask a question. *Chris started first grade this year. I wanted a steady place for him. Plus, my mother needed me home. She's lost her sight.*

This was the most information I'd ever gotten out of her. All I'd known previously about her family was what I could find from doing a Google search. She was one of four Lanigan siblings who had inherited part of their father's billions after his death. Edward Lanigan had built an empire making long-distance trucks. His children had sold the company, as no one wanted to run the business. Now they were all worth a lot of money. When I'd asked Teagan about her family, she'd shut down and told me that I was breaking our casual rule by prying.

I texted back.

I'm sorry to hear about your mother.

Thanks. Take care, Wyatt.

Before you go, I have something to say. After you left, I missed you more than I thought myself capable. I know you're not into long-term relationships, but I wanted you to know I think about you. A lot.

Seconds later, another text arrived. *That's sweet of you to say, but we both know you had another woman in your bed five minutes after I left.*

Five minutes was an exaggeration. More like five days. But I'd quickly realized that after Teagan, no one else would do. Women had continued to throw themselves at me, but I'd lost my womanizing ways. I'd found the one I wanted. No one else would even be close.

If only she thought the same about me.

No one like you. God broke the mold when he made you.

I could almost hear her rolling her eyes, substantiated by her reply.

5

Do women actually fall for your trite one-liners?

I found myself smiling as I texted her back. *Tell me the truth. Do you ever think about me?*

Once in a blue moon.

I nodded, as if she could see me. *Blue moons happen more often than anyone thinks.*

No, they don't.

Like twice a year, at least. I had no idea if that was true or not but I hoped she'd admit she thought about me once in a while.

Seriously, are you going to be all right? Are you writing songs?

No. I just feel...broken. I'm not sure I'll ever go on stage again.

You will. Give it some time. And therapy.

I'll think about it. I would not think about it. Men like me don't go to therapy. That's what we have whiskey for.

Are you drinking a bunch?

Crap. How had she read my mind? *Some.*

Meaning a lot?

I'm not the healthiest I've ever been, no. I caught a glimpse of myself in the mirror that hung next to my fireplace. Bags under my eyes and a shaggy beard proved my point. I'm not even sure when I last showered. Days probably. My dark blond hair looked brown. I was wearing a pair of sweats with holes in them and my Bud Light T-shirt that I'd had since I was sixteen. *I suppose you're as gorgeous as ever?*

I'm freaking hot as hell. You know that.

I laughed. *I do.* God, did I know. An image of her legs wrapped around me as I carried her to my bed woke my body in ways that it hadn't in weeks. *I recall you enjoyed me as much as I enjoyed you.*

Yes, we were good together. In the bedroom. But you and I both know that a man like you and a woman like me are a recipe for the biggest disaster of the century. Anyway, I've got to go. I'm at the pickup line at my son's summer camp, and they just let the kids out. Chris will be here in a second. These women get ferocious if you linger a second too long. You can't believe how scary some of these moms are. Makes Hollywood seem like a picnic.

Teagan Lanigan in the school pickup line? Somehow I couldn't imagine it. She'd always looked so glamorous and sophisticated in her designer clothes. Even without the trimmings, she was a classic beauty. Masses of copper hair tumbled around her shoulders. A thousand freckles decorated her white skin. Small features and enormous green eyes that could cut a man down to size with a dart in his direction. God, I loved her. The ache in my chest that accompanied my memories of her forced me to hunch over my legs. As if that would help.

One more text came through.

To answer your earlier question, yes, I think about you. More than I care to if you want to know the truth.

Enough that you'd see me again?

I held my breath as I waited for a reply.

My life is completely different than when we spent time together. I'm just a regular mom in Idaho with her family breathing down her neck every other minute. We don't belong together. Take care of yourself, okay? The world needs your music.

You take care, too. I stared at the phone, hoping for one more reply. I dared not send another one. If she blocked me, I'd have no hope of contact.

I stared at the phone for at least five minutes after her abrupt dismissal. Then I ordered Chinese and went to take a shower. This was the best I'd felt since it all went down. Which told me one thing and one thing only. I needed Teagan in my life. And dammit, I was going to convince her she needed me. Four hours later, with a full stomach, clean jeans, and a T-shirt that was only a few years old, I had my bags packed and my truck loaded. This country boy was going to Peregrine, Idaho.

FOUR AFTERNOONS LATER, I PULLED INTO PEREGRINE, IDAHO, AT about half past three. I'd booked a room at the only inn and found it easily, as there weren't more than a dozen buildings in the entire town. Brick buildings in a row and the mountains as a backdrop, I could easily have believed I'd driven into 1900. The inn was in the only Victorian in town, painted a bright shade of purple with white trim. I parked in back and walked around the stone path and up the stairs to a wide porch. Temperatures were in the high seventies, which felt cooler to me because of the dry air. I was used to humidity in Nashville. I breathed in deeply and scanned the sky, enthralled by the shade of blue. Everything seemed more vivid here, as if there were a flattering filter.

I took off my cowboy hat as I opened a screen door and walked into a dim lobby. The scent of snickerdoodle cookies filled the room. My stomach growled with hunger. I'd pushed hard today, stopping only once for gas and a pepperoni stick. A woman dressed in the same shade as the house sat behind a desk. She looked up from her computer as the screen door slammed behind me.

"Welcome, Mr. Black." The ample middle-aged woman with wide hips and a large chest smiled and held out her arms as if she wanted to hug me. Had there not been a desk between us, I might have been compelled to do so. Her dewy skin and bright eyes looked like an advertisement for plant-based eating and drinking a lot of water. She seemed familiar to me, as if I'd known her all my life. "Right on time. I'm Moonstone, your proprietress. I used to say proprietor until a certain young lady you love scolded me."

"Someone I love?" Her statement unsettled me, as if I'd blocked out an important detail from my past or maybe suffered from short-term memory loss. *Did* I know her from somewhere? Had I forgotten?

"Teagan, of course."

My stomach fluttered at the sound of her name. "You know Teagan?"

"Yes, I'm very good friends with the entire Lanigan family. I'm practically family myself." Moonstone reached behind her for an old-fashioned key. Had I fallen into 1900? "I realize you don't know this, but today's her birthday. She's having a party."

Her birthday. How did I not know this? How would I have a chance to win her heart if I didn't know the day of her birth?

"Don't be discouraged that you didn't know." Moonstone slid the key across the desk. "You can't be expected to know things of that nature unless the woman tells you. This is the whole problem with our feisty Teagan, isn't it?"

"Ma'am?" I had no idea what she was saying. Maybe I needed to drink water, because her words didn't make sense.

"Have a seat, Mr. Black. You're looking pale."

I did as requested, sitting in a high-backed antique chair covered in burgundy velvet. Were the walls also a shade of purple? A light lavender, or was it white and my eyes were playing tricks on me?

She popped up from her chair like a jack-in-the-box and crossed over to a pitcher of lemon-infused water. Ice clanked as she poured me a glass. "You're probably dehydrated from the drive," she said as she placed the glass in my hand.

"Thank you." I sipped the water. The lemon was surprisingly refreshing. I downed the rest like a man who'd spent a week in the desert.

Moonstone settled herself back behind the desk and typed into her computer. "I have you booked for a week, but if that changes for any reason, let me know. If my visions were correct, you won't stay even one night here. A pretty redhead will make sure of that."

What? How did she know I was here to see Teagan?

"However, my psychic abilities don't pay the rent, so I'll have to charge you for tonight at least."

"I'm confused. How did you know I came to see Teagan?"

She waved a hand in front of her eyes. "Visions. They're especially strong when it comes to the Lanigan siblings. I've known when their true loves come to town every time now. You were the last. Until the children are grown, obviously."

Obviously?

"Now listen carefully," she said. "You're to go to that party tonight and tell Teagan your intentions." She ripped a sticky note from a pad on her desk. "Here's the code to the gate. Their turnoff is just a few miles north on the highway. Just drive through town and keep going until you see the Lanigan sign, then turn left."

Lulled into her strangeness, I asked, "What time?"

"Get cleaned up right away and head out there. Time's wasting away as we speak, young man." She reached under her desk and presented a bouquet of pink roses. "Give her these."

"How did you have those ready?"

"I knew you were coming." She tutted and shook her head as if she felt very sorry for my inability to understand reality. "Don't question. Just do as I say."

2

TEAGAN

On my thirty-fifth birthday, I sipped a glass of wine on my patio and watched the party go on around me. The event was a success. Laughter, chatter, and the background of Hawaiian guitar music filled the pleasant summer evening. Earlier the temperatures had risen into the eighties but had fallen cooperatively around six as guests arrived. They now mingled on my patio eating and drinking from the catered feast and open bar. My family was all here. What was left of us, anyway. Minus two Lanigans. My father and brother Finn were gone. I crossed myself and said a silent prayer. My remaining brothers, their wives and children, my young son, plus my mother were alive and well. All here to celebrate me.

Why did I feel bereft then? Jittery and hollow? As if something or someone were missing.

This was what I'd wanted, I reminded myself. To be home with my family. For my little boy to be with his cousins.

I knew what it was. Of course I did. Denial only gets a person so far. Wyatt Black. As much as I wished it were not true, I wanted him here. The man had wormed his way into my heart. And it really pissed me off. Who fell in love with someone they were supposed to be having a casual fling with?

Apparently, me.

Since the text exchange with Wyatt, my fingers practically twitched with the desire to continue communication with him. And the dreams. They were killing me. Dreams that would make a lady of the night blush. I woke drenched in sweat and aching for that stupid man.

Focus on what you have, I chided myself. *Your family. This house.* Designed by architect David Perry—the brother of an actress friend of mine—it was my dream home. Built in a style that merged farmhouse and modern, it had big windows that faced Blue Mountain. A large stone patio with a square pool lined with green tiles paid homage to the wild times I'd once had by the Mediterranean Sea. Those days were long past, I thought, as I glanced around the party. Nothing exciting would happen tonight.

In what felt like a prior life, during my time as a film costume designer, I'd worked with famous directors and actors. I'd often been invited to parties so wild they'd have made my sister-in-law Charlotte faint. No longer. Now I was the mother of a six-year-old living in nowhere, Idaho. The nowhere I loved.

My mother was currently sipping her signature vodka martini and talking to my brother Ardan's high-tech billionaire friend named Ashton Carter. The way she was shamelessly flirting with him, one would never know that her eyesight was almost completely gone. Only months ago she'd still seen shadows. Now, she'd confessed to me last week, even those were gone.

My brothers Ciaran and Kevan sat at a table by the pool, drinking scotch and arguing about politics. Their wives, Bliss and Blythe, stood by the food table, chatting about who knows what. Sisters, they always appeared to have more to say to each other, no matter how much time they spent together. Only in

Idaho, I often teased them, would two brothers marry two sisters. The sisters resembled each other, both with honey-colored hair and pretty eyes. However, Bliss was tall and athletic, whereas Blythe was smaller and more delicate.

My older nieces, Lola and Clementine, both blonde beauties, were playing in the shallow end of the pool with Ciaran and Bliss's baby daughters.

Sweet, dark-haired Charlotte huddled with Hope under a blue beach umbrella. Since she married my brother Ardan, Charlotte had become much more than just a sister-in-law. She was my best friend. The best one I'd ever had. Charlotte had recently become a best-selling mystery writer. She and Hope loved to talk about movies and books. Hope, who'd grown up with us out here in the wilds of Idaho, was an actress. The two of us had actually worked together a few times. Blonde and stunning, without an ounce of fat on her, she was like dressing a doll. One with a big, sassy mouth.

I wandered over to where a DJ had set up his equipment on one corner of the patio. He'd introduced himself to me earlier as Ryan Chambers. Now he looked up at me and asked if the music was all right.

"Great," I said.

"Awesome. You had me worried with that sad face." I guessed him to be in his late twenties. Tattoos ran up his neck. More than a few piercings decorated his ears.

I smiled at him politely. "Not at all. Everything's wonderful. Later, after the food, maybe play some dance tunes."

He gave me the thumbs-up. "Killer."

I thanked him and crossed over the patio toward the kitchen to check in on the caterer and her staff of two. I caught a reflection of myself in the window. I'm the only redhead in the family and the only one with a temper. I got all the bad stuff—hair the color of a new penny, freckles galore, and a long, gawky body. My legs are the problem. They're stretched really skinny. I'm a giraffe. Meanwhile, my brothers are all gorgeous. Kevan and Ciaran take after my father, dark hair and skin that tans a golden brown. Ardan is fair like my mother. Even in her seventies, Mother is a beauty.

"Everything all right?" Jodi Sapp asked as I entered the kitchen. Jodi was a new resident of Peregrine and member of a newly formed book club, thanks to Charlotte. Nice woman, although I had the feeling she was unhappy. From what I'd heard in town, she'd come from the city. Which city, no one knew. In Peregrine, one city person was the same as the rest.

"Yes, everything's great," I said. "The food is wonderful. The kids devoured the pot stickers."

Jodi smiled as she rubbed her hands against her black apron. "I'm glad they enjoyed them. That's a recipe my mother passed on to me."

"Miss Lanigan?" Paula Neal, one of the women working for Jodi, looked over at me with an expectant gleam in her eyes. "Do you think I could meet Hope Manning tonight? I brought my headshot to give to her."

"I told you not to ask about that," Jodi said. "I'm sorry," she said to me.

"It's fine," I said. "But Hope is here to relax, and I'm sure she'd rather just be a guest. If you wanted to leave your headshot on the counter, I'll be sure to give it to her."

"That would be awesome," Paula said.

"Right now we're focusing on work," Jodi said, with a hint of irritation in her voice. "And please, keep your hair pulled back in a ponytail. It's not sanitary."

"Sorry. I forgot." Paula stepped away from the sink, where she'd been washing cherry tomatoes, and tugged plastic gloves off her hands. With a quick flip of her wrist, she tied back her hair. In their black pants and white shirts, the two women kind of looked alike. They both had long brown hair and were about the same height and weight.

My son, Christopher, came running toward me. Thankfully, he hadn't inherited my red hair. He looked like Ciaran. They even had the same mischievous brown eyes. "Mom, there's someone at the door. He says he's a friend of yours."

A friend at the door? All the invited guests were already here. How would anyone have gotten through the gate without the code? Unless someone had followed a car in, which happened sometimes. The gate closed slowly. I should probably have that fixed. "Did you talk to him?" I asked Chris. He knew he wasn't supposed to talk to strangers.

"No, Mom. Effie answered the door." Chris looked up at me with his innocent eyes. "She sent me to tell you because she didn't want to let him in since he wasn't on the guest list."

"Very wise of her." Effie, who normally worked for Ardan and Charlotte, was on loan for the evening. Nothing and no one would hurt the Lanigan family while on her watch. Her loyalty to Ardan, who she said rescued her from a terrible fate, extended to the rest of us.

I followed my son into the wide front room. The shades were partially drawn over the floor-to-ceiling windows in order to filter the late-afternoon sun. My home was not the typical Idaho rustic style. I preferred light colors and a kitchen separate from the great room instead of the rough beams-and-log look so many favored.

Still damp from swimming, Chris's shorts made a swishing sound as he shuffled across the dark hardwood in his bare feet. He spent a lot of time outside traipsing through the property with Ardan and Ciaran as well as swimming in the creek and the pool. His skin had browned during these long days of summer. The color suited him.

Like my brothers, he seemed made from this particular piece of land as if it had birthed him instead of me. From the moment we'd come home, he'd adjusted seamlessly into country life, emulating my brothers. He snowshoed and skied with Ciaran, fly-fished with Ardan, and rode a horse like his uncle Kevan. I sometimes longed for a real father for my only son, but God had blessed me with brothers who filled part of that hole in his life.

We reached the foyer. My legs weakened when I saw the identity of this uninvited guest.

Wyatt Black, cowboy hat in hand, stood just inside the door. Effie had her arms folded across her middle, glaring at him suspiciously. She must not listen to country music, I thought, or she'd know who he was.

Flabbergasted, I stared at him. He wore his typical faded jeans and worn cowboy boots. In juxtaposition, he had on a shirt that matched his ice-blue eyes. For a moment, I wondered if I was seeing things. Had I conjured him up because I'd wished for him?

"Hey, Teagan. Happy birthday," Wyatt said in that Southern drawl that melted me. Never in my life had I been as drawn to a man, both physically and mentally. Which was exactly the problem. He was bad news. Women, wine, and song. Wasn't that how the saying went? Only it would be women, whiskey, and song.

I manage to keep my voice steady and my expression bland. "How did you find my house, and how did you get through the gate?"

"I'm staying at the inn. Moonstone gave me the code. She seemed to think you'd welcome my company."

"Moonstone gave you the code? Unbelievable."

"She said she was practically family."

"That sounds like her." I narrowed my eyes, taking Wyatt in. He looked haggard and thinner than the last time I saw him sprawled out naked over the hotel bed. Although he appeared freshly shaven and his hair perfectly combed, as it always was, his eyes had a hollow look to them. His cockiness level seemed to have dropped a notch as well. "You look like crap."

He placed his hat over his heart. "Yes, ma'am, I'm aware."

Effie continued to watch him with wariness.

16

"It's all right, Effie. Wyatt's a friend of mine."

"Nice to meet you, Effie," Wyatt said.

She raised one eyebrow but didn't say anything.

I remembered Chris, who was currently staring at Wyatt as if he couldn't believe his luck. Wyatt Black at his mother's birthday party was a dream come true for my little guy. Chris loved music and most especially Wyatt's. My fault. I should never have started playing his music in the car.

The hairs on the back of my neck stood up as my mama bear instinct kicked in. I didn't want my kid anywhere near this man. Wyatt was charming and funny and supersmart. He could probably charm Mother. He was that good. Two days in and my entire family would be in love with Wyatt Black. They'd be heartbroken when he sniffed the wind and wandered away. Down the road to the next party. That's what men like him did. They were ramblers. Always in search of the next place to play their tunes and woo a woman.

"You must be Christopher." Wyatt knelt to his level. "I'm Wyatt."

Chris shook his hand. "Nice to meet you. Are you here for Mom's birthday?"

Wyatt grimaced as he stood and drew a hand through his hair. "That depends on your mother." He looked at me. His eyes were different. They'd once been full of life and humor. Now they were as dull and sad as a beaten dog's. "I don't want to invite myself."

I couldn't even get mad at him. He was obviously not in his right mind. "Did you drive here from Nashville?"

"I sure did. Took me four days. Reminded me of the old days with the band. Back when we were still nothing to nobody. Staying in fleabag hotels and eating the cheapest thing we could find."

"Did you bring your band with you?" Chris asked a little too hopefully.

"No, sir," Wyatt said. "They're taking a break right now."

"Oh golly, that's where I know you," Effie said in her clipped English accent as her eyes widened in horror. "I just saw you on the telly. Charlotte's a big fan."

"Charlotte?" Wyatt asked.

"My boss. She's married to Teagan's brother." Effie covered her mouth with both hands and spoke through her fingers. "I thought you were one of the locals trying to crash the party."

"No, ma'am. I'm sorry if I scared you." Wyatt turned to me. "Moonstone assured me you'd like to have me at your birthday party."

"Moonstone's psychic," Effie said.

He rocked back slightly on the heels of his boots. "That so?"

I turned to Effie. "Would you mind taking Chris outside to the party? Wyatt and I need to have a little talk."

"Sure. Come along, love," Effie said. "Let's get you a plate of food."

"Okay." Chris grinned at Wyatt. "Wyatt, after you and Mom talk, come out to the pool."

"Thank you kindly, Christopher," Wyatt said.

"You can call me Chris. All my friends do." My son's eyes were fixed on Wyatt, all soft and adoring. Damn Wyatt. "If you want, I can show you my room later."

"If it's all right with your mother," Wyatt said.

"You may go now," I said to Chris.

"See you later," Chris said.

I bristled as they grinned like idiots at each other. Who did he think he was coming here and disrupting my life? All Chris needed was some man to mess with his mind. He was already asking me why he was the only one at school without a dad.

The two scurried off, hand in hand.

"You mad?" he asked. "If so, I'm sorry."

"Moonstone's known for being interfering as well as psychic."

"She's kind of spooky."

"You have no idea." I sighed, fighting my internal instinct to either slap him or kiss him. "Seriously, what are you doing here?"

"I needed to see you."

Needed? Strong word. "And you just drove out here on a whim?"

He set his hat on the side table, then shoved his hands into the pockets of his jeans. His T-shirt stretched across his muscular chest. I knew just what his muscles felt like under my hands. "I haven't been able to write or play, and I thought a change of scenery might help. Plus, you said you missed me once in a blue moon."

More than that. "So you showed up here, uninvited?"

"It was risky, I know." His voice lowered, sounding husky and more vulnerable than I'd ever heard him, other than when he was performing some song about his lost dog and an old truck. "I knew if I asked if I could visit, you'd say no. Driving here, I prayed you *might* be happy to see me."

I softened. Again, the problem with Wyatt and my stupid, misguided heart. "I'm not *unhappy* to see you. It's just that this is my real life. My son and my family. They won't understand why you're here. They're old-fashioned."

"So am I."

I croaked out a dry laugh. "I don't think so. Have you forgotten the nature of our relationship?"

"What was that exactly?" He leaned one shoulder against the wall and watched me. Even when he looked like hell, he was still the sexiest man alive.

I drew closer, making sure to keep my volume low. "We were a month-long booty call. My family is the 'marry your soul mate' type of people. They would not understand this thing between us. The way you've shown up here—they'll take that as a grand gesture, like in a sentimental movie. They'll have us married off in their heads before your hat's back on your head." That's *exactly* what they would do. Charlotte would be planning the wedding before we were done with introductions.

He straightened and brushed his knuckles against my bare arm. "Listen, I'll get on down the road tomorrow. But since I'm here, I'd like to help celebrate your birthday with a present." My skin prickled under his touch. And God help me, his cologne smelled sinfully good and reminded me of the nights we'd spent giving each other ridiculous amounts of pleasure. I could still taste the salt of his skin.

Wyatt lifted my chin with the tips of his fingers, forcing me to look into his eyes. "Let me give you the kind of present I'm so good at." His voice was low and seductive in my ear. "I know everything you like."

I shivered as a bolt of desire coursed through every nerve ending in my body. "This is a bad idea."

"Why?"

Because I would fall hard, and when he left I'd be undone. All the ways I'd protected myself from hurt could be obliterated by one kiss from his full lips. I'd barely escaped intact the last time.

"Teagan, who's this?" Charlotte asked.

I jumped away from Wyatt as though someone had stabbed me with a hot poker. She would see right through this. I turned to look at her. She had a glass of wine in her hand and a copy of her latest mystery in the other. Someone must have wanted an autographed paperback. Charlotte's big brown eyes inspected Wyatt as if she were one of the detectives in her novels.

"Um, this is Wyatt," I said. "Charlotte's my sister-in-law."

"I know who you are." Charlotte flashed one of her heart-melting smiles. "We've heard a lot about you."

"You have? That's interesting." Wyatt winked at me.

"From television, not from me," I said.

Charlotte clicked her tongue sympathetically. "I'm so sorry about what happened. How are you feeling?"

Wyatt's eyes misted over. "I'm having some troubles. I can't sleep or eat or write songs. Thanks for asking."

"How awful for you." Charlotte touched his shoulder. "I can't imagine how difficult it must be. You were right to come here."

"I was?" Wyatt asked.

"Absolutely," Charlotte said. "You'll be able to heal here. Peregrine's so quiet, and our summers are absolutely beautiful. Are you staying in town at the inn?"

"Yes, ma'am," Wyatt said.

"He's *not* staying." I crossed my arms over my chest. "Wyatt's just passing through and stopped to say hello."

"I *could* stay." He grinned at me. All hints of sadness had magically disappeared. "Charlotte thinks I should."

"I promise you that staying for a few weeks will be good for you," Charlotte said. "Spend time outdoors. Teagan and Chris can take you around to all their favorite swimming holes. Ardan would love to take you fly-fishing. My mother lives here, and she's the best cook. Her meals will cure whatever ails you."

I made a mental note to throttle my best friend later. She knew exactly what she was doing. Charlotte knew about my fling with Wyatt. She also knew that I essentially ran away before I got my heart broken.

"Did you finish filming the movie?" Charlotte asked. "The one where you and Teagan met?"

The woman had no boundaries.

"Yes, last year. I only had a small part. It'll come out at the end of the summer."

"How fun," Charlotte said. "Our friend Hope Manning's here tonight. Do you know her?"

"Not all famous people know each other," I said.

Charlotte flushed. "I know. I just thought maybe he'd run into her at the film studio or something."

21

I immediately felt bad for making fun of her.

"As a matter of fact, I have met her," Wyatt said. "At an awards ceremony last year. She was there with a buddy of mine."

I inwardly winced. His buddy had been another country performer who'd dumped Hope and sent her into a spiral of self-destruction. She'd come home to Peregrine swearing she'd never return to Hollywood. That lasted a few months, and then she was back to her usual ways. "Your buddy treated her terribly. Like musicians do. Love them and leave them."

"Not all," Wyatt said.

I raised an eyebrow. "Not any I've met."

"It's not good to stereotype," Wyatt said.

"True," Charlotte said.

I glared at her.

Charlotte took the hint, finally. "I'll let you two finish talking. But then come outside. We have a ton of food to get you eating again. I'm sure a cold beer sounds good, doesn't it?"

"Thank you kindly," Wyatt said. "A cold brew would hit the spot."

He was laying the Southern charm on thick.

"I'll see you later then." Charlotte gave us a nod and then scooted out of the foyer on her cute little legs.

"She's about as sweet as sweet iced tea." Wyatt's mouth curved up into a sexy smile. "Your brother's a lucky man."

A twinge of jealously slapped me upside the head. I didn't like thinking about him with other women. Hadn't that been the reason I ran away in the first place? No man would hold me hostage. But damn, he was so sexy it was sinful. I took him in as though I was thirsty.

"What?" Wyatt asked.

"Listen, you can stay for the party, but after that, I want you out of here."

"You can't make me leave Peregrine if I don't want to. Charlotte thinks I should stay. Why not you?"

I snapped. This was not a game. "Of all the people you know, why did you come to me?"

"Because I like you the best of any human in the world."

Liked me best? What the hell? The minute I'd left town, he'd hooked up with one of the bit-part actresses on the movie. The pictures were in the tabloids sooner than I could get his scent off my hands. "You're so full of crap."

"I'm here to win your heart."

"Are you kidding me with this?" I crossed my arms over my chest and sucked in a deep breath. "I saw the photos of you and several women since you and I had our little fling."

"Pictures aren't truth. Not always, anyway." He held out his hands. When I ignored them, he shoved them back in his pockets. "Come on now, Pretty Girl. Give me a chance. I've been doing a lot of thinking since everything went down. I don't want to spend the rest of my life alone or wondering, what if I'd gone after you like I wanted?"

"I have a little boy, Wyatt. He has to be number one in my life. When you get bored and decide to hit the road, there are real consequences to those you leave behind."

"Don't you think I know a little about that? My mama sacrificed everything for me. But if there had been a man to come along who loved her, I sure as hell would've wanted her to have the chance to be happy."

I had no idea what to say. Nothing had ever surprised me more than this man showing up on my doorstep.

He reached out for me once again. This time I let him take one hand in his. "What do you say? Let me stay for the party. I'll be on my best behavior. And on my mama's grave, I'm here with only good intentions."

I reached up to brush the side of his face with my free hand.

"You can stay if you promise you'll eat something and get some sleep tonight."

He captured my hand that cupped his cheek and pulled me against his chest. I peeked up at him, sure he would kiss me and unsure what I would do if he did. Instead, he surprised me. "You're all I've thought about, Teagan Lanigan. I love you. All I need is some time to prove how much."

"You can stay for the party, and we'll go from there." Amazed at how calm I sounded considering that my heart was beating so fast I thought I might pass out, I stepped away from him and held out one hand. "I'll introduce you to my brothers. If you're still around after that, we can talk."

3

WYATT

Charlotte, true to her word, had me hooked up with a cold beer seconds after I walked out to the patio. Teagan was called away by a woman dressed in black and white who I assumed was the caterer, so Charlotte took me over to meet the Lanigan brothers.

"Guys, this is Wyatt Black," Charlotte said. "Teagan's friend."

She introduced me to the brothers, Ardan, Ciaran, and Kevan. They offered me a chair at their table. Charlotte gave me a friendly wave before walking away to greet another guest.

"Welcome to Idaho," Ardan said.

"What a trip to meet you," Ciaran said. His dark hair was on the longer side and had one of those carefully tousled styles. He looked vaguely familiar to me but I couldn't place from where. Teagan had told me next to nothing about her family. "We're all huge fans of yours."

"Thank you," I said. Compliments about my work from people in my real life, so to speak, always made me feel odd. I often had the sense that I should have an equally kind thing to say about their vocation.

"What brings you to Idaho? Did you make the trip just for

Teagan's birthday?" Kevan asked. Given the lines around his mouth, he was obviously the oldest of the three. Mama always told me that a person's eyes told you everything you needed to know about their character. His dark blue eyes saw right into a man. Not much got by him, I suspected. Yet there was depth and calmness in his demeanor. He was like a long walk down a woodsy path. What would it be like to have a father like this man? I'd never know.

I wiped condensation from the bottle of my beer. "I'm sure you heard about the shooting. Since then I've been going through a rough patch. I thought a change of scenery and a visit with my favorite woman in the world might do me good."

"I'm so sorry." Ciaran's brown eyes were soft and sympathetic. He wasn't a man to judge another, as if he'd had enough pain in his own life to give everyone the benefit of the doubt. "I can't even wrap my head around what happened."

Ardan nodded as he reached for the cross that hung in the hollow of his throat. "Something that horrific doesn't seem real when you see it on the news. To have gone through it, no wonder you're struggling."

I scratched the nape of my neck and moved my head like a yoked horse that wanted to run free. "I can't stop thinking about the people. They were there because of me."

"No way, don't blame yourself," Ciaran said.

"I can understand how you'd feel," Kevan said. "But you have to let it go. Sometimes terrible things happen and we have to accept that there was nothing we could have done differently and move on."

"Not that it's easy," Ciaran said. "Our brother was murdered, and it took us a long time to accept it and figure out how to think about his life rather than his death."

This was news to me. I hadn't realized Teagan had lost a brother. "I'm sorry to hear that. Teagan never told me much about her family."

"That's Teagan," Ardan said. "She's not really the best at sharing her feelings."

"It's our fault," Ciaran said. "Too much testosterone in her childhood."

"Regardless, we're glad you're here," Kevan said. "If anything can fix what ails you, this is it. Spend some time outside."

"I've been basically wallowing around on my couch," I said. "Anything would be an improvement."

"Did Teagan suggest you come here?" Ciaran asked, sounding surprised and a little skeptical. He was right. Teagan would never have invited me.

I glanced behind me to see if she was in earshot but didn't see her. "Truth is, I invited myself. I didn't think she'd agree to a visit, so I just showed up. I'm staying in town at the inn."

Ciaran laughed. "Dude, that was brave."

"Brave or stupid, I don't know which," I said. "But tragedy like I saw tells a man what's important. What he should fight for."

"Amen," Ardan said as he patted my shoulder.

"Tread carefully," Kevan said. "She's like a wild animal. Scares easily."

"I know," I said. "She skipped out on me in the middle of the night. Vanished from my life."

"Ran away. That's her way." Ardan's eyes were those of an old soul, equal measures of sadness, hope, and wisdom. "And now you've come for her."

I looked down at my hands. "I'm in love with her for real. I'm hoping to convince her to give me a chance."

Kevan's features softened but he didn't say anything.

"Does she know that?" Ciaran asked.

"I told her just now. Declared my intentions like my mama taught me." I tipped back the beer and took a deep drink.

"Holy crap. What did she say?" Ciaran leaned forward in his chair.

"That I could stay for the party but that's it," I said.

"She's really bossy," Ciaran said.

"And prickly," Kevan said.

"Plus the sharpest tongue in the West," Ciaran said. "That's why God gave her that red hair, to warn people that she's coming. Don't take it to heart if she acts like she doesn't want you here. Mostly she's just trying to protect herself."

"She told Charlotte about you," Ardan said. "That's something. She's never told us about any man."

My spirits lifted. "Really? That is something. A little something, anyway."

Ardan nodded. "This is coming secondhand from Charlotte, who tends to romanticize most things. She thinks Teagan had real feelings for you, which scared her."

"Like an animal in the forest," Kevan said.

"Can I ask y'all something?" I set my beer on the table. "What happened with Chris's dad?"

"We don't know," Ardan said. "We don't even know who he is. One day she told us she was having a baby and not to ask questions."

"She was our dad's little princess," Ciaran said. "So that didn't go well. They had a big fight, and he died shortly thereafter."

"Whoever he was, he hurt her really badly," Ardan said.

"Which is why she's so skittish," Ciaran said.

"Don't take this the wrong way," Kevan said. "But your reputation is kind of...how should I say it?"

"Playboy?" I asked.

"Right, yeah. Maybe that has her worried," Kevan said.

"No offense," Ardan said. "But musicians don't have the best reputation."

"True and usually deserved." I shrugged, embarrassed. He was right. "However, the past is the past. That was all before I met Teagan."

"Sure, people can change," Ciaran said. "Like me, for instance. I was a total man-whore before I met Bliss." He gestured toward a tall, pretty, honey-haired woman holding a baby on one hip. "She tamed me."

Teagan approached, carrying a bucket of beers. "You guys need another?"

Everyone nodded. She placed it in the middle of the table. "So, I see you've met my brothers?"

"Yes, ma'am," I said.

"Kevan's been grilling him," Ciaran said. "But Ardan and I have been very nice."

"There's no need to grill him," Teagan said, her green eyes flashing with temper. "I'm a grown woman."

"I have *not* been grilling him," Kevan said. "He's been very forthright about his intentions."

"Yes, we approve," Ardan said.

"Even if we did warn him about your temper," Ciaran said, chuckling.

"They think I'm still twelve years old," Teagan said to me. "Which is annoying."

Ciaran laughed. "You are to us, Copper Penny."

"Do not call me that," Teagan said through gritted teeth.

"Copper Penny? That's cute," I said.

"That is not cute. Not at all. In fact, bringing up my least favorite feature is rude." Teagan squinted as she looked at each of her brothers. "In case any of you get any romantic notions, Wyatt's a friend who's staying in town, not here at the house."

"That cluster of buildings is hardly a town," I said.

"True enough," Ciaran said.

The DJ on the other end of the pool spoke into the microphone. "Good evening, everyone. Teagan asked if I'd play her favorite song to kick off the dancing portion of the night. Pick a partner and come on out to the dance floor."

Teagan backed away from the table. A look of panic crossed

over her face. She raised her hand as if to halt the DJ, but it was too late. The first notes of my song "Blue Bird Calls" played through the speakers.

I rose to my feet and leaned close to whisper in her ear. "This is your favorite song?"

"Shut up," she said.

"I'm flattered. I didn't think you liked my music."

"I don't know what gave you that impression. I'm not a gusher, if you haven't noticed."

I chuckled. Sparring with Teagan had me feeling like the old me. "Come on, take pity on me. May I have a dance with the birthday girl?"

She glared at me. "One dance. That's it."

"I'll take whatever I can get." I offered her my hand. The pool deck had filled with a half-dozen couples, including the Lanigan brothers and their wives.

The tennis bracelet she always wore on her left wrist sparkled, catching my eye as I led her over to an empty corner of the patio. I pulled her into my arms. Where I'm from, a man held a woman's hand in his and put the other arm around her waist. Instead, she wrapped both arms around my neck. If this was the way they danced out in the West, I was all for it. Feeling the soft skin of her arms against mine was like sliding into silk sheets. Her silky hair tickled my cheek.

To distract myself from what I'd like to do to her, I asked her, "You've never told me about your bracelet. Was it a gift from someone special?"

"My father. He gave it to me when I graduated from college. I never take it off except to have it cleaned."

"It's beautiful." I'd like to give her diamonds. Thousands of them.

Damn, I thought, *I wish I'd written a longer song.* We were already to the second chorus. I would hold her all night if I could. Teagan was a tall woman, just a few inches shorter than me with legs that went on for a long summer day. She was on the slender side and had no chest, which I found refreshing, given the number of boob jobs I saw on a regular basis. Tonight, her long hair hung in loose waves down her back. I loved seeing her tresses unleashed. They were as wild as the girl herself.

I glanced around at the other couples, pleased that everyone was dressed casually for the party. Thankfully, since I wore my usual jeans, T-shirt, and cowboy boots. Regardless, Teagan had a way about her that screamed glamour no matter what she wore. Her sense of aesthetic leaned toward the whimsical, with bright colors and soft material. This evening she wore a pair of distressed jeans with thick cuffs paired with strappy sandals. Her top was a halter with a tie around the back of her neck. One quick twist of my fingers was all it would take to untie it.

"You smell good," I said. "I've missed this."

Her chest rose and fell with a sigh. "We never danced."

"That's not true. The first time we ever went out, I took you to my favorite country bar."

"We drank too much, as I recall."

"That's not my strongest memory of the evening." Images of her wrapped around me in my hotel room shuffled like post-cards through my mind.

"The first of many mistakes." She nestled closer, even resting her cheek against my shoulder as we swayed to the music. Could she feel my heart beating faster than it should?

"Why's this your favorite song?" I asked.

"I don't know. I like it, that's all."

"I wrote it super-fast, like it just came to me all at once."

"Your talent is massive," she said softly and without the edge she'd had since the moment I walked in the door. "Don't let what happened ruin your creativity. The world needs your music now more than ever."

The song ended, and another ballad came on. I expected her to withdraw from me, but she held on tighter.

31

I drew in a deep breath and splayed one hand through her thick hair. "I don't know if it's coming back. My hands shake when I try to play."

"You've been through a trauma. You'll be back. Just give it a little time."

"I hope so."

"Did you bring Mabel?"

"Yeah, she's out in the truck." I'd teased Teagan that Mabel was the only woman in my life who'd put up with me for long. In hindsight, I should've kept that to myself.

"You want to play tonight?" She lifted her head from my shoulder to gaze into my eyes. "We could ask the DJ for his mic."

"Like I said, I'm not sure I can play."

"That's impossible." Her forehead wrinkled. "You can't let this thing beat you."

"I wish Mama were here. She'd know what to do to get past this."

"Think about it. What would she say to you?" Teagan asked.

An image of my sweet mama came to me. She'd been such a pretty woman, delicate and small-framed. Light blue eyes like mine that still twinkled no matter how tired she was at the end of the day. An undetected heart defect had taken her from me unexpectedly five years back. My first record had gone platinum. I'd bought her a house in Nashville. I was so proud of that. Six months later, she died in her sleep. The hole she left had never been filled. "She'd say how sorry she was for those people." My throat ached as I gathered myself. "And for their families." I stopped, unable to go on without tearing up. I didn't want Teagan to see me this way. Yet being in her arms made me more myself than anything in this world.

"This wasn't your fault. You have to stop thinking that way."

"I don't know how," I said.

"What else would your mother say?" Teagan continued to look me in the eye. As much as I wanted to look away, I couldn't. This was what I'd longed for all these months. She was here now. She wanted me to talk to her.

"She'd fix me some tomato soup and open a package of saltines and put on a record for me to listen to. That was my favorite when I was a boy. She'd sit across from me and tell me to remember how much I loved making music and that God had given me a talent to share with others. But it all feels so stupid now. And selfish."

"Music gives people joy," she said. "We need you. Especially now."

"There's all this stuff in my head all the time. I can't escape from my thoughts. What if it's all over? What if my hands never stop shaking and the words won't come? Who am I without music?"

Her eyes snapped. "You're not without music. You're going to get over this, and your songs will be even deeper and better. Play for us tonight. There's nothing that can hurt you here. No guns. No danger. Go get Mabel and come back out here and play for my friends. Do it for my birthday, please."

The song ended and another, more up-tempo one began. I took her hand and led her to the edge of the patio and onto the grass. As far as I could tell, the Lanigan property encompassed much of the valley and a good portion of the slope of Blue Mountain. Teagan's home was perched in the foothills above a grassy meadow. From this height, I could make out the dirt road that snaked through the property. The setting sun cast the meadow in shades of orange.

"I can see why you love it here." I wasn't sure I'd ever seen a more beautiful setting than the one before me.

"Do you see why I had to come back here? For Chris?"

"I do. He's a lucky little boy."

"My brothers make up for his lack of a father." She said this quietly, with more than a hint of sadness.

"I'm sure they do."

She wandered over to a pair of Adirondack chairs. "Sit with me?"

"Sure," I said.

"I picked this part of the property because of the elevation," she said, as if I'd asked. "I wanted to be able to see the whole valley."

After a few seconds of silence between us, I turned to her. "You know you've never asked me for anything? Nothing. Not once. Most people I meet these days want something from me. You're independent. So sure of yourself. You don't need me."

She let out a breathy laugh. "Does that hurt your male ego?"

"Not at all. It's a relief. I know if I ever win your heart it will be because you want me, not the money or lifestyle. You're like my mama that way. She never asked anyone for a favor. She always said, 'Nothing's free.' If you ask for something, you better know it comes at a cost. Somewhere along the way, anyway."

"I'm asking for something now. I'm asking you to play a few songs for my birthday. Talk about an epic party. Wyatt Black live in my backyard."

"You're trying to appeal to my huge ego, aren't you?"

She laughed again. "Maybe. Seriously, though, I think this is the perfect place to prove to yourself that you're fine."

The sun had lowered all the way behind the mountain, leaving streaks of pink and orange. White lights strung over the pool came on, sparkling in the twilight. For the first time since everything went down, I felt like myself. This woman made me feel alive and invincible even though I knew there was no such thing. Not even for a guy who had been on top of the world. I now understood my own mortality in a way I hadn't before. "I'll do it for you, but don't hold it against me if I'm awful and get booed off stage."

"You won't be." She touched her fingertips to my wrist. "Don't let him take anything more from you."

"Remember, Mama said nothing's free." I grabbed her hand

and made circles in the palm with my thumb. "What do I get for playing?"

Her mouth widened into a smile. "The dances were your up-front payment. There will be nothing more."

But the way the skin on her arm had turned to goose bumps told me differently. No one could deny the heat between us. Why would they want to?

The answer came, as if Mama were standing next to me. *She's trying to protect her heart.* Teagan wanted me but didn't trust me. I wasn't leaving Idaho until she changed her mind.

With that, I strode across the pool deck and around the house. As I passed by, I noticed the two catering ladies sneaking a cigarette at the far end of the driveway. With their backs to me, they didn't notice my presence.

I grabbed Mabel from my truck and plopped down on Teagan's front steps to tune her. How many times had I tuned this old girl in my lifetime? Most every day over the last twenty years, I figured. I fiddled with her for a few minutes, talking to her. "Don't let me down, Mabel. I need you to carry me this time. Got it?"

For years it had been just Mabel and me and a dream. When I finally hit it big, my manager had tried to talk me into a fancier brand of guitar. I'd refused. I was loyal to my first love, my Mabel. I'd learned to play on her, practicing until the tips of my fingers bled and finally calloused over. She understood me. She coaxed the melodies and words from my subconscious into music. Lately, though, not even Mabel could penetrate my dark-ness. She would have taken a bullet for me had it come to that. But she couldn't fix the hurt in my heart. Not even Mabel could do that.

I looked out to the circular driveway, crammed with cars. A sliver of moon had risen in the sky, and a few stars twinkled. The night air had cooled and smelled of roses and fir trees. The noise of the party around back penetrated the quiet, yet I could sense how silent it must be here at night. I'd never lived in a quiet place. As a kid, the trailer park where my mother and I lived had always been noisy. No matter what time of day, the sounds of a couple fighting, a baby crying, tires on gravel, and even the good sounds of laughter had been the background melody of our lives.

Being here, I was already starting to understand Teagan better. There was an independence to her that reminded me of the scene before me. Untamed and left to grow tall and beautiful underneath this clear sky. A fluttering of wings caught my attention. I squinted into the light from the lampposts, looking for the source. A falcon had landed on one of them. He went still, his magnificent wings tucked close to his sides.

I stared at him as a feeling of tranquility washed over me. A feeling I hadn't had since that awful night. The line of a verse came to me. *All that's been will be again.*

I rose to my feet and gave the falcon a nod. "I got this," I whispered. "Me and Mabel are supposed to be the light, not the darkness."

The bird cocked his head to the side, staring back at me. Another line came to my head.

Remind her of what was. Be her light.

The magnificent creature spread his wings and flew up into the night. For at least another minute, I stood there, watching for his return, but it was only the sliver of the moon and a few stars that winked back at me. I held Mabel against my chest and whispered, "I'll do my best, Sir Falcon."

With Mabel slung over one shoulder, I went back around the side of the house. One of the catering women remained, just finishing a cigarette. She turned toward me. A slow, sneaky smile lifted the corners of her mouth. "Well, hi there. I've been waiting to talk to you all night." With two wide steps, she was upon me. Then she hurled herself at me, knocking Mabel aside to wrap her arms around my neck.

"Whoa there, that's not necessary." I placed my hands on both sides of her hips pushed her away. She stumbled backward but didn't fall. Thank God. With Mabel as my shield, I backed away.

The kitchen door opened and the other caterer appeared. Clearly she was the boss, given what came next. "Paula, what are you doing?" She turned to me. "Is she bothering you?"

"No, ma'am. I'm just making my way to the patio."

I slipped past her into the kitchen, praying Teagan hadn't seen the young woman's antics and thought they were anything but an unfortunate lack of boundaries.

4

TEAGAN

W hile Wyatt went to fetch Mabel, I went into the kitchen to pay Jodi the remainder of what I owed her for the evening. Jodi and Paula were just coming in from outside. I caught the scent of cigarette smoke.

I set the envelope with the check on the counter. "Thanks so much for your great work tonight. The party's still going strong, and it may be a long night, so I threw in extra. You've both done a fantastic job."

"Thanks, Ms. Lanigan," Jodi said. She was soft-spoken and reserved. Once I'd seen her flinch from a loud noise in a way that made me think of someone who'd been hit a lot as a child.

"I put my headshot next to the phone," Paula said. "In case you want to give it to Hope before the end of the night."

"Great, thank you," I said. This poor girl. If she thought Hope was the way into Hollywood, she didn't have a good understanding of how the industry worked.

Paula's face lit up. Now that I took a better look at her, there was a predatory nature in the set of her mouth, like a hungry coyote. "I totally appreciate it. I'm trying to make connections for when I leave this hillbilly place and go to Hollywood."

Jodi busied herself with the leftovers. "Help me with this, Paula, and let Teagan get back to her party."

"Well, anyway, thanks again for your help," I said as I turned to go. Paula's next question caused me to turn back.

"Is Wyatt Black your boyfriend?"

"A friend," I said. This girl would not be working for me again.

"There's no reason to get huffy," Paula said. "I just wondered if he was available."

"He's a tad old for you," I said, more kindly than I felt at the moment. This was exactly the problem with Wyatt. He was irresistible to almost all of the female population. Young women just like this one threw themselves at him at every turn. What man would be able to resist? Even if he had a wife at home in Idaho, as an example.

Charlotte entered the kitchen, carrying a tray of dirty glasses. Clearly she'd heard Paula because she said, "Definitely too old for you, Paula."

"I've been on my own since I was sixteen," Paula said. "I'm twenty now."

I wasn't sure how that was relevant. Wyatt Black was thirty-seven. Much too old for this woman who was clearly not yet mature.

"Why were you on your own?" Charlotte asked. "What happened to your parents?"

"Dead," Paula said flatly. "I was in foster homes until I ran away. Now they can't do anything to me."

I wanted to ask who *they* were but for once I kept my big trap shut. Trouble followed this type of girl. I shot Charlotte a look. She seemed to get the hint, because she didn't ask any follow-up questions. That was hard for her. As a writer, she was curious about everything and everybody. One had to be careful around her, or they might end up in a book.

Jodi's other staff member, a young man named Ralph Jones,

came into the kitchen carrying a stack of silver serving dishes. "Where should I set these, boss?" he asked Jodi.

"By the sink," Jodi said. "We can wash them. Can you pull the van around to the side door?" Jodi tossed him a set of keys.

"Sure thing." Ralph sprinted out of the kitchen.

"You'd think he won the lottery by how much he loves this job." Paula rolled her eyes.

Charlotte and I exchanged an amused glance. "Okay, we'll leave you to it," Charlotte said.

Charlotte and I walked out to the patio with our arms linked. Mother, who looked lovely in a white dress and pink sweater, was sitting next to Ardan on one of the outdoor lounge chairs.

"How's Mother tonight?" I asked Charlotte. "I haven't had time to speak with her."

"She's well," Charlotte said. "I took her into town to have her hair fixed, which always cheers her up."

"We should go talk with her," I said.

"She'd like that," Charlotte said.

Only Charlotte could say something so loaded without causing offense. She was quite aware of my tenuous relationship with my mother. Mother and I had been slowly moving closer as the months wore on, but there was still a tension between us. One born from years of snipes and criticism, which, if I were honest, went both ways. Now that I'm a mother, I understand my own so much better. We all do the best we can for our children, but often we fail them. Forgiveness and grace appeared to be the secrets to creating loving relationships in families. In the past, the Lanigans hadn't been good at either one.

Ardan gave us a smile as we approached. "Mother, Charlotte and Teagan are here."

Mother put her nose in the air and sniffed. "I can smell their perfume. Too much, I might add."

"Behave yourself, Riona," Charlotte said as she swapped

places with Ardan. He pointed toward the house, where Hope and Ashton Carter were talking on the couch. "I better check on Ashton before Hope lures him home."

"She'll eat him alive," Mother said.

"See you all later." Ardan leaned down to kiss Charlotte on the cheek before scurrying away.

We all took turns with Mother, knowing it was best to ration our time with her. Other than angelic Charlotte, shorter visits seemed to work out best for everyone involved. Even Ardan, who was the best of the Lanigan siblings, lost his patience with her.

"Teagan, give me a hug," Mother said gruffly as she rose to her feet. "You're still my baby, even if you're thirty-five today."

I put my arms around her, dismayed by how small and fragile she'd become. Her tongue, however, was as sharp as ever.

"You're practically naked." Mother ran her fingers up and down my arms.

"It's a halter top, Mother. I'm hardly naked."

I eased her back into the chair and sat next to her. "Are you having a nice time?"

"Delightful." Her dry tone told me she was displeased with me. As usual, I couldn't fathom why.

"What's the matter?" I held in a sigh.

"I hear your boyfriend's here and I have yet to meet him." This was all said in a tone of deep disappointment.

"He's not my boyfriend. The man just showed up here with no warning."

"That means something," Mother said.

"That he's in love with Teagan," Charlotte said.

"For goodness' sake, not everything's a fairy tale, Charlotte," Mother said. "There's no such thing as Prince Charming."

"Not true. I present Ardan as exhibit A," Charlotte said.

"You're a silly young lady and you know it," Mother said.

"Now tell me what Teagan's wearing in addition to the handkerchief she calls a halter top."

Charlotte described my outfit. "She looks beautiful with her hair down and styled in waves."

"Jeans for a party?" Mother tutted. "In my day, women dressed like women."

Charlotte looked over at me and grinned. We'd heard this same line many times.

"And what about this Wyatt?" Mother asked. "What does he look like?"

"He's totally dreamy," Charlotte said. "A cowboy type and very muscular. Nice butt. The most beautiful light blue eyes and one of those full, sexy mouths."

"Charlotte, you're a married woman," Mother said.

Charlotte laughed. "I was simply describing him for you."

"Who does he look like that I would know?" Mother asked. "From my era."

"I'd say a mixture between Robert Redford and Clint Eastwood," Charlotte said. "He's pretty like Redford but has the ruggedness of Eastwood."

"And the body of a bull rider," I said, getting into their game despite myself.

"Oh yes, totally," Charlotte said.

"He sounds like quite the fox," Mother said.

Charlotte and I laughed.

"And what's the trouble with him exactly?" Mother asked. "Why are you sending him away?"

"How did you know?" I asked.

"Your brothers have big mouths," Mother said. "I think you should invite him to stay. It sounds like he needs a respite from the world. Your father always said this part of the country was a place to rest one's mind and body."

I was surprised to hear her advice. I'd assumed she would lecture me about not giving away the milk for free or whatever the saying was. Charlotte's influence was becoming clearer by the day. Mother had softened.

"I don't want to lead him on, Mother, by letting him stay at the house. Not to mention that Chris is already besotted."

"I see." Mother sniffed. "You don't believe in love and all that. Same old routine. It's boring, dear."

"Whatever, Mother," I said.

"Now, don't fight." Charlotte frowned. "We're having such a nice time."

"I want to meet him even if you're casting him aside," Mother said.

"I'll bring him over to meet you after he sings for us," I said.

"He's going to perform?" Charlotte asked, with a girlish squeal. "This is such an exciting night."

"He said he hasn't been able to play since the shooting," I said. "I thought I'd push him a little to see if performing in a safe environment might help him. He can't avoid performing forever."

Mother chuckled and patted my arm. "Right, but you don't care about him at all."

"Very funny, Mother," I said. "Anyway, I don't want him around for a month and then taking off. Chris will get attached to him and then Wyatt will leave and he'll be brokenhearted."

"Just Chris?" Charlotte asked.

"You two are impossible," I said.

"Charlotte is, not me." Mother gave me an impish smile and then asked for another martini.

5

WYATT

The guests sat around tables, all watching me as I adjusted the microphone. Teagan had had one of the guys bring out a stool from the kitchen for me to sit on, which I appreciated. My legs were shaking as if this were my first time in front of an audience. I hugged Mabel to my chest and asked God to help me get through this without embarrassing myself.

"Hey, y'all. I'm Wyatt, a friend of Teagan's."

A few twitters from the audience made me smile. Someone called out, "We know who you are."

"Teagan, happy birthday. I have a new song to share with y'all that's not yet recorded. Birthday Girl, this one's for you." I strummed the first chord of a song I'd written right after she vanished from my life. "I call this one 'Pretty Girl.'"

I sang the first line. "Woke up to lipstick on my towel, the only hint you were there."

And then I shut out everyone, even Teagan, and Mabel and I shared what we had to give. Maybe it wasn't enough to make the world better or to drive away evil, but it was all I had. By the end of the song, my legs had stopped trembling. I still had it. Me and Mabel could still belt out a country song.

We played through a few hits. With only Mabel to take the place of my band, I was reminded of the old days when I'd played in bars that smelled of beer and lost dreams. During that time my songwriting was prolific. I'd recorded a lot of them later after I got a record deal. Yet they'd never been as pure as back in those days before bright lights and cheering crowds and women waiting in my dressing room to do whatever I wanted. The music had been enough, even when I could barely make rent every month. Had I lost that part of myself? Could I find it again?

Under a few stars and a sliver of moon and in front of the woman I loved, I connected to a place in my heart long frozen. Even before the shooting, I'd been on automatic pilot, skirting it all. Had I enjoyed it as much as I should have? Was there something missing in my music now? Had I become my image instead of an artist?

As I played, more and more stars appeared overhead. A few children, including Chris, started dancing in the space between me and the tables. "Y'all, get up and dance too," I said between songs. "I'll play a ballad for all you lovebirds out there." I strummed the opening chord. "This is a song about my mama. The Christmas I was ten years old, I asked Mama for a guitar so I could learn to play like the guys on the radio. I was such a dummy back then, I had no idea how much it would cost, and my single mama didn't exactly have cash lying around. I can't tell you how she scraped up the money, but she did. I named this guitar Mabel and she's been with me all this time, even though Mama's in heaven now. But I got to sing this one to her when I played the Grand Ole Opry for the first time. This is called 'Blue String.'"

I'd written it about my sweet mama's love for music and how she'd passed that on to me when she bought my first guitar. *Blue*

String was a metaphor for the ties that bind us as family but also the sacrifices a mother makes for her son. To this day, I couldn't sing it without choking up.

Everyone clapped between songs, but this one received the loudest applause of the night. Of all my hits, this one had been the biggest. Music lovers knew when something was from your heart. There was no faking that.

After a dozen songs, I decided it was wrong to hog Teagan's whole night, so I signed off by singing "Happy Birthday" to her and asked everyone to join in. Charlotte brought out a cake lit up with candles. Teagan blew them all out with Chris by her side, looking at her with such love that it choked me up all over again thinking about my mama and me. We'd been like the two of them, without the loads of cash, of course, but bonded. Two against the world, she used to say.

I often wondered why Mama never remarried. I hated to think it was probably because she was so protective of me. However, knowing her, that was the most likely scenario. She'd never been married to my father but had lived with him from the time she graduated from high school. Her mother had died when she was in high school and she didn't have anyone. She'd moved in with my father and gotten pregnant. Only months in, he started hitting her. "I didn't know any better," she'd said to me once. After I was born she had new incentive to run away from him. "If he'd hurt a hair on your head, I would've killed him. And I didn't want to go to prison and leave you at the mercy of the state." That's the extent of what I knew. I figured the man was dead, or he would have come sniffing around for money.

I set Mabel inside near the fireplace. She looked good against the stone. The house was a nice mix of rustic and modern with vaulted ceilings and dark wood floors. It wasn't huge, maybe a little over four thousand square feet. I'd have expected more of a mansion given Teagan's net worth, but maybe she was trying to keep it real for her little boy.

I stopped for a moment to look at the pictures set out on the baby grand piano. There were several of Chris at various ages and one of the two of them in the snow. A few older pictures were of her and her brothers on horses somewhere on this property if I had to guess, given the trees in the background. I picked up a formal photo of the entire family. Teagan looked around eighteen. Her deceased father and brother had still been alive then. They looked like the perfect family. Tragedy doesn't care how perfect you are.

I set that one aside and peered closely at a photo of Teagan and her father. She was probably ten years old. She stared up at her dad with an adoring expression. He had his hand on the top of her head and smiled back at her. I shivered as a cold, empty feeling came over me. An image of the falcon from earlier flashed before me.

Shake it off, I told myself. *You're having a good time. You were able to play music.*

I turned away from the photos to see Chris standing in front of Mabel. "Hey, bud, what's up?" I asked him.

"Nothing too much. Nana wants you to come see her. She liked your singing a lot."

"That's good to hear." I ambled over to him and sat on an ottoman to be on his level. He was cute as all get-out with his round face and big brown eyes. "Should I be afraid of her, though? I've heard some tales."

Chris shook his head. "Aunt Charlotte says she acts grumpy but inside she's soft and squishy. That's the same way with my mom. Did you know that?"

"I've noticed that, yes. But I still like her a whole lot."

"I heard Aunt Charlotte say something about how you want Mom to be your girlfriend. Is that true?" He fixed an unblinking gaze on me.

I studied him. Which way was this going? Did he like the idea or hate it? "It is true. I'd like to take her on a date."

He lifted one finger to his mouth and nodded, as if contemplating a scientific question. "Where to?"

"I don't know. What's good around here? Like for dinner."

"There's only one place, and Mom says it's terrible even though the whole family goes there all the time. I like their french fries though."

"I could take her there, I guess. Or maybe I could cook her dinner."

"She'd like that. She hates cooking. Sometime I hear her say bad words and she clangs pans around and stuff. One night she caught her apron on fire."

I chuckled and scratched the nape of my neck. "That doesn't sound too good."

"My aunt Blythe is a really good cook. She's always making the family dinners when we all get together. There's a lot of us so it's hard work. I help with the dishes."

"Do you like living here?" I asked.

He grinned and lifted his hands in a gesture of disbelief. "It's awesome here. Can't you tell that already? I've got a best friend now. His name's Martin and he lives in town. The other town. The one where I go to school. It's a long drive and there's no bus. But Mom doesn't mind driving me. She said she likes to listen to music on the way home, after she drops me."

"What kind of music?"

"Sometimes she listens to you." He narrowed his eyes and gave me a good once-over. "Did you really write a song for her?"

"Yep, sure did. Your mom has a way of getting under a man's skin and not ever letting go."

"There's a girl like that at my school. Her name's Nora and she's really pretty. I'm going to give her a Valentine next year. Like a really big one."

"I think that's a mighty fine idea."

"You talk kind of funny," Chris said.

"That's because I'm from the South. We have a lot of sayings and such where I'm from."

"Will you teach me some?"

"Sure. But for now, I better go see your grandmother."

"Good point. She doesn't like to be kept waiting. I'll take you to her." He held out his hand and I took it, moved by this adorable kid. Just like his mother, he was easy to fall in love with.

MRS. LANIGAN SAT BEHIND A LARGE DESK IN THE STUDY, LIKE THE head of a Mafia family. If she kissed both sides of my face, I knew I was goner.

"Nana, Wyatt's here," Chris said. "He's going to sit in the seat across from you." He pointed at one of the two chairs on the other side of the desk. "She likes to know where a person is in the room."

"So I can direct my gaze at you, even if I can't see a blasted thing," Mrs. Lanigan said.

"Got it," I said. "I'm happy to sit wherever you tell me to."

"Chris, you may be excused," Mrs. Lanigan said.

"Okay, Nana," Chris said. "You let me know if you want me to come get you."

"I will, sweetheart." Mrs. Lanigan waited until the door shut before she directed her sightless gaze toward my direction. "My children count out all the steps for me to get from one place to another in their houses, but since I'm afraid to fall, my grandson and Charlotte escort me around."

"He's a great kid," I said.

"Agree. However, that's not what I want to talk to you about. Not yet, anyway."

I braced myself for questions. She probably thought I was a derelict showing up this way, unannounced.

"I hear you've had some trouble." She tented her hands under her chin. "I was terribly sorry to hear about the shooting. Such a horrendous thing to have happened. Teagan and I were together when the news broke." She paused for a second before continuing. "My daughter was frantic when she heard you were on the stage."

I leaned back into the cushion of the chair as I took this in. Teagan had been worried about me. That had to mean something.

"When they reported that you were fine, she abruptly left the room," Mrs. Lanigan said. "I heard her crying in the bathroom. My hearing is better than ever now that I can't see."

"Crying?" Why would she cry that I was all right?

"The kind of crying that happens after you've been really scared and your fears haven't come to be."

"I see." I didn't exactly, but I stored it away to examine later.

"That's all I'm going to say about that," Mrs. Lanigan said. "Now, tell me how you've been."

"I've struggled. I can't lie."

"Questioned your own worth? Thought why them and not me? Feeling as if it were your fault because they were there to see you?"

I stared at her. "Yes, exactly. How did you know?"

"Because I lost a son and a husband, both of them better people than I."

"I'm sorry, Mrs. Lanigan. I lost my mother five years ago, and I'm still not over it."

"One never gets over it, does one?" Her unseeing eyes reddened. For a moment I thought she was going to cry, but instead she straightened her spine and took in a breath. "Anyway, I'd like to understand exactly why you've come here. Is it because you needed a place to get away, or is it because of my daughter? Just tell me the truth. I'll know if you're lying either way."

"The truth is that when it happened and I thought I was going to have a breakdown of some kind, I wished for one person and one person only."

"Teagan." Not a question.

"Yes, ma'am."

"And now?"

"I've come to try to win her heart."

"How extraordinary," Mrs. Lanigan said. "Old-fashioned."

"Yes, I guess it is. I want another chance to show her who I really am. The way we left things had me wishing I'd done some things differently."

"Like what exactly?"

"You know, acted less like a jackass. Less like I didn't care if she came or went."

Mrs. Lanigan laughed. "I've had a few of those myself."

"Yeah, I'm not real good with women, especially ones who are smarter than me, like Teagan. I should've been a little more forthright about my feelings. Then she ran away, and I never had the chance. Honestly, it wasn't until she was gone that I realized what I'd lost."

"That happens." She nodded, surprisingly sympathetic. I sensed an ally in Mrs. Lanigan.

"So I was lying around feeling sorry for myself, and Teagan texted to see how I was. I decided she might just miss me a little and that maybe I had a chance. Right then and there, I decided to do something about it. I got in my truck and drove to Peregrine. The surprise part maybe wasn't the smartest decision. Especially since it's her birthday and I didn't know." I stopped. Babbling in front of the matriarch of the Lanigan clan wasn't exactly smooth.

"May I give you some advice?"

"Sure, yeah."

"My daughter takes after me, for better or worse. We're sharp-tongued, especially when we care about something or someone. Chris's father broke her heart. I don't know who he is or what the situation was, but he damaged her. She'd never admit it to be true, but it is. She's terrified to get hurt, and she doesn't want Chris to become attached to a man who leaves. She'll push you away, but don't let her fool you. I can hear it in her voice when she talks about you that she cares for you. She told Charlotte and me all about you when she came home last year. She left you before you could leave her."

Was this true? Did I have a chance? Please, God, let Mrs. Lanigan be right.

"This time around, if you really want her, keep showing up. Be steady as a rock. If it's meant to be, she'll start to trust you."

"She told me to leave town after tonight."

"Don't you dare. If you do that, you'll simply prove that her suspicions were correct. She's wonderful at self-sabotage."

"If you say so." Could it be more than just her body that had responded to me? Was her heart in there somewhere too?

"Now, tell me what you're going to do about your career," Mrs. Lanigan said.

"I'm a mess. I canceled my tour."

"I heard." Her mouth curved downward.

I tugged at my shirt collar. The room had grown increasingly warmer during the course of our conversation. "The thought of going back on stage terrifies me. I can't stop thinking about all those people. And their families."

"Give it some time. Have you considered therapy?"

"Yeah, I don't know."

"Men," she said with a laugh. "Always so afraid that talking about your problems means you're weak."

"Is that it?"

"I suspect so. Anyway, I'm glad we had this little talk." She lifted her hand as if to stop me from leaving. "Also, one more thing. Christopher comes with Teagan. If you're not interested in becoming a father, then this isn't for you."

"Mrs. Lanigan, I was raised by a single mom. She worked at the local diner, penny-pinching and cutting coupons from the paper to keep us going. I would never in a million years mess with that kid's head. I show up when I say I will. Both for the small stuff and the big stuff."

"I like people who show up." She lifted her chin. "Would you care to escort me back to the party?"

"I'd be honored." I got up and went around the desk to help her to her feet. As I used to with Mama, I tucked her arm into mine.

"Quite some muscles you have there, young man."

"Thank you kindly. Vanity keeps me working out."

"Ah yes, my old friend Vanity. I know her well. I have a cane," Mrs. Lanigan said. "But I'm too vain to use it at events such as this. Isn't that awful?"

"Maybe, but who cares? A person can choose how they want to live, even when crappy circumstances cut you deep." I guided her across the room to the doorway.

"I suppose that's true. Something you might think about when you're deciding whether or not to walk up to the microphone in front of your fans."

I smiled as we crossed the living room toward the back patio. "Mrs. Lanigan, you remind me of my high school principal."

"Was he mean and grouchy?"

"No, *she* was the type to tell you how it was and to straighten up or get out. She had to tell me that a few times during my high school career."

"My kind of woman."

Mrs. Lanigan was *my* kind of woman, as was her daughter.

6

TEAGAN

It was nearing midnight, and I was feeling no pain. Charlotte had offered to take Chris for the night so I could enjoy the rest of the party. Hope was currently inside with Ashton. They appeared to be arguing or at least debating a point, given the way Hope's hands were gesticulating. I'd invited them to stay over, as they'd had a lot to drink.

Jodi and her two staff members were in the last stages of taking down tables and loading equipment into the catering van. Ryan Chambers was doing the same with his speakers and equipment.

And me? Well, I was in the very place I shouldn't be, spread out long on a double chaise next to Wyatt. If he was in my proximity and my son wasn't around, I was going to sleep with him. I'm a weak, weak woman.

With our legs intertwined and holding hands, we stared up at the stars.

"Not kidding, that's the prettiest sky I've ever seen." Wyatt's voice was as low and smooth as a fine Washington state cabernet. "How come you didn't come back here sooner?"

Wyatt's enthusiasm for how bright the stars were warmed

my heart. My family had spent every summer here from the time I could remember. This land and sky were etched into my cellular makeup. When my father died, I couldn't fathom coming back to our family property. Everything here reminded me of him—the scent of wildflowers, dew that sparkled on the grass in the early morning, creek water tumbling over rocks, and most especially the bright stars. I'd thought being here would be too painful, a reminder of our last exchange. To this day, I cringed anytime I recalled the argument we'd had about my unwed pregnancy. The words we'd said to each other in anger and hurt haunted me. Since my return, however, I'd sensed his presence more than once. With it had come a feeling of peace. He'd forgiven me and was as sorry as I was about our last interaction.

I didn't say any of this to Wyatt. Instead I answered his question with a partial truth. "Career ambition, I guess."

He turned his head to look at me. His breath smelled sweetly of whiskey. "You know what's happened to me since the shooting?" He didn't wait for me to answer. "I can tell now when someone's bullshitting me. There was a reason you didn't come back here for all those years. I won't pry, but if you'd ever like to tell me, I'd be happy to listen."

"Let's just say my father and I didn't see eye to eye about my unwed pregnancy." I paused to stop the hitch from happening in the back of my throat. "He died, and I never got the chance to say I was sorry for the things I said."

I hadn't meant to say so much. It was the tequila. The warmth of his hard body helped, too.

He turned on his side and trailed a finger down my neck toward my breasts. I shivered under his touch. My nipples strained against the fabric of my blouse. *Jesus, give me the strength to walk upstairs and lock the door.*

Apparently Jesus was busy with other things, because I didn't do that. Instead, I turned on my side to soak in the beauty that was Wyatt Black. I tugged on his bottom lip with my thumb and index finger. "Why does your mouth have to be so sexy?"

Said mouth turned upward into a smile. "I'm glad you think so."

I rolled my eyes. "You know I do."

He wrapped an arm around my waist and tugged me closer. "Do you have any idea what I want to do to you tonight?"

I surged with desire, intoxicated by him. "I think I do, because you've done it before."

He chuckled as he reached under the waistband of my jeans and ran his thumb across my back. "How's the little dragonfly? Has Belle missed me?" When I was in college, I'd gotten a tattoo of a dragonfly just above my tailbone. My mother referred to it as my tramp stamp. Wyatt, however, did not share her opinion. He'd once traced his tongue along the wings and named her Belle. I'd almost burst into flames.

"She's fine," I said, huskily.

He brushed his mouth against mine. I breathed in the scent of him and the taste of the whiskey on his tongue.

"What's happening here?" I asked. "Did you mean what you said earlier?"

"Every word of it. Don't you see? I fell for you the first night we were together." He kissed me again, drawing me close. A tightening in my chest made it hard to breathe. I'd felt the same way. My feelings had scared the hell out of me. Why did he feel like the place I belonged? How could that be? After all these months away from him, it was as if no time had passed.

"What do you want, Wyatt? For real."

"I want a family. A place to belong. I want you."

He thought it was here? With me? With Christopher? Did he have any idea how much responsibility he would have to take on as a stepdad? There was my family, too. The big, messy lot of them.

"I know what you think," he said. "That I'm not the type to be a good stepfather, but you're wrong. I know what it means."

"This is all too sudden," I said. "You don't know what you're saying."

"I do." He kissed me, deeper this time, as if his mouth searched mine for answers. When he pulled away, he brushed my hair away from my cheek. "The night it happened, I went back to the hotel. I couldn't sleep. All I could think about were the people who died and how easily it could have been me. I thought about what I would've regretted if that had been my last day on earth. Was there anything I wanted that I hadn't achieved? Had I made mistakes? Walked away when I should have stayed? The only one on that list was you. Everything else I've ever wanted came true. I didn't have any wrongs to set right. I took care of my mama like I should have. The guys in my band are the best friends anyone could have. But there was a big hole. One I realized couldn't be filled by anyone but you. I'd been such a chicken. I didn't tell you how I felt. Instead, I hid from it because I was afraid to lay it all on the line. I'm not going to live that way any longer. I'm here at your mercy. All I know is if I died tomorrow, at least I'd have told you how I felt. Even if you don't return the feelings, I was brave enough to tell you."

I smiled and swallowed the lump in my throat. The lights around the patio were bright enough that I could see into his eyes. What I saw there was as raw and tender as I'd ever seen on a man.

"Say something," he said. "I just poured my heart out to you."

"I'm not sure you understand how I am."

"How are you?" He caressed my cheek with the backs of his fingers. "Other than beautiful, smart, and funny?"

"I'm like a skittish cat. One who doesn't want to get hurt or locked out of the house to be eaten by wolves."

"Am I the wolf in this scenario?"

"No, you're the one who locks the door. The wolf is my broken heart when you leave."

He studied me for a few seconds. "What happened with Chris's dad?"

My gaze flickered away from him. I rolled on my back and nestled into the crook of his arm.

"Did he lock the door?" Wyatt asked.

"Not only did he lock the door, he burned down the house." An image of Oscar floated across my mind. French and artistic with an eccentricity I'd found fascinating. I'd worked for him on a project filmed in a castle in the Loire Valley. The historical costumes had been a dream job, and a sexy, mysterious head designer made it even more so. I fell in love for the first time, hard and swift. We'd had an intense affair for six months. When I'd found out I was pregnant, I'd told him, all wide-eyed and stupid, sure we'd marry and live happily ever after like the characters in the movie we'd helped make. That's when he told me he was married.

"I've never told anyone who Chris's father is."

"Why?"

The question floated between us as I decided whether to open up to him. "He was married. I didn't know until I told him I was pregnant. He's French." I added that last part as if it explained everything. Maybe it did.

"What an ass," Wyatt said.

I let out a dry laugh, more like a cough. "He said he would support the baby financially, but I couldn't possibly expect him to be in Chris's life. I laughed hard over that. He had no idea about my family."

"It takes only a Google search," Wyatt said. "Even a hick like me knows that."

"Right. He wasn't really interested in me. I was a fling during a movie. That's all. Pathetic, really, that I didn't see him for what he was. I was young and didn't know any better. I thought all men were like my dad and would treat me like a queen."

"The right man would."

Wyatt was silent for a few moments. "Is that why you were sure we were just a fling? The same scenario? Only you were the one who left before I could leave you."

"You're kind of the cowboy version of him."

"I'm not married." His eyes glittered under the lights.

"No, but you have a girlfriend in every city."

"I don't. Maybe when I was younger. Not now. Not since you."

My heart leaped. Was it true? Could he really feel that way about me? I propped myself up with one hand and looked at him. "I'm exactly like my mother. Destined to be bossy and cranky. You're looking for a girl like Charlotte. Not one like me."

"How about you let me decide that?"

Still propped up on one hand, I stared at him for another moment before resting back on his chest.

He stroked my hair as we lay there looking up at the stars. From inside the house came the sound of Hope's laughter. The DJ and Jodi's staff were no longer on the patio. Soon, we would hear the van drive away and I would have no more armor. If Wyatt wanted to stay, I would let him.

"We never did this," Wyatt said. "Hanging out instead of having sex."

I didn't comment. What could I say? He was right.

"Not that I'm complaining," Wyatt said. "But this is nice."

The glass doors off the kitchen opened, and Jodi stepped out to the patio. "Ryan and Ralph already left. Paula and I are leaving now too. Unless you need anything else?"

"No, thank you, Jodi. Drive home safely. There are deer this time of night."

"I will."

She disappeared, closing the French doors behind her.

"Do you want to stay?" I asked.

"You know the answer."

A scream pierced the calm of the night.

We both leaped from the chaise and headed toward the house. As we reached the kitchen, Jodi stumbled in through the side door. She was visibly shaking. Tears streaked down her face. "It's Paula. I think she's dead. Her head's…bashed in. Oh God, I think I'm going to be sick." She rushed to the sink and vomited.

My stomach churned. I grabbed Wyatt's arm as my legs turned to mush. Jodi slumped onto the floor and drew her knees to her chest.

"Stay here," Wyatt said.

He sprinted across the kitchen and out the door. Hope and Ashton entered the kitchen. "What the hell's going on?" Ashton asked. "Was that a scream?"

I nodded, unable to speak. Still on the floor, Jodi rocked back and forth.

Wyatt returned with his phone pressed to his ear. "We need an ambulance. There's a young woman in the driveway. She was hit with something on the back of the head. No, ma'am. No pulse."

7

WYATT

The world moved in slow motion between the time I made the 911 call and when the police arrived. Teagan and Hope huddled together on one end of the couch with Jodi on the other. Pale and still shaking, she hadn't said a word. Ashton sat quietly in one of the armchairs.

I could not get the sight of the girl's bloodied, dented head out of my mind. Brains and blood. Brains and blood.

A blunt object had been used. I'd watched enough crime shows to think it was a baseball bat or golf club. But when I'd done a quick scan of the area, using my cell phone flashlight, I'd seen no weapon. Whoever did this had gotten rid of the murder weapon somehow.

Finally, the police and ambulance arrived, sirens shrieking in the night. Jodi started to cry silently.

Had it occurred to anyone else that we were all going to be suspects? When I'd come through the gate earlier, I'd noticed a security camera. The authorities would know who had been here during the time of the murder. That included the people in this room in addition to Ryan and Ralph. I wasn't sure exactly when they left, but I had a feeling their exits would be in the window of time.

Looking around at the four other people in this room, it was hard to believe any of them could have murdered someone. However, I didn't know Ashton or Hope. They could have ghosts in their pasts, perhaps connected to the dead young woman. For that matter, Jodi could have murdered her employee. Maybe they'd had a fight over money. Or a man. Who knew? The list of motives was endless. Except I didn't know enough about any of them to make an educated guess.

I knew only this. Teagan Lanigan had not murdered the girl. She'd been with me during the entire time in question. However, the cops wouldn't have any reason to believe me or her. What if this got out to the press? All I needed was more death connected to my name. Hope wouldn't like that kind of publicity either. Teagan stood as the sirens ceased. "What do I do now?"

"Go out and greet them," I said. "I'll go with you."

I took her hand, and we walked through the kitchen and out the side door where the body lay only twenty feet away.

Several men in dark suits were already squatting near the victim. A photographer snapped photos of the crime scene. I tried to look at the situation through the lens of a cop. Would they see evidence of what had happened?

One of the detectives approached and introduced himself as Detective Cryer. He looked to be in his middle to upper thirties, wide-shouldered and muscular. He wore a crumpled suit and a tie that hung loosely around his neck. No wedding ring. His eyes were like a sniper's, sharp and focused. Not much got past him, I suspected.

Teagan shook his hand. "I'm Teagan Lanigan. This is my home. We were having a birthday party. Most of the guests had gone home. There were just two friends and the catering staff left."

"For how long?" Cryer asked.

"I'd say an hour," Teagan said. "Give or take."

"Tell me their names," Cryer said.

I put my arm around her trembling shoulders as she rattled off the names of the catering staff as well as Hope and Ashton.

"I'll need to talk to everyone," Cryer said.

"The men, Ryan and Ralph, had already left when Jodi discovered...the body," Teagan said. "I think I heard them leave about ten minutes prior."

"Do you have their contact information?" Cryer asked.

"No, but I'm sure Jodi does. I'd never met any of them before tonight. She hired the DJ as well."

"Does your security camera work?" Cryer asked.

"Yes. Everyone coming and going tonight had the code," Teagan said.

"Is there a place I can conduct interviews?" Cryer asked.

"Yes, you can use my study. There's a desk and chairs." Teagan gestured toward the side door. "I can show you."

"Good, thank you."

I had a feeling Cryer knew what he was doing. This was good, I thought. The sooner this was solved, the better for all of us. Still, I had a sense of deep foreboding. Who was the murderer among us?

THE NEXT FEW HOURS WERE A BLUR. PAULA NEAL WAS pronounced dead on the scene, killed by a blunt object to the back of her head. A cigarette butt near the body indicated that she'd been smoking right before the attack. Paula's back had been to the murderer. She wouldn't have seen what was coming. Not that it mattered now. She certainly couldn't identify the killer.

"Did you know the victim prior to this evening?" Cryer asked.

We were sitting in Teagan's study. Cryer had taken the seat behind the desk. He had a small notebook in front of him and held a silver pen in his left hand. I was reminded of the time I'd been sent to the principal's office in high school. I'd been falsely accused of starting a food fight in the cafeteria. Like then, I was innocent yet felt guilty as hell under the scrutiny of sharp-eyed Cryer.

I shook my head. "No, sir. I only arrived in town this afternoon. I checked in at the inn and then came out to the party."

"How is it that you know Teagan Lanigan?" Cryer was unshaven. Bloodshot eyes and the way his thick brown hair stood up in the back told me he'd woken from a deep sleep. In the light of the study, he appeared older than he had outside. Lines around his eyes told me he was closer to forty than thirty.

"We're friends," Wyatt said. "We met through work."

"Are you sleeping together?" He turned the page of his notepad while continuing to stare at me. Ink stained the side of his left hand. My best friend growing up had been left-handed. He'd constantly been washing his hands to get rid of the ink or pencil.

"No, sir. Not tonight, anyway. We were together before. A year ago now." My throat constricted. I hadn't done anything, so why did I feel guilty?

"You came to restart the flame?" Both sides of his cheeks pulsed, as if he were grinding his teeth.

"That's correct." Not that it was his business.

"Did you come specifically for her birthday party?" He scribbled something in his notepad.

"No, sir. I wasn't aware it was happening until I got to town." Did I tell him about Moonstone?

"You came uninvited?" Cryer asked.

"Kind of."

"Either yes or no."

"I wasn't invited." I pulled on the collar of my shirt as I'd done earlier when being interrogated by Mrs. Lanigan.

"How did you know the code to get in through the gate?" The silver pen in Cryer's hand caught the light. It was a strangely delicate, thin pen for such a large man.

"Moonstone gave it to me. She owns the inn and is a good friend of the Lanigans. She thought it would be fun to surprise Teagan."

He squinted as he looked at me. "If I ask this Moonstone that same question, will she give me the same answer?"

"Yes." Yes, because it was the truth. This guy was starting to tick me off. How could he think I had anything to do with this?

"I'm aware you were at the shooting in California," Cryer said.

"That's right."

"You've canceled your tour schedule." He said this as fact, not a question.

I swallowed and tried to think of what to say next. "I've had some trouble since the shooting. I needed some time off."

"Have you experienced PTSD after the shooting?"

"Yeah, sure."

"What happens to you?"

"Mostly nightmares. I wake up in a cold sweat, usually screaming." I knew what he was implying. He was prying into my mental state, thinking I might have had some kind of meltdown and murdered a girl because of PTSD. People who'd been to war or had other trauma sometimes came back violent or suicidal. I knew more about this than I should because of my neurotic search on the internet after the first nightmare. "I was with Teagan for the last several hours of the party. We didn't leave each other's side."

"Was there anything you noticed tonight that seemed odd?"

"No, not really. Honestly, it was a busy night for me. Teagan has a large family, and they all wanted to get to know me. I was pretty focused on them. Then, after everyone left, I was focused on getting Teagan to let me stay with her tonight."

"How was that going?"

"Pretty well...until, you know." Until a poor girl was beaten to death. Quite a damper on the libido. "Tell me what you know about Teagan Lanigan. Prior to tonight."

"She's a costume designer for movies and a mom to Chris, who's six. Comes from a large Irish American family. Her father was Edward Lanigan of Lanigan Trucking and made a zillion dollars. All of his kids and his widower live here on the same fifty-acre property."

"I could read that on the internet. I mean, what's she like as a person? Temperament? Any addictions? That kind of thing."

"No addictions." I prickled from the questions. How could he even ask such things about Teagan? "She's a devoted family member and mother. There's nothing there, sir."

His eyelids flickered. He jotted something in his notepad before turning his gaze back to me. "Jodi Sapp told me that the victim hit on you earlier tonight."

I leaned forward and gripped my knees with my hands. Alarm bells sounded between my ears. This was the kind of thing that would make me look guilty. "Sort of, yes."

"What happened?"

"She hurled herself at me. You know, like girls do sometimes."

"No, I do not know. Describe it to me."

"She put her arms around my neck. I put her aside like a second later. Then Jodi came out and scolded her. I got out of there as fast as possible."

"Did Jodi seem overly angry?"

"No, more annoyed."

"Did Teagan know all this?"

I shook my head. In hindsight, a little too vehemently. I probably looked guilty as sin. "She was somewhere else at the time."

"Did you tell her later?"

"No, I didn't think it was relevant. That kind of thing happens to me a lot. I'm pretty sure Teagan doesn't want to hear about it."

"Because she's a jealous girlfriend?"

"She's not that way."

"She's not the jealous type?"

"No way. Teagan's too badass to get jealous. She knows she's the best there is."

One eyebrow rose before he scratched in his notepad. What did he think? What was he writing in there?

"All right. That's all for now." Cryer stood. "But as far as you leaving town, we need you to stay until we have this settled."

"Fine." Any reason that kept me in Peregrine, Idaho, was fine with me. The next second, I burned with shame. *A girl is dead, you insensitive, selfish bastard*, I told myself.

I got up and went to the door. Did I thank him? What was the protocol when one was a murder suspect? Mama would have told me to mind my manners, even if the cop thought I was a murderer. I turned back. "Thank you, sir."

"Thank you. I'll be in touch."

8

TEAGAN

The police detective, who had come from Hailey, had obviously been woken in the middle of the night and hadn't bothered to brush his hair. Everyone who had been in the house at the time of the murder was interviewed separately. This included Hope, Ashton, Jodi, Wyatt, and me. I was the last to go. We'd been at it for fifteen minutes already. It was nearing five by the time I'd described the events leading up to the scream. Tentacles of sun sneaked through the blinds and hurt my itchy eyes. I yawned and tried to focus.

"Are you certain you know the time the young men left?" Cryer asked.

Cryer. Such an unfortunate name.

I thought for a second. Had I heard a car engine? "I can't remember hearing a car leave." My blouse clung to my back as perspiration dribbled down my spine. "But I was preoccupied with Wyatt and not paying attention. Do you think one of them could've done it?"

He blinked and looked at me as if I were purposely dense. "Ms. Lanigan, everyone in this house from midnight to one are suspects."

That had been the catering staff, Hope, Ashton, Wyatt, and me. "Including me?"

"That's correct." He tilted his head, then looked around the study as if clues were written on the walls. "And if you're guilty, then so is Mr. Black. Your stories match up perfectly. Who's to say you didn't do it together?"

"That's absurd. What would be our motive?"

"There are a lot of different reasons to kill someone."

Knowing Wyatt and I hadn't done it, my mind raced ahead to the others. "Did Ashton and Hope give you the same story?"

"Their stories were similar but not exact. Hope, who confessed to being inebriated, said she went to the bathroom without Mr. Carter at some point, but she had no idea when that was within the time frame. So you see, either of them would have had time to kill and return to the living room without the other knowing anything about it."

"Hope's been my friend for thirty years. She's not a murderer."

"Time will tell, Ms. Lanigan. Now, if you'd escort me to the living room, I have a few things to go over with all of you."

Hope and Ashton were slumped on either end of the couch. Jodi was curled up in an easy chair with her arms clasped around her knees. Her makeup had long since been cried away, and her eyes were red and swollen.

I sat next to my supposed partner in crime on the love seat. Instinctively I inched closer to him. Wyatt took my hand.

"As I said to Ms. Lanigan, everyone in this room is a suspect in the murder of Paula Neal," Cryer said. "Which means none of you can leave the area until we've cleared you of suspicion. Mr. Black, is that clear?"

"Yes, sir," Wyatt said.

"I have a movie shoot to get to," Hope said.

"You'll have to postpone it," Cryer said.

"That's not the way the business works." Hope glared at him. "They'll replace me."

Cryer seemed to look right through her. He was clearly unimpressed with her fame. "Mr. Carter, I understand this is a vacation home for you. That said, if you try to flee the state, it will make you look very guilty."

"I have nowhere to go," Ashton said as he nudged his glasses up his nose. "I'd planned to be here all summer. I retired early."

"Right. Retired at thirty-two. You mentioned that," Cryer said with a bitter edge to his voice. I suspected he hoped the murderer was one of us rich bastards and not one of the young men who'd been working for Jodi. "I'll be going now, but I'll be in touch very soon. Get some sleep. You're going to need it."

I walked him to the door. "My son is sleeping over at my brother's house. Can I bring him back here in the morning?"

"Your driveway's a crime scene. It's up to you if you want to expose him to that or not."

I swallowed the bile that had risen to my throat. Such a simple sentence that implied so much. Not only was I a murder suspect but also a bad person. Perhaps to influence his opinion to the contrary, I said, "My understanding is that Paula didn't have family. I'd like to pay for her funeral."

He narrowed his eyes, studying me. I wanted to look away even though I hadn't done anything. As a kid, when someone had misbehaved and the teacher was trying to figure out who did it, I'd felt guilty even when I was innocent.

"That's kind of you," he said without inflection or facial expression. Did they teach you how to train your facial muscles not to move at police school? "Unless you did it, which then makes it heinous."

With that, he walked out and down the steps. I shut the door and pressed my forehead against the cool wood. My stomach churned. A young woman had been murdered in my driveway.

I remembered something Paula had said earlier. *They can't do anything to me anymore.* Were "they" a killer? Had they come to get her? I made a mental note to tell that to the detective. For now, I had to get some sleep.

I'd sent my entire family a group text telling them what had happened. There had been no response because they were all still asleep. In a few hours, all hell would break loose. Until this was cleared up, should I leave Chris with Ardan and Charlotte? Would seeing yellow crime tape upset him? What would my mother have to say about all this? Most likely, she'd add this to a long list of my failings. Only I could have a murder occur on my thirty-fifth birthday.

I thought about my father. What would he do if he were here? He'd been such a strong man, both physically and mentally. Would he have let the detective intimidate him as I had? I'd always acted so tough as a kid, running around these woods with my wild brothers. Inside, though, I'd often been scared. Like the time Ciaran had dared me to hold that stupid garter snake. I'd done it because I'd rather have died than show weakness, but not without a mental battle.

My thoughts went next to Finn. He'd been murdered six years ago, and there wasn't a day that my stomach didn't twist in rage. As hard as Paula's life had obviously been, perhaps it was an act of kindness that she didn't have family to mourn her.

They will get this sorted out, I told myself. *The killer will be caught.* At this point, the only thing I was certain of was the innocence of Wyatt and me. The rest? Who knew? Like the detective said, people had secrets. Still, I couldn't fathom how any of us had any connection to Paula Neal.

When I returned to the living room, Jodi was crying into her hands and Hope was attempting to comfort her. The men were sitting with their arms between their knees. Both looked as if they'd been on a two-day bender, unshaven and disheveled.

"Can I get anyone anything?" I asked. "Food? I could make coffee."

No one answered, other than weary shakes of their heads.

"I have the guest rooms made up," I said. "If anyone would like to rest."

Jodi lifted her head from the arm of the chair. "Thank you, but I'll go back to the inn."

Hope had her hands clasped together in her lap as if she were willing herself not to fall apart. "I'll go home and get some sleep. And then call my agent and tell her I'm stuck in Idaho because I'm a suspect in a murder."

"Will they replace you?" Wyatt asked.

"Probably," Hope said. "There's always someone younger and prettier waiting to take my place."

"Maybe they'll solve this quickly," Ashton said.

"This is ridiculous." Hope raised her petite hands. "Do these look strong enough to bludgeon someone to death?"

That was a good point. One I hadn't thought of. How could any of the women here tonight have hit someone hard enough to kill them? Didn't it take tremendous strength? They hadn't yet discovered what kind of blunt object it was, though. Maybe it had been a sharp rock and the murderer knew just how to strike. I shivered. I glanced at Ashton's hands. They were large. His arms looked strong as well. Could he have done it? But again, why? What connection could he have to the lost young woman?

"Teagan, are you all right?" Ashton asked, sitting forward. "You're looking pale suddenly. Are you all right? Can I get anything for *you?*"

"You're sweet to ask, but I'm fine." My voice betrayed me, all shaky and breathy.

"I could use a drink," Wyatt said. "A double shot of whiskey."

"I'd like one too," Hope said as a flicker of a smile crossed over her perfect features.

"Where's your booze, baby?" Wyatt asked me.

I pointed in the direction of the liquor cabinet. "Go for it. I'll take one too."

"Me too, please," Jodi said. "This is all my fault."

"Of course it's not," Hope said. "This had nothing to do with you."

"What if one of those men killed her? I hired them," Jodi said. "I did background checks, like I do with any temporary staff before I bring them into people's homes. Nothing came up from their pasts, other than Ralph had bad credit. But Paula didn't have any money to steal or anything."

"Being broke doesn't make you a murderer," Wyatt said.

"True," Hope said. "But what other motives do people have for murder?"

"Statistically, they're committed by someone the victim knows," Ashton said.

"I'm the only one who knew her before tonight," Jodi said. "I know I didn't kill her."

I couldn't imagine sweet, timid Jodi killing a spider, let alone a human.

"How long had you known her?" Hope asked.

"This was her second job for me," Jodi said. "She'd been moving around before this, taking jobs where she could find them."

"A grifter type?" Wyatt asked as he set glasses and a bottle of whiskey on the table.

"No, not that I could tell." Jodi tucked her long, shiny brown hair behind her ears as she reached for a glass and held out her hand for Wyatt to pour her a drink. "And I've seen some criminals in my day. She was just young and, frankly, obnoxious. The type who sought attention. From men, especially."

Sunlight pierced my large windows and hurt my tired eyes. Morning felt wrong after the awful darkness of the night we'd just endured. Today would be another beautiful summer day. Only there was one less person in Peregrine this morning.

I accepted the glass of whiskey from Wyatt.

"How do we know it's not someone who came in from the outside?" Jodi asked, with a hopeful lilt to her voice.

"Security cameras," Ashton and I said at the same time.

I nodded. "The detective told me they'd already looked at the tape from my cameras. There was an hour gap between the last guest and when you and your staff were ready to pack up. Given our statements, they believe she was murdered sometime between midnight and one. It has to be one of us or one of the two men who worked for Jodi."

"I'd met her before." Hope stared into her whiskey glass. "A couple of days ago. She basically accosted me outside the coffee shop, trying to get my photo. I wasn't in the mood and put up my arm to shield my face and accidentally hit her. There were at least a half dozen witnesses looking through the coffee shop windows."

"Did you tell that to the police?" Ashton asked.

Hope lifted her blue eyes to look at him. "I did, yeah. Figured it was better to tell him myself than have someone else tell him when he starts snooping around town."

"As far as that goes," Wyatt said, "I had a little trouble with her tonight as well. She hit on me on my way back from my truck."

"She did?" I asked. How come he hadn't told me this earlier?

Wyatt's glance slid to me. "It was nothing. I didn't want to upset you."

"Only now it could seem like a motive," I said. "Jealousy."

"Or one for me," Wyatt said.

"That's stupid," Hope said. "No one would kill a girl for hitting on their boyfriend."

"If someone were unstable," Ashton said. "Psychotic."

"I'm not psychotic," I said.

"I know," Ashton said.

Had that been fear in his voice? Did he actually think I was capable of murder? I didn't know much about him as far as that went. Maybe he was psychotic.

"I don't like it when people lunge at me like that," Jodi said as if she were a few sentences behind us. The tone of her voice had a tinge of panic. I'd had a friend in high school who was claustrophobic. They'd sounded like that whenever anyone talked about small spaces.

"It wasn't any big thing," Wyatt said. "I just picked her up and set her aside."

I threw back my shot of whiskey and tried to calm my thoughts, which were bouncing around like the early-morning bees on the honeysuckle outside the windows.

"She asked Teagan about you," Jodi said to Wyatt. "In the kitchen."

"That's right," I said. "It irritated me at the time, but I didn't think she'd actually accost you."

"Did you tell the detective?" Ashton asked.

"I hadn't thought to tell him," Wyatt said. "But there was no need. Jodi here had already spilled the beans."

"He asked me if I'd seen anything odd." Jodi eyelids fluttered. "I thought that was odd."

The way she looked at Wyatt made me think she suspected him. I could almost hear her finishing the sentence with, "And gives you motive."

"Wyatt was with me the entire time," I said. "Plus, he has nothing to do with Paula. In fact, you're the only one who really knew her."

"She was my employee," Jodi said. "For a short time. I didn't know her well either."

"What motive would any of us have?" I asked. "Unless we have secrets."

"Do you think I got you in trouble?" Jodi asked Wyatt.

"I don't have anything to hide," Wyatt said. "I'm not worried about what you told him. Anyway, it was the truth."

"Do you think any of the rest of us are in danger?" Jodi asked.

That was a strange thing to say. "Why would we be?" I asked.

Jodi fluttered her hands, almost manic. "I don't know. I mean, what if he or she is a serial killer and they come after another one of us?"

Her logic didn't make sense, but I was tired and she was devastated. I put it aside to think about later. I looked over at Wyatt, who seemed to be fading fast. "I think it's time to get some sleep."

Ashton and Jodi both rose from the couch and said goodbye, then headed for the front door.

Hope gave me a quick hug. "This is all going to be all right," she said. "They'll figure out it was one of the staff. None of us could do anything like this." Hope took her purse from where she'd left it on the table so many hours ago. "I'll call you later."

When Hope had gone, I placed my hand on Wyatt's knee. "Will you stay? Chris is going to stay with Charlotte for today and tonight. We have the place to ourselves."

A lazy smile took over his face. "Lead the way, Pretty Girl."

9

WYATT

The sun was low in the sky by the time I woke that afternoon. Teagan was no longer in bed, and I heard the shower running. I looked at the clock on her dresser. Five in the afternoon. We'd slept most of the day. I lay on my back staring up at the ceiling fan. Set on low, it gave off only a slight breeze, which felt good on my face.

We'd fallen into bed, not even bothering to brush our teeth. My mouth was dry, and I needed something to drink. On the bedside table, a glass of water with ice waited. Teagan must have put it there for me. I guzzled the entire glass, then crunched through a piece of ice.

The shower shut off. A few seconds later, Teagan came out of the bathroom in a robe with a towel wrapped around her head.

"Hey," she said. "You're awake."

"Sure am. Thanks for the water."

"I left a toothbrush in there for you if you'd like to get cleaned up."

I swung my legs off the bed. "I'll just be a minute."

"Take your time. We've got all night to do whatever we want."

I did a double take before entering the bathroom. Had that been an invitation? Because she knew exactly what I wanted to do to her. But she was already in her closet, probably getting dressed. Too bad. I would have liked to take the robe off her and toss her back into bed.

The shower was exactly what I needed. I scrubbed and washed my hair and felt like a new man by the time I'd brushed my teeth. Looking in the mirror, I rubbed my hand over my scruff. Not ideal for kissing Teagan. Maybe she wouldn't mind?

The next moment, I felt bad again. A woman was dead, I reminded myself.

A wave of remorse came over me, remembering all of the souls who'd left the earth that horrible day. Here I was still alive and as selfish as ever.

I tied a towel around my waist and wished I had some clean clothes to change into. No sooner had I thought that than I noticed my jeans, boxer shorts, and shirt neatly folded on the counter. Teagan had washed them for me while I slept. She'd folded them into perfect squares, as my mother used to do. Strangely, that small act moved me to tears. I leaned against the sink and took in a few deep breaths.

There's hope, I thought. *She cares about me.*

I didn't dress in my clean clothes. Instead, I wrapped the towel tighter around my waist and entered the bedroom. This master suite, decorated in soft green and cream, faced Blue Mountain. As in the rest of the house, large windows took up most of one wall. A king-size poster bed made from walnut was at the center of the room. Several soft armchairs were arranged by the window with a table among them. A stack of paperbacks and a vase with fresh flowers were on the bedside table. Across from the bed, a gas fireplace decorated one wall.

But none of that kept my attention for long. Teagan was

standing by the bed dressed in nothing but a T-shirt and a thong. She'd dried her hair while I showered, and the copper strands shone in the soft light of the room. The familiar scent of her perfume weakened any resolve I had left. I was instantly ready for her. "Teagan," I said, hoarsely. "What are you trying to do to me?"

She beckoned to me with her finger. "Come here."

I crossed the room like a kid walking on hot sand. I couldn't get to her fast enough. The shades were drawn, but sunlight peeped through, casting a glow on her skin. I wanted to push her onto the bed and take her that instant, but I held back, stopping inches from her body. So many nights I'd thought about her, wishing for just one more time. Finally, the time had come, and I wanted to savor her long limbs and the curve of her hips. I traced my fingers along her soft, silky skin from her shoulder to her forearms. Her small, perky breasts pressed against the fabric of her shirt. I knew they wanted my mouth and fingers on them, teasing. She might not have admitted to an emotional attachment, but her body knew exactly what she wanted.

"I've missed you," I whispered as I planted a kiss under her ear. "More than you know."

She sighed but didn't say anything.

"Raise your arms," I said.

She did so, and I lifted her T-shirt over her head. My breath caught at the sight of her. I grabbed her around the waist and lifted her onto the bed, then we fell backward together. My towel slipped off as I stripped her of her thong. "I don't know why you bothered with that," I said before leaning in to kiss her.

She let out a throaty laugh. "I haven't had anyone to wear them for."

I growled as I trailed kisses down her neck. "The male pig in me is happy to hear that."

"I won't ask about you," she said.

I teased one nipple with my tongue and grinned with satisfaction when she gasped and arched her back. "There's no one like you."

Her hands explored my chest and back. This was going to be a quick one. It had been too long.

Her hands were in my hair. "Don't wait too long. I want you now." She pressed her hips against me and wrapped her legs around my backside. I couldn't have been more ready. I plunged into her, and she let out a soft moan that almost finished me off right then and there.

She said my name, which I loved, as I slowed down, trying to make it last as long as I could. The grip of her legs tightened as she brought me in deeper. I thrust into her harder, finding our rhythm. Only seconds later, she arched her neck and cried out. I followed her seconds later.

We lay together, breathing heavily and holding hands. I turned slightly to get a better look at her. "I guess that answers that question," I said.

"What was the question?"

"If it was as wonderful as I remembered. The answer is yes."

She gave me a slow smile. There was a softness in her eyes that I hadn't seen before. "Yes, it was. But you're different."

"I am?"

"I can't explain what it is exactly, but something." She turned on her side, facing me. "Did you mean it when you said you were in love with me?"

"I meant it."

"You really want to be off the market?" she asked.

"If you want me, I'm here."

She traced her finger down the side of my face. "I don't know yet. You've surprised me."

"Will you let me stay?"

"Not here in my house, unless Chris is gone for the night."

"But in town? At the inn?" I asked. "And let me woo you? Chris gave me some advice about where to take you on a date."

She laughed. "He did?"

"Sounds like the bar and grill is the best we've got," I said. "To me, there's nothing better than a dive bar, so that suits me just fine."

She played with the hair on my chest. "Wait until you see it before you say that."

"I'd go anywhere with you."

Teagan lifted her gaze to meet mine. "Let's go out and try to forget all the ugliness for the evening. None of this has anything to do with us." Her voice trembled. "But I can't stop thinking about that girl. It happened in my driveway at my party."

"I know, baby. I get it, trust me. I've got thirty-four souls on my conscience."

"I understand better than I did last night what that must feel like." She cupped my cheek with her cool hand. "Everything about performing is now tainted."

"Do you know it only lasted like fifteen minutes? He did so much damage in such a short time." I pushed a stray hair from her damp neck. "That's the part I can't stop thinking about. How easily everything can change. There's nothing to hold on to that makes me feel safe. Before this I was just another young, clueless guy who thought he was invincible."

"You know differently now. I wish you didn't." She smoothed one finger over my eyebrow, then kissed my cheekbone.

"I preferred being clueless."

"I think a better word would be *innocent*. After Finn was murdered, I remember thinking I'd never feel innocent again. I knew too much now." A tear traveled down her cheek. She brushed it away. "I'd have given anything to feel that way again."

My chest ached as a surge of tenderness and love overtook all reason. All I wanted was to fix everything for her. Erase all pain. Take her burdens as my own. Bargain with God on her behalf. Was this what love did to a man?

Her forehead wrinkled. "What is it?"

"Nothing. Everything."

She smiled as she traced my bottom lip with her thumb. "How about we go on that date?"

"You got it, Pretty Girl."

TEAGAN HAD NOT EXAGGERATED ABOUT THE STATE OF THE Peregrine Bar and Grill. Cushions in the booths were held together by duct tape. Tables with spindly legs looked as if they'd been there since the 1970s. Peanut shells decorated the bar's floor. The joint even had one of those jukeboxes from the eighties. No fancy streaming device here in the Peregrine.

I loved every inch of the place.

A white-haired woman wearing jeans and a flannel shirt greeted us without looking up from the plastic menu she was wiping with a damp towel. "Bar or dining room?" She spoke in the flat tone of a woman who'd said that same phrase way too many times in her life. When she lifted her gaze from the sticky menu, her eyes widened. If she recognized me, she was either too polite or too reticent to say anything. "Ms. Lanigan. What'll it be tonight?"

"Hi, Trish. Bar, please. How's your husband?" Teagan asked.

Trish made a disgusted noise at the back of her throat. "Mean as ever, but his blood sugar's been regular since I got him to give up soda."

"That's great news," Teagan said.

"You know what they say—only the good die young." Trish took two menus from the pile on the table and handed them to me. "I heard there was some trouble out your way last night. They know who did it?"

"Not yet," Teagan said, a slight edge to her voice. "Have you heard any gossip?"

"No, other than that lunatic Moonstone was in here this

afternoon telling anyone who'd listen that she'd had a foreboding feeling just an hour before it happened." She made air quotes when she said *foreboding*. "My money's on her being the killer." Trish's mouth puckered with disapproval. "Back in my day, we didn't have Moonstone types in this part of the country. Simpler times with normal people."

"Moonstone *is* colorful," Teagan said. "But she wasn't there during the time of the murder. I'd consider it a favor to the Lanigan family if you didn't repeat your theory around town."

Trish's mouth turned downward, giving her an even more sour expression. "None of my business, anyway. Sit anywhere you like. The special tonight is beef stew."

We sat at a small table by the window. There were four guys playing poker at a table in the corner, plus two other couples. No one had even glanced our way. "It's nice how folks don't bother me here," I said quietly. "Such a relief not to have to be 'on.'"

She leaned across the table and spoke through her teeth. "It's the Peregrine way. There's a certain mistrust of anyone rich or famous, along with an insecurity. If they don't acknowledge you, then they can pretend they're not intimidated." She'd put her hair into a messy bun before we left the house. With little makeup and those freckles on her nose and cheeks, she appeared much younger than her thirty-five years.

"Well, I like it," I said.

"I can see that." Teagan peered at me with more intensity than usual.

"Do I have something on my face?" I asked, teasing.

"No, you just look different today. Rested."

"I like it here," I said. "A man can breathe."

She flinched, as if a loud noise had gone off near her ear. "Father always said that. *A man can breathe here, Teagan. And when you can breathe, you think straight, and when that happens, you can figure out who you are and what your job is in this world.*"

"I can see what he meant. You must, too, or you wouldn't have come home."

"We're like homing pigeons, the Lanigans. We always find our way back here."

A young bartender with tattoos on every visible part of his body and a long, thick beard dropped off a pitcher of beer at the table of poker players before greeting us. "Hey, Teagan." His eyebrows shot up when he recognized me, but he didn't say anything. Peregrine and the people here were endearing themselves to me at a rapid rate.

"Hi, Derek. How's business?" Teagan asked.

"Actually, not bad. We've had a lot of people around lunchtime passing through on their way to the resort towns."

"Glad to hear," Teagan said.

"What can I get for you?" Derek asked.

I ordered a beer. Teagan asked for a vodka and soda.

"Anything to eat?" Derek asked.

"Give us just a minute to look over the menu." Teagan gestured toward me. "We've got a newbie to town."

"Welcome." Derek put both hands in the back pockets of his jeans and rocked back on his heels. "I heard what happened last night out at your place. You guys all right?"

"We're fine," Teagan said. "Shaken up, though. Have you heard anything?"

Derek drew a little closer and lowered his voice. "I don't like to spread gossip, but that DJ guy was in here a week or so ago. Bad vibe, if you ask me."

"Did he do or say anything that makes you say that?" I asked.

"Not exactly. He sat at the bar and asked me a lot of questions like we were long-lost best friends or something. He wanted to know if there were any single ladies here in town." Derek glanced behind him. The poker players had started arguing about politics and didn't seem to be paying any attention. "Another super weird thing—he asked if I knew any divorcées. He told me he liked women with a little experience. Also, he said Moonstone wouldn't let him stay at the inn and did I know of anywhere else to rent a room."

"Why wouldn't Moonstone rent him a room?" Teagan asked.

"You know how she is," Derek said. "She gets ideas about people."

Teagan glanced out the window before turning back to Derek. "Let me know if you hear anything else."

"Will do. Now I'll get you those drinks." Derek hustled over to the bar.

I turned my gaze to Teagan. She looked out the window as her eyes filled with tears. The blue neon beer sign that hung in the corner suddenly lit up, gave a few friendly blinks, and then went back to its dormant state.

"You all right?" I asked.

Her slender fingers reached for a napkin from the holder. The thin paper ripped as she tugged it out of the tight space. "I was thinking about that girl. She doesn't have anyone to mourn her." She dabbed at her eyes. "I find that beyond sad."

"I do too. No one should go out of this earth without someone loving them." I placed my hand over hers. "But don't forget that up there her mama is waiting. Maybe her dad too." I pointed toward the ceiling.

"Do you really believe that?" Her eyes were even greener when she cried. God help me, she was so pretty I thought my heart might stop.

"I have to. Otherwise, the world's too sad for me to bear." I brought my hand back to my side of the table. "When I lost Mama, the only thing that gave me peace was knowing I'd see her again."

She nodded as she dabbed at her eyes once more. "I know what that's like." The pain in her eyes shot a dart through my chest.

"I'm sorry about Finn. I can't imagine how hard that must have been."

"Well, that's just life, isn't it? A bunch of bad days with a moment of joy thrown in every once in a while to keep you wanting to live."

"Teagan. Is that how you really feel?" I asked, shocked at the bitterness in her voice.

"Not all the time."

I couldn't think what to say. Instead of answering, I looked out to the street. Every few minutes, a car would drive by, but other than that, the town was quiet. There wasn't even a stoplight in this town. Fodder for a song without a doubt.

"I'm scared," Teagan said, breaking the silence.

"Oh, baby, it's going to be all right. We have to trust that Cryer's going to get this solved. Then we can breathe easier."

"What if Ryan Chambers hit on her and she rejected him? Maybe he killed her because she didn't like his advances? Maybe he's a predator. And he was in my house. If he's some kind of serial killer, it could have been any of my sisters-in-law."

Derek approached with our drinks, cutting off the conversation. "You guys ready for food?"

"I'll have the barbecue chicken," Teagan said.

"Burger for me."

"Won't take but a minute," Derek said before scurrying back to the bar.

"Should we pick some music from the jukebox?" I asked, mostly to distract her from the subject of murder. I'd hoped for this to be an escape from reality for a few hours. However, in Peregrine, it seemed impossible. Everyone knew everything in this town.

She gestured to the jukebox. "Everything on that thing is from the eighties. There's no Wyatt Black. And it only takes quarters."

I grinned as I dug in my pockets for loose change. "Hold on.

I'll be right back." I went to the jukebox, delighted at the selection and the vintage machine with its glass dome. The songs were from the eighties: Waylon, Willie, Johnny, some Emmylou and Dolly. I picked a dozen songs, and the first notes of "Blue Kentucky Girl" started before I got back to our table.

"Derek came back and wondered how you wanted your burger cooked. I told him medium rare," Teagan said.

"You remembered?"

"It's not that hard to remember how a guy likes his beef."

A blue jay landed on a streetlamp just outside the window for a second before flying away.

"Mama loved this song," I said. "She always said she wanted to go to Kentucky every time we played this song."

"Did she ever get there?"

"Yeah, much later. She toured with me before she died," I said. "We went all over the country."

"In the bus?"

I chuckled. "Yeah. Mama, the boys in the band, and me. It was awesome. Everywhere we went, she bought a refrigerator magnet as a souvenir and hung it in the bus."

For the entirety of my childhood, Mama had never been able to afford a vacation. We were lucky to make the rent on the mobile home. She'd kept this scrapbook of places she wanted to go, cutting out images from magazines. I'd made a pact with myself that someday I'd take her to all those parts of the world and more.

"After that first tour, I was able to gift her with a trip all over Europe. She snapped thousands of photographs. Every meal we ate. Every famous sight. I teased her at the time, but now I'm glad I have all those memories to pull out whenever I want." We'd checked off all the places on her list. Those had been some of the best days of my life.

"What was she like?" Teagan asked. "Tell me about her."

"She was the best. Kind and hardworking. A little shy until

she got to know you. When I was a kid, everyone loved her down at the diner. She was a fixture in the place, always with a pot of coffee in her hand, filling a cup before it was empty. When she announced her retirement to go on the road with me, they threw her a party. The whole town was there, giving me a hard time about stealing her away."

"How did she die?" Teagan pushed around the ice in her glass with the cocktail straw.

"Heart condition. She went peacefully in her sleep. That's given me comfort." The coroner told me the condition had been there since birth. Undiagnosed because we were poor. He didn't say that, but I knew it to be true. "Doc told me there was nothing I could've done or any way we'd have known." I took a slug from my beer. "It's been five years and damned if I don't pick up the phone to call her before I remember she's gone."

"You gave her some good years," Teagan said.

I smiled. "Yes ma'am, I did. I'm prouder of that than anything I've done."

Her eyes misted over. She reached for my hand. "You really are a country song."

"Is that a bad thing?"

"No. Not at all. Unusual, yes. Bad, no."

Derek arrived with our dinners, setting them down in front of us with more of a flourish than I would have expected. The sweet scent of the barbecue sauce on Teagan's chicken wafted up from her plate.

"You guys need another round?" Derek asked.

"Why not?" Teagan asked. "We're on a date."

"Cool. Coming right up," Derek said.

"So, this is a date?" I asked, teasing. "Should I be hopeful?"

She leaned over the table and spoke just above a whisper. "Given our bedroom antics, I guess it has to be."

"Ouch." I grinned. "I feel so cheap."

She laughed as she cut into her chicken. "It'll be all over

town in about five seconds that Teagan Lanigan is dating Wyatt Black. You'll be obligated to marry me or head out of town."

"I have no intention of leaving unless it's to buy you a ring."

She flushed and looked down at her meal. "Be careful. I might start believing you."

"I'm not perfect, but I never say anything I don't mean. You'll see."

She peeked up at me through her lashes. "I guess only time will tell."

I smiled and picked up my burger. "And I've got nothing but time."

10

TEAGAN

In the middle of the night after our date at the bar, I woke with a start. I'd been dreaming of my dad standing in the meadow by Ardan's house. He'd been pointing up to the sky as a peregrine falcon flew overhead, circling and circling.

"Do you see?" Father had asked me in the dream.

"Do I see what?" But I woke before he could answer.

I rolled over to look at Wyatt. In the dark room, I could only make out his form. He slept on his stomach with his arms overhead and stuffed under his pillow. I snuggled closer and went back to sleep.

I woke again sometime later to the gut-wrenching sound of Wyatt's scream. I bolted upright, heart pounding. He thrashed about and made a sound like a horse being whipped. I turned on the lamp next to the bed, hoping that might wake him. Somewhere in the back of my mind I remembered someone saying you should never wake a man during a nightmare. Or was that sleepwalking?

"Wyatt," I said, touching his shoulder. "Wake up. You're having a bad dream."

He opened his eyes and stared at me for several seconds as if he didn't know me.

"You're all right," I said. "You were having a nightmare."

"Teagan?" He blinked a few times, then sat up, drawing his knees to his chest. "I'm sorry I woke you." He dropped his forehead onto his knees. His back lifted as he drew in a long breath.

I stroked the spot between his shoulder blades. "Don't worry about me."

He remained with his head pressed against his knees. "The dream's always the same. I'm on stage, watching all the people fall."

"Let's go back to sleep," I said, continuing to rub his back.

"Give me a minute. I want to wash my face."

I waited, listening to the sound of the toilet flushing followed by water running. After a few minutes, he came back to bed smelling of fresh soap. He grabbed the pair of boxer shorts he'd abandoned earlier during our frenzied unclothing and put them back on before getting into bed.

We lay on our sides, facing each other.

"I don't know if I'm ever going to feel normal again," he said. "I've never been the type to have nightmares."

I brushed his cheekbone with my fingertips. "You had an experience that forever changed you. You can't expect to feel normal."

"I used to feel invincible."

"The song of youth," I said.

"When I think back, I can't believe I had the guts to head to Nashville after graduating from high school. I was too young to know how ridiculous it was. I arrived in Nashville on the Greyhound bus with nothing but Mabel and five hundred bucks stashed in my boot. That first night, I wandered Broadway and looked at the flashing signs and lights of the bars and honky-tonks frightened out of my mind. It occurred to me to give it up and go home. Maybe get a construction job and attend community college."

"What made you stay?" I asked.

His mouth twitched into a smile. "Mama. I knew if I went back with my tail between my legs, I'd have let her down. She'd spent my whole life building me up even when the world told us we were scum. If I went back after everything she'd done to be a louder voice than the world's, it would've broken her heart. So I stayed. The next day, I got a job busing tables at one of the bars that featured new talent. Every night, burgeoning songwriters came and auditioned their songs in front of a live audience. I listened and watched, learning what types of songs resonated with the listeners. During my time off, I'd work on my own songs. My homesickness went away, and Nashville became the place where I belonged. It took three years before I asked the manager if I could have a slot. I was so nervous I puked in the bathroom before I went on. But I did it."

"And the rest is history?"

"Not exactly. It took another couple years before I got noticed by a producer named Bo Camps. My song about Mama was the one that caught his attention. He left his card and told me to call him to talk about possibilities. I'd figured he wanted to talk about buying a few of my songs, but he surprised me by saying they were interested in making a recording with me. Bo's a genius. If it weren't for him, I wouldn't be where I am today."

"Does he know you're here?" I asked.

"No. We're not scheduled to cut a new record until next year. If I have any songs written, that is."

"You will."

I smiled and twisted around to switch off the lamp. Wyatt rolled onto his back and I snuggled against his chest.

"Chris comes back tomorrow," I said.

He stiffened. "Does that mean I go back to the inn?"

"It does."

"I could come for a visit. Hang out tomorrow for a swim and a cookout."

Was that a good idea? I didn't know how Chris would interpret that. Would spending time with Wyatt get his hopes up that the man would stick around?

"We can't play with Chris's heart," I said.

"I'm not playing. With you or him."

"I want to believe you, but it's hard."

"Do you know what my mother used to say when I found a bug in the salad? *Good for you, extra protein.*"

"My son is not like a bug," I said, chuckling.

"Okay, not the best metaphor. What I mean is—I don't see Chris as a deterrent but a bonus."

God, please let him mean that.

"Fine, let's do swimming and a cookout."

He kissed the top of my head. "You won't regret it. I promise."

"Promises aren't just words."

"I know what it feels like to be Chris. I'd never give him false hope if I wasn't one hundred percent sure of my feelings for his mother."

"You're such a smooth talker." I closed my eyes. His hand smoothed my hair, lulling me to sleep.

Before I fell asleep, my thoughts drifted to the investigation. Had the detective discovered anything yet? I hoped so. The sooner that was over and done with, the sooner I could focus on what was happening between Wyatt and me. For now, I'd sleep. Tomorrow was another day.

THE DOORBELL RANG JUST AFTER EIGHT THE NEXT MORNING. I'D already showered and was in the kitchen making coffee. Wyatt was still upstairs taking a shower.

It was Detective Cryer, looking as rumpled and disheveled as he had the first time we'd met.

"Ms. Lanigan, may I come in?"

"Sure. I was just making coffee. Would you like a cup?"

"Always."

I took him back to the kitchen. The soft morning light flooded my white kitchen. A sweet scent from the bowl of ripe peaches mixed with that of the freshly brewed coffee. A pleasant scene. If not for the police detective here about a murder in my very own driveway.

"Have a seat," I said, gesturing toward the island. "Do you take anything in your coffee?"

"Black is fine, thank you."

I poured him a cup and one for myself. Instead of sitting next to him, I rested my elbows on the countertop and waited for him to speak.

He sipped his coffee before asking me, "Is your son here, Ms. Lanigan?"

"No, he stayed the night at my brother's house."

"Mr. Black is here?"

"Yes. He's taking a shower but should be down at any moment." I drank from my cup and watched him do the same. He was an odd man, I'd decided. A loner who didn't necessarily play well with others. Handsome, though, other than his sloppy attire. His eyes were a strange color, somewhere between muddy water and green.

"I've done some checking on both you and Mr. Black."

"Did you find anything?"

"He's squeaky-clean. Not even a traffic ticket," Cryer said. "Unless you count the number of women he has ties to."

"Nothing I don't know about, Detective, if you're working up to me turning on him. Not that there's anything to say. I stick with my story because it's true."

Cryer's thick brows scrunched together. Several wayward

94

hairs stuck out as if they'd been electrocuted. He needed Bliss to make him over, I thought absently, as I waited for what was next.

He continued scrutinizing me. Again, I felt guilty even though I was innocent. "Did you know Wyatt had an affair with Hope Manning?"

My stomach dropped. I set my cup down on the counter before he could notice that my hand shook.

"Ah, I see you didn't," he said.

I swallowed before answering so as to steady myself. "I didn't know. What he did in his past doesn't concern me." Despite my calm demeanor, inside, my mind reeled with this new information. How could he not tell me that? What about her? She never thought to mention it when he showed up at my house?

I replayed the party. Had they interacted much at all? I couldn't remember either of them acting strangely when I'd introduced them.

"Are you sure?" I asked.

"I found an old photograph of them from a movie magazine, looking cozy. Some paparazzo had taken it of them at the beach. They were obviously involved." He pulled his phone from his front pocket and slid it across the table. "See for yourself."

The photograph had to be at least ten years old because the headline read: Hope Manning Seen with a New Man in Santa Monica. The article went on to say that the man was Wyatt Black, a newcomer taking the country music scene by storm. I could see clearly that it was him—a less buff, younger version, but his face left no doubt. I couldn't be certain the woman was Hope. She was blonde with a similar figure, but not necessarily her.

"How do we know for sure it's her?"

"The magazine would've fact-checked, don't you think?"

"Depends on the magazine," I said.

"Do you find it strange that neither of them mentioned it to you at the party?"

If it was her, I did find it strange. However, there was no way I was admitting that to Cryer. I could see what he was doing. He wanted to chip away at my loyalty to him.

"If they lied about this, what else would they lie about?" Cryer asked.

"Even if that is her, having had a short affair hardly makes them murderers," I said.

"Maybe. Maybe not." Cryer snatched his phone back and stuffed it in his pocket.

"Anyway, none of it ties them to Paula Neal."

"If there's a connection, I'll find it."

"Is there anything else?" I regretted giving him coffee now.

"How well do you know Jodi Sapp?"

"Not well. We met at book club and she mentioned she was looking for clients. I liked her and asked if she'd do my party. Why? Did you find something on her?"

"Nothing I can share."

He looked like a satisfied cat. I wanted him out of my house. "I need to go pick up my son."

He stood. "I need to talk to Wyatt. Since he's here, I might as well do it now."

I heard footsteps coming down the stairs. "Good timing," I said as pleasantly as I could. "Sounds like him now."

"Do you mind if I talk to him here in the kitchen?"

"Not at all. I'll go get my son now. Tell him to lock up when he leaves."

I didn't wait for him to arrive in the kitchen. As angry as I was, it would only get ugly in front of the detective. God didn't give me red hair and expect me to keep my temper. I said goodbye to the detective and grabbed my purse from the counter and sprinted out to the garage.

I held my breath as I backed out, trying to calm myself. I'd

96

just started trusting him and now to find out he omitted something like this from his past was puzzling and infuriating. *If it's her*, I thought. *It might not be.* I drove down my driveway slower than usual to give myself a second to think. Had he known before the party that I was friends with Hope?

I turned out of my driveway and headed down the dirt road to Ardan's house. We lived about five minutes from each other, but the houses were not visible because of forest. A few minutes later, I pulled up to the house. The sun beat down on my head when I hopped out of the car and went around back. They were often on the patio this time of morning. Ardan and Charlotte both swam in the early mornings for exercise, then had coffee and breakfast before going up to shower. I envied the ease they had with each other and how perfectly they fit together. Since Wyatt's appearance the other night, I'd actually let myself think there was a chance I could have that too. What an idiot.

Ardan, Charlotte, and Mother were all sitting around the outside table. Chris, wearing nothing but a pair of shorts, sat cross-legged under the awning, reading a book.

"Hello, Lanigans," I said.

"Mom's here," Chris called out as if no one else had noticed.

"Teagan, you're here so early," Charlotte said, beaming at me. "Sit. Effie made a quiche and we have fresh fruit." She had a cover-up over her bathing suit. Her damp hair curled around her face.

"I couldn't stay away any longer." I hugged my boy. His bare skin was warm and tanned. "I missed you."

"I missed you, Mom, but I've had so much fun."

"Go back to your book, sweetie," I said. "I want to hang out for a bit before we go."

"Okay, Mom." He scurried back to his favorite chair and opened up the book.

"Do you want coffee?" Ardan's hair was also damp and slicked back from his forehead.

"Yes, please." I had been too upset to finish mine at home. "Good morning, Mother. You're looking lovely." Mother wore a simple polo-style dress and a hat and sunglasses. She turned her head in the direction of my voice.

"Thank you, dear," Mother said, and lifted her cheek for me to kiss, which I did. She smelled of her perfume and talcum powder. She'd gotten so good at getting around and taking care of herself. When Charlotte had first come, she would hardly get out of bed and refused to learn how to do anything on her own. Fortunately, Mother's stubbornness and cleverness had come back to life. "Is there something wrong?"

How had Mother known? She'd always been discerning, but now that she'd lost her eyesight, she was even more so.

"Is there?" Charlotte asked. Her kind eyes studied me for clues. "Did they learn anything more about the murder?"

I plopped down in the chair next to Mother. The table was under an umbrella so I didn't have to worry about burning. "I'll tell you later," I said quietly.

As she always did when someone needed any little thing, Effie appeared. "Morning, Miss Teagan. I've brought you a plate and a cup."

"Bless you, Effie," I said.

Effie scooped a wedge of quiche onto the plate, then poured me a cup of coffee, all so quickly I didn't have time to protest. She gestured toward Chris. "Shall I take the wee one in and have him pack up?"

"Thank you, yes," I said.

After the two of them went inside, I turned to Charlotte and Ardan. They were both looking at me, concerned.

"The detective was by this morning," I said. "And he told me something about Wyatt that I didn't know." I proceeded to tell them about my conversation with the detective. "He never said anything about knowing her before."

Charlotte's big brown eyes were wider than usual. "It can't be her, then. He wouldn't lie to you."

"How do you know?" I asked.

"He's not stupid," Charlotte said. "Not telling you he dated a friend of yours would be suicide."

"Is it possible neither of them remembered?" Ardan asked. "Hope's been known to be a partier."

"Unlikely," Mother said. "I agree with Charlotte. It's not her. Who wants to bet me ten dollars?"

"Mother," Ardan said. "We're not betting on Teagan's love life."

"We like Wyatt," Charlotte said. "He's a good man. I have a good sense of people."

"Not true," Mother said. "You simply like everyone."

"No, remember that guy who cut in the line at the grocery store last week?" Charlotte frowned and crossed her arms over her chest. "I gave him a real piece of my mind."

"Then you apologized to him almost immediately," Mother said. "All the way home you talked about how he might have just had a cancer diagnosis and was preoccupied and why had you spoken so harshly to him?"

Charlotte shook her curls and smiled. "All that could be true. That's why you should always be kind." She turned to me. "Anyway, Teagan, don't do one of your knee-jerk reactions before you hear his side of the story. I can tell you're into him, despite your protests to the contrary."

"I don't know," I said. "I'm no good at this love stuff."

Mother harrumphed as only she could. "God knows that's the truth. But the good Lord might've actually made someone for you. It's a miracle."

"Thanks for the vote of confidence," I said, rolling my eyes.

"What if he's the one?" Charlotte asked. "He's not intimidated by you, and let's face it, you're intense."

"Why does everyone always say that?" I knew the answer.

Thankfully no one answered, even though Mother's mouth twitched.

"He really put himself out there, showing up the way he did," Ardan said. "I admire him for that."

"He reminds me of Charlotte," Mother said.

"Really?" Charlotte asked, clearly delighted. "How?"

"He's a genuinely nice person, which, as you know, dear, we only have one of those on the Lanigan side of the family."

"You mean Ardan?" I asked.

"Who else could it be?" Mother asked.

"Not you," I muttered under my breath.

"I'm blind, not deaf," Mother said.

"The three of you are getting on my nerves." I'd been grouchy before, but my family had pushed it up a notch. "I'm taking Chris home."

"You know, you should leave him for one more night," Charlotte said. "Take some time to talk with Wyatt."

"I've already invited him to swim and have dinner," I said. "He wants to spend time with Chris." Damn, I really hadn't wanted to tell them that part.

"Oh, really?" Charlotte's eyebrows were raised almost to her hairline. "You do like him if you're letting him spend time with Chris."

I rose to my feet too fast and knocked the edge of the table with my knees. "I'll see you all later, dearest family. Thank you for having Chris."

"Send me a text later," Charlotte said. "I want to know everything."

I didn't answer as I walked inside to get my son. Since I'd moved home, I'd had to adjust to my brothers and their wives in my business 24-7, but sometimes they bugged me. I glanced out the window from the kitchen. The three of them were chattering away like three gossipy hens. They were annoying as hell, but they were mine and they loved me.

11

WYATT

I drove back into town with a heavy heart. The photo Cryer had dug up from ten years before would surely cause trouble between Teagan and me. Would she believe me if I told her it was just a woman who resembled Hope? I wasn't sure, even though it was the truth.

Teagan had a temper. She might dismiss me from her life without hearing my side. Things between us had been going so well. Now all my progress could be lost. She was going to come whizzing in here mad as a hornet. I needed to come up with a strategy to get her to listen to me.

I parked in the back of the inn and walked into the cool lobby. Moonstone, wearing a bright purple caftan and multiple rings on her fingers that sparkled under the lamplight, sat behind the desk chewing on the end of a pencil. She looked up and greeted me with a friendly smile.

"Wyatt, good to see you. Did you come to get more clothes for Teagan's?"

I swear to God, I flushed bright red. "Yes, ma'am. If she lets me, that is."

She leaned her head sideways and narrowed her eyes. "What did you do?"

"Nothing, really." I had a sudden impulse to ask for her help. "You're supposed to be psychic, right?"

"No 'supposed' about it." She raised one eyebrow and tapped the eraser end of her pencil against the top of the desk.

I suppressed a shiver. The woman scared me. Was she a witch in addition to being psychic? Would she cast a spell on me if I somehow crossed her? "I don't suppose you can look in your crystal ball and tell me the best way to handle my situation with Teagan?" I flashed her my red-carpet smile.

She frowned and crossed her arms over her ample chest.

Okay, then. She was having none of that. Moonstone wasn't susceptible to my charms. Unfortunate as that was, I plodded onward.

"The detective pulled out a photograph from ten years ago of me and a blonde on the beach. The blonde looks like Hope Manning, which the tabloid ran with."

"And it's not her in the picture?"

I thought she was supposed to know these things, but I didn't ask questions. "No. Her name was Lucy. I think. Just some girl I picked up at a bar and spent a few days with. That was how I rolled back then."

"He showed this photo to Teagan?" Moonstone asked.

"Yes, this morning." I explained how he'd come by to interview us again. "He told me he'd mentioned it to her and that she was visibly shaken and pissed."

"That detective is a troublemaker," Moonstone said. "Don't worry. You can explain it and all will be well."

"You know how she is, though. What if she won't listen?"

"I do know how she is. I haven't seen a couple more willing to let true love pass them by than you two."

"What do you mean? I'm trying as hard as I can to convince her I'm worthy."

"My psychic abilities are particularly strong when it comes to the Lanigans." Her long purple-painted fingernails played with a dangly earring. "You don't have to convince me. I can see by your aura that you've come to get her. Finally." She waggled a finger at me. "You're going to have to be inventive. Teagan Lanigan's a hard case. The hardest one of all the Lanigans. First, it was the Frenchman leaving her, then her father's death after their terrible argument. Combined with your all-inclusive generosity to women in the past, she's going to find any excuse to push you away."

"All-inclusive?" I asked, fairly certain it was an insult.

Her eyes flashed with impatience, as if I were purposely not understanding. "You haven't exactly been a choirboy. Am I right?"

My toes curled in my boots as I plastered a fake smile on my face. Getting nailed for my dalliances with women wasn't exactly what I'd come here for. "Well, that's not really the point."

"For her it is. She's waiting for you to smell a fragrance in the wind and take off down the road."

"You make me sound like a dog."

"This thing with Hope is a real setback." Moonstone shook her head sadly.

"It's not a thing with Hope. Lucy, remember?"

"Right, yes. The best thing to do is tell her all about it with as many details as you can remember. That way it sounds more truthful."

"It *is* truthful."

"You're going to have to dig deep here. Teagan's looking for a reason to run. Your job is to make sure she can't find one."

"How do I do that?" I asked.

"Be yourself."

"I'm not sure that's going to work." I grimaced. "I mean, all the women from my past are working against me." That photo was just a symbol of who I'd been. Now Teagan had been reminded of exactly that. Even if it wasn't Hope, it was someone similar.

"You best get upstairs and shave. When was the last time you had a haircut?"

I ran a hand over my head. It was shaggy and a little long. "Since the concert."

"Go down to the salon and get a haircut. Did you bring anything besides cowboy clothes?"

I looked down at my faded jeans. Teagan had washed them and my T-shirt at her place yesterday. "Teagan likes me in jeans."

"Wouldn't hurt to dress up a little, but that's merely my opinion." She continued without a pause for breath. "In all the time you two were messing around, did you ever take her someplace or was it all just happy times in the sack?"

"Happy times," I mumbled.

Moonstone reached for a pad of paper. "I'm going to write down a few places in Hailey where they serve a nice dinner. Going out for a real date would be good for her. Taking her to the bar last night doesn't count."

"You knew about that?" I asked.

She smirked as she scribbled something on the paper. "What part of psychic don't you understand?"

"Right. Sorry."

She tore the paper from the pad and thrust it at me. "I'll call the gals down at the beauty shop. They'll get you fixed up. Meanwhile, I'll talk to Teagan and see if I can get her to listen to reason."

"Yes, ma'am." Taking instruction from a purple-obsessed psychic? Up in heaven, my mama must have been laughing her cute little head off.

I TEXTED TEAGAN AFTER MY HAIRCUT TO ASK IF I WAS STILL invited over for the afternoon. She must not have been too mad because she answered back right away that, yes, I could come and would I stop at the grocery store for some chicken, fresh vegetables, and fruit.

I replied yes and that I'd be there at three. Since she didn't mention the photograph, I figured it was best to wait until we were together in person.

The grocery was small and smelled of damp concrete and fresh fruit, as they all had before the big chains took over. I grabbed a cart and meandered through the produce section. I breathed in the scent of peaches and strawberries that were currently being doused with a fine mist. Quart pulp containers of blueberries and blackberries looked as if they'd been picked locally. Six different varieties of apples in hues of pink to green to red took up an entire display. Their names jumped out at me: Gala, Honeycrisp, Fuji, Jazz, Pink Lady, Ginger Gold. The last three names sounded like strippers. Best not to mention that observation to Teagan, I thought.

I picked up one of the Jazz apples. Which apple type was Chris's favorite?

One time when I was young, my mother had come home from the diner with a surprise. A boutique soda supplier had come by with some samples. The owner had quickly shut him down. "Folks around here like Coca-Cola products, not the fancy stuff." Mama had felt sorry for the crushed salesman and had slipped him a free piece of pie. To thank her, he'd given her a few bottles of his soda offerings: a root beer, an orange, and a ginger ale. She'd brought them home, and we sampled them all to decide which we enjoyed the most. Orange soda had won. Such a small thing, but I'd never forgotten that evening.

Which gave me an idea for something to do with Chris. I'd buy one of each variety of apple and we'd have a taste test. I knew Teagan would never go for the soda idea unless they had one made from kale. But apples? Everyone could get behind an apple.

I gathered them into my basket, feeling stupidly excited. Maybe I wasn't that much older than Chris. A kid in a man's body. There were worse things to be, I guess.

I wandered around the store, taking it all in, enjoying the simplicity and quiet. A few women nodded at me but left me alone. In the meat section, I looked into the glass counter at the chicken. Should I do breast or thighs? Both, I decided. A butcher wearing a white apron over his round belly greeted me with a wide grin. "I'm Bog, your friendly neighborhood butcher." Bog had a receding hairline and a small mouth in a wide face. His laugh lines told me he was a man who enjoyed life. "I was real sorry about what happened. Must have been rough."

This was the first time since I'd arrived that anyone had acknowledged who I was. Yet it felt neighborly rather than intrusive. "Thank you kindly."

"How the heck did you find your way to Peregrine?"

"Just visiting a friend," I said. "She's sent me for chicken."

"You got it," Bog said as he reached a beefy arm inside the case. "How long you staying?"

"Not sure. I needed some downtime. A place to think."

"You'll find that here but not much else. You fish?" Bog asked.

"No, sir. Is it true folks out here kiss them and throw them back?"

"Some do. Rich tourists mostly. People from here, we fry them up and eat them." Bog pulled a piece of butcher paper from the wheel that hung on the wall. "Who's your friend? I know most folks around here."

I hesitated, not sure Teagan would want me to tell him.

"Small town gossip's rampant here," Bog said, clearly sensing my apprehension. "But whatever you tell me stays here."

"Teagan Lanigan's my friend," I said. "We've known each other for a while now."

He grinned as he set the wrapped chicken on top of the display counter. "That little firecracker's been causing trouble in this town since she was a tiny little thing. She and her brothers used to come in here to buy ice creams on summer afternoons, all dirty and wet from swimming in the river, just like the local kids. You wouldn't have guessed they were rich. Their daddy was like that too, rest his soul. Salt of the earth. Terrible thing about Finn. My wife taught all the kids piano when they were here for the summers. He was the only one with any talent."

I smiled, imagining a little Teagan trying to play piano.

"The locals haven't always been friendly to the Lanigans, but I got no beef with them. Good people. You say hello to Teagan for me. Tell her Bog wants to know why she hasn't come in for ice cream yet this summer."

"I surely will," I said. "Thanks for the chicken, Bog."

"Don't be a stranger. I've got some grass-fed local beef coming tomorrow. Best steaks around."

"Will do." I gave him a friendly wave and took off, pushing my cart and smiling to myself.

This town felt like home. Now I just needed to convince Teagan to let me stay long enough to show her I could be her forever home.

I HEARD THE HAPPY SHRIEKS OF A LITTLE BOY AS SOON AS I GOT out of the truck. With the grocery bag in one arm and a bouquet of flowers in the other, I strode across the yard and around the side of the house. The police tape was still around the crime scene and made me shiver, despite the warmth of the afternoon. How long until they took it down? The murder seemed surreal still, as if it had happened to other people instead of us. However, the yellow tape was a reminder of just how real it was.

I put those thoughts aside, ready to focus on Chris and Teagan. As I rounded the corner of the house, Chris waved from the side of the pool. "Hey, Wyatt. I'm practicing my diving. Do you want to watch?"

"You bet," I said.

He dove into the water as sleek as a dolphin. When his head popped out of the water, I whooped. "That was a good one."

"Thanks," he said, treading water. "Want to see another one?"

I gave him the thumbs-up as Teagan came out from the kitchen, looking sexy in a bikini top paired with cutoff jean shorts. I liked it when she got her country on. "Hey," she said.

I smiled and held out the flowers. "These are for you."

"Thank you." She didn't make eye contact. Not a good sign.

"The woman in the photograph wasn't Hope." I blurted it out like an idiot. Moonstone *had* cast a spell on me.

She turned toward me. "She's not?"

"I would've told you something like that. The rag had it wrong."

"Who was it, then?" She lifted her gaze to meet my eyes. What I saw there surprised me. Not distrust but jealousy. Teagan Lanigan was jealous. Go figure. *And thank you, God,* I said silently.

"A girl name Lucy. I don't even remember her last name."

"Was it a relationship?"

"Not at all. More like a weekend fling."

"So not really even dating?" Teagan asked.

"Heck, no." I clutched the bag of groceries against my chest. "Blondes aren't my type anyway."

"They must have been at one time."

"I'm more of a redhead man myself."

"I'm sorry I doubted you. I immediately went to the bad

place." Her glance flickered toward Chris, who was climbing the ladder to the slide. "The stakes are high here."

"I know, baby. They are for me too."

She held out her arms. "Give me the bag."

"No, thank you. Show me where to put it."

She gestured for me to follow her into the kitchen. "Put it there," she said, pointing to the island.

I set it where she asked, then reached in for the chicken. "I brought some apples. All different kinds. I thought it would be fun to have a taste test. The three of us, that is." I set the individual bags on the counter. I'd labeled them with the type of apple so I wouldn't forget.

She stared at the apples as if they were something she'd never seen before.

"If it's a stupid idea, that's fine," I said. "My mama did it once with sodas but I didn't think you'd like that because of the sugar."

Her mouth turned up in a slight smile. "It's great. Chris will love the idea."

I breathed a sigh of relief. I'd thought for a moment I'd flubbed up again. Truth is, I didn't know anything about kids, other than I used to be one. I was hoping that would pull me through.

"What made you think of it?" she asked.

"I thought it would be a thing to do, you know, to get to know each other. I'll label them by numbers, that way you guys won't know which is which until you've voted on your favorite."

"Very wholesome of you," she said.

"I'm a mama's boy, what can I say?" I took her hands. "I can remember what it was like to be six and to worship my mama. I'll do my very best." I settled onto one of the stools at the island and pulled her between my legs. She placed her hands on my bare thighs, which distracted me for a split second from my mission. "I wish Mama had met someone, but she always put me first and was too afraid to risk harm to me if she chose poorly. I'm not a poor choice. I know you don't see that yet, but give me a chance to prove it to you."

She nodded, but the wary look in her eyes hadn't gone away. Not yet, I thought. I just needed to keep chipping away at her shell.

"I'm ready for a swim," I said.

"Yeah, me too. But I have an idea. I want to take you and Chris down to our old swimming hole. The water should be warm enough by this time in the summer."

"Lead the way." The old swimming hole? Now this was progress.

TEAGAN

D ust trailed behind Wyatt's truck as we bounced down the dirt road. Chris sat between us chattering away to Wyatt about the elk, who were nowhere to be seen today but were often spotted in our meadows. The temperatures were pushing ninety, so they were probably down by their watering hole staying cool and hydrated.

"When Aunt Charlotte first came here, she got stuck in her car because the elk wouldn't move," Chris said. "Uncle Ardan had to come rescue her. That's when they fell in love."

"Is that so?" Wyatt looked over Chris's head to twinkle his eyes at me.

Damn, this man was so sexy. He'd never looked better than right now, wearing swim trunks that hung low on his waist and a faded blue T-shirt. Other than when we were in bed, I'd never seen him without his boots. Today, he wore flip-flops and damn if he didn't pull those off, too. He'd gotten his hair cut in town and looked a hundred times better than he had when he first arrived.

The relief I'd felt after his explanation about the photograph had made me almost giddy. I'd also felt stupid and petty. Why had I believed something bad about him so easily? The woman wasn't Hope, even if it was some girl he'd had a fling with. But it was ten years ago, I reminded myself. He didn't know me then. I'd certainly had enough meaningless flings of my own that judging him would be hypocritical. He was doing all he could to gain my trust.

Yet there was another part of me that remembered he'd been through a trauma. Were his feelings from that, or were they real? Was I a crutch he leaned on for now but once he felt better would toss aside?

"Are you going to stay for my birthday?" Chris asked.

"When's that?" Wyatt asked.

"July twenty-fourth," Chris said.

"Wait a minute, are you kidding me?" Wyatt smacked the steering wheel with one hand.

Chris shook his head and laughed as if Wyatt had said the funniest thing he'd ever heard. "No, it's my real birthday."

"That's my birthday too," Wyatt said.

"No way." Chris bounced up and down. "Mom, did you hear that?"

"I did." How had I not known he shared a birthday with Chris?

"That's a real knee-slapper," Wyatt said.

"What's that?" Chris asked.

"It means something's funny." Wyatt smacked his own knee. "Like so funny you have to slap your knee to keep from....well, now that I say it, I'm not actually sure what would happen if you didn't slap your knee."

"Maybe you'd explode from laughing so hard," Chris said. "One time at school me and my best friend started laughing in class and we couldn't stop. We got in big trouble. Had to stay in for part of recess."

"That's the worst," Wyatt said. "When you should stop laughing and you can't."

"Totally. I'm going to be seven. How about you?" Chris stared up at him with a look of delight and adoration.

"I'm going to be thirty-eight." Wyatt grinned at me.

"Wow, that's old," Chris said.

"Yes, it is." Wyatt released one of his belly laughs.

"Turn left up here," I said, pointing to the T in the road. "It's just a little farther."

Wyatt slowed and steered left onto another dirt driveway.

"If you'd gone right, that would be Ardan and Charlotte's place," I said. "Ciaran and Kevan's homes are farther down the main road a half mile."

We traveled in silence for a few minutes until we reached the end of the road. "This is it," I said.

Over the years, the parking near our favorite swimming hole had been flattened by our truck. Not surprising. For fifty years, my family had been coming here to swim. I loved it as much as I had as a child.

I hopped out of the truck and turned back to get Chris. He, however, was already crawling over the seat after Wyatt. My stomach clenched. Was I doing the right thing by my boy? I shook my head, shoving the thoughts aside. Today would be a good day. *Don't ruin it with worrying.*

Leaves in the row of aspens that grew tall and slender along the creek rustled in welcome. The air was dry and hot under the bright sun. I put on both my straw hat and my sunglasses.

Ardan had a smaller swimming spot within walking distance of his house, but I preferred this one. The creek widened into a natural deep pool here, still and safe.

Wyatt grabbed the backpack with drinks and snacks and handed it to me. "I'll get the chairs." He gave me one of his easy smiles before leaning close to steal a kiss. "It's pretty cool to see you in your natural habitat."

I didn't know what to say, embarrassed. He was right about one thing. This spot on the creek was the place of my heart.

Every memory here was a good one. Most of them were of my brothers and me on lazy summer afternoons, swimming, diving for rocks, teasing a crawdad with sticks just to watch it scuttle under a rock. Ciaran had had a fascination with lizards and snakes. He'd pick them up in his bare hands and talk to them as though they were his babies.

Chris had already run ahead. The path, like the place we parked, was packed down from years of running feet.

We strolled toward the water. I breathed in the familiar smell of minerals from water that had washed over rocks and dried in the sun in combination with evergreen trees, wildflowers, and dried grass. This was the scent of the creek. The smells of my childhood.

Dragonflies and bees flew from flower to flower that grew on either side of the path. This time of year, the yellow grasses swayed peacefully in the soft breeze, resigned to their fate. They'd had their spring, green and fresh with droplets of dew and rain.

I loved every season here, but summer was my favorite. Despite my fair Irish skin, I loved the feel of the sunshine as if it were life itself. Thankfully, my vain mother had insisted on sunscreen and hats for me or I'd be shriveled by now. Even with sunscreen, my freckles popped like sprinkles of cinnamon on vanilla ice cream.

We passed through a row of aspens to a sandy area. Wyatt let out a gasp of appreciation when he caught sight of the green pool. "It's the same color as your eyes."

I nudged his ribs with my elbow. "Not really." Still, I flushed with pleasure. My father had always said my eyes were the color of the creek as if Idaho had birthed me. Mother had always laughed and reminded him of her eighteen-hour labor.

On either side of the deep pool, shallow rapids stole the water to make the music of the creek. I closed my eyes and leaned my cheek against Wyatt's shoulder. "Can you hear it?" I asked.

"You mean the water over the rocks?"

"Yes. Isn't it beautiful?"

He didn't answer, but it wasn't necessary. The softening of his shoulders told me he agreed. A bird chimed in, as if to remind us that they, too, made music.

Chris pulled his shirt and sandals off and jumped into the water. He splashed with his hands and shouted for us to hurry. "It's not cold, Mom, I promise."

"Is he all right swimming alone?" Wyatt's brow crinkled.

"He's been able to swim since he was three," I said. "He took to it like my brother Ardan. Anyway, the water's calm here. But we'll keep an eye on him." I motioned toward the shade of an oak. "We usually sit there."

Wyatt took the beach chairs from their bags and unfolded them, then set them next to each other in the shade. I spread the blanket near them and set the backpack in one corner. Sweat dribbled down my lower back and stuck to my shirt. I shimmied out of my jean shorts and tank top.

He shook his head as his gaze swept over me from head to toe. "Good Lord, girl. You make it hard for a man to breathe."

He made me hotter than the summer sun. If we'd been alone, I would have made good use of that blanket. I looked longingly at the water. "You want to go in?"

"I'm afraid of this cold water," he said, teasing. "In the South, the water's warm and brown."

"You'll be surprised. The water warms here in this pool because it doesn't travel very fast."

He pulled his shirt over his head and tossed it on a chair. "Last one in's a rotten egg."

I snatched my hat from my head and lobbed it toward the other chair. My aim was off. The traitorous thing landed on his shirt, like long-lost lovers. "You're on."

I raced him to the water, yelping as the hot sand burned my feet. We plunged into the water at the same time.

I dived in headfirst. The cold water immediately cooled my hot skin. I surfaced, wiping the water from my eyes as I found the sandy bottom with my feet. Wyatt had not yet appeared. I turned to look for him, frightened. Had he hit his head on a rock? I made a full turn.

I screamed as he grabbed my legs and lifted me into the air.

I smacked his shoulders, laughing. "You scared me, you jerk."

He had his arms wrapped around my bottom. "Kiss me and I'll let you down."

"Not in front of Chris," I said, speaking through clenched teeth.

"It's okay, Mom. You can kiss. I'll just look the other way so I'm not grossed out."

Wyatt chuckled as he set me down. "You heard the kid."

I smacked him again but let him give me a quick kiss. "You don't play by the rules."

"That's the secret to my success." He smoothed back the fine hairs plastered to my forehead and chin with his fingers.

"Wyatt, Wyatt, watch me," Chris shouted from the shallow edge of the creek. "I can stand on my hands."

"I'm watching," Wyatt said.

Chris dived into the water. Seconds later his feet appeared, wriggling hello. A bee hovered near his big toe, seemingly curious about the creature that stuck up out of the water. I expected the pretty insect to take a rest on his feet, but Chris did a backflip and disappeared for a moment before his head popped up. "Did you see? Did you see?"

"You looked great," Wyatt said.

We swam around for a few more minutes until I got cold and headed toward the blanket and chairs, where I plopped down and reached for the backpack. I'd stuffed turkey-and-cheese sandwiches plus drinks inside the insulated backpack. I wasn't sure about the boys, but I was ravenous.

For now, Wyatt was teaching Chris how to skip rocks. I ate my sandwich and watched them. Chris's first attempt was more of a toss and plop than a skip.

"It's all in the wrist," Wyatt said. "See here, how I turn it toward the ground." He flicked his hand, and the flat rock skipped across the creek seven times like a flying saucer unsure whether to land.

By the sixth try, Chris managed to get two skips and the next time three. "I did it. Mom, did you see that?"

"Way to go, honey."

After a few more, they dived back in the water and splashed each other, giggling as if they were both six going on seven.

As a single mother, I'd considered myself lucky to have my brothers. They'd always been willing to spend time with Chris, especially since I'd returned to Idaho. He adored his uncles, but especially Ciaran. They shared a similar sensibility. Both loved to be outdoors playing more than anything else. Whatever they were doing, it always seemed to be like a party. People were drawn to them. At school, Chris was popular with everyone. The kids wanted him at their table at lunch. Girls fought over him for attention. Like my brother, he seemed oblivious to it, gliding through life happy and carefree and always looking for fun.

He was nothing like me.

I was like my mother. Intense and driven. Never satisfied.

Looking at him with Wyatt, though, made my heart ache. He knew his uncles were his uncles. They would never be his father. Kevan and Ciaran had children of their own. It was only a matter of minutes before Charlotte was pregnant. Seeing him with Wyatt, I understood for the first time how desperately he wanted a father. The need was practically coming out of his pores.

A tinge of guilt bothered me, like a mosquito you can hear but you can't find. Had I been wrong to assume Chris was better off with just me? I'd told myself a thousand times that his uncles were all the father figures he needed. Plus he had his aunties, who showered him with affection. Charlotte and Blythe were always there for him with hugs and snuggles on the couch. Bliss was a great role model, teaching him that loving a strong woman was the way to a happy life. His big cousins treated him like the little prince, especially since he was the only boy in that generation. The kid was beloved by the entire family. He would never doubt that.

But this. This was different. Having a dad of his very own was what every little boy deserved. Could Wyatt be that?

"Come eat," I said. "I have sandwiches."

They turned at once, with the same grin on their tanned faces.

And the same birthday. That was weird.

I put all that aside so I could get them to eat and hydrate. Chris sank onto the blanket and took a sandwich from my outstretched hand. Wyatt grabbed his own before sitting next to me in the other chair. His muscular legs stretched out in front of him as he settled into the chair as if he did this every day.

I gave them both juice boxes. "Drink these. It's hot and you need to stay hydrated."

"Awesome." Wyatt tore the straw from the carton and plunged it into the sealed hole on top. "Apple juice is my favorite." He sucked through the straw from one corner of his mouth.

"This is the best day ever, Mom." Chris mimicked the way Wyatt drank from the straw. I'd never seen him do that before.

Chris took a break from drinking and grinned at Wyatt. "She only lets me have juice once a week."

"She's wise," Wyatt said. "Water's much better for you than all this sugar."

"But sugar's so good." Chris resumed his sucking motion.

"Eat your sandwich," I said, sounding gruff to hide my emotion. "Not just juice."

Chris set aside his drink and picked up the sandwich and took a bite. While he ate, he wandered down to the creek's bank to examine a water bug dancing along the shore.

"He's perfect," Wyatt said quietly. "Right?"

"I'd have to agree. He's the best of my creations."

He grabbed a second sandwich and resumed eating. The dark smudges under his eyes had disappeared since he'd been here. His skin had tanned quickly under our Idaho sun. My land was already working its magic on him.

After he finished his sandwich, he got up from the chair and lay on his back with his head resting on his folded-up T-shirt. He perched his cowboy hat over his face and crossed his arms over his chest. "Just resting for a minute, Pretty Girl."

I smiled to myself. A nap after a swim in the creek was a long family tradition. Whether I cared to admit it or not, he fit in here. With my family. With Chris. With me.

I reached into the backpack and pulled out a copy of *Vogue* with the actress Lisa Perry on the cover. She was gorgeous and glamorous, with alabaster skin and sapphire-blue eyes. They had her dressed in a low-cut silk dress that matched her eyes. Her white-blond hair and understated makeup gave her an ethereal look. The headline read: Lisa Perry. Reclaiming Her Life after Unthinkable Tragedy.

I opened the magazine and began to read. About a paragraph in, my stomach dropped. Lisa Perry had been in the audience on the day of the shooting. A woman standing next to her had died as Ms. Perry tried to stop her bleeding.

The piece was a flattering profile of Ms. Perry as a kind, thoughtful humanitarian who'd been deeply affected by the shooting. She'd grown up in Iowa with her twin brother and their parents. Witnessing the shooting had sent her into a spiral of anxiety triggered by loud noises. She was currently trying to work through the trauma with a therapist. I was surprised by her candor.

That day had such far-reaching repercussions. No one there would ever be the same. Nor would the families who'd lost loved ones. What were we supposed to make of this? The church had told us everything happens for a reason, but I didn't buy it. How could we find any meaning in a tragedy like this?

I set the magazine aside and watched my son trail a stick in the water as he walked up and down the creek bed. His brown hair had dried and glistened under the sun. This boy had been my heart from the moment he was born. I hadn't thought there would ever be a man I trusted enough to let into our life. My gaze flickered to Wyatt, still sprawled out on the blanket. He was different than he'd been last year. Maybe I was, too. Was it true that timing was everything? Or was it just that hardships changed our hearts, made us understand how love was truly the only aspect of life that mattered?

Love? Did I love Wyatt? Had I always loved him?

I shooed away a fruit fly and turned to watch my son. Was my mother right? Had the good Lord made someone just for me?

13

WYATT

After supper that evening, Chris and I each took a modest dish of ice cream out to the patio. Teagan remained in the kitchen, cleaning up our dinner. She'd insisted on cleaning since I'd grilled the chicken, made Mama's potato salad, and steamed green beans. I hadn't cooked much in the last few years, usually choosing the takeout option. When alone, cooking a meal always seemed silly and a little pathetic. But growing up, as soon as I was old enough, I'd taken over cooking dinner for Mama and me. She was always exhausted after a ten-hour shift at the diner. The last thing she wanted in the evenings was anything to do with food. Around age nine, I'd asked her if I could make spaghetti one night. After that, I started going through her recipe box, making all the old family dishes. My grandmother had written them on index cards in old-fashioned cursive. At first, the dinners weren't great. Who knew, for example, that spaghetti noodles had to be stirred or they'd stick together? My grandmother hadn't thought to write down those kinds of specifics. In her day, maybe everyone knew these things, but a nine-year-old boy did not. Mama, bless her heart, never complained. She said, after a bite of the stuck-together spaghetti, how interesting it was that I'd made them that way. "Most people like them the other way, but I think this way is very innovative. You're always doing things just a little different." She'd beamed at me then, as if I were the most clever boy in the world.

Regardless of my first disastrous meals, cooking had become my thing. Even in high school when I was busy with sports or music after school, I'd come home to put a meal on for her. She'd change out of her uniform and take a quick shower while I finished dinner. Then she'd sit on the couch and I'd turn on the soaps I'd recorded for her during the day. I'd put our plates on TV trays and we'd watch the two soaps back-to-back. I knew the stories of those characters as well as she did. Not that I'd ever have admitted it to my buddies.

After we finished our recordings, we'd turn on a sitcom or whatever else was on and watch until it was time for bed. Unless I hadn't finished my homework, in which case, I went to the kitchen table and studied until I was done. She didn't ask for much, but she insisted I do well in school. Even if I ended up making it with my music, she would say, there's no excuse not to take advantage of school if you could.

This might sound like a bleak existence to those who lived in fancy houses and had fathers, not just a worn-out mama. But to us it was normal. We were as happy as the next folks. Maybe more so, because there was never a doubt how much we loved each other.

When I was a junior in high school, a local bar hired me to play music on Friday and Saturday nights. That's where I really earned my chops. I learned all the current country hits and sang them as best I could to sound like the originals. I suppose most start out that way, imitating their heroes until they find their own unique style and voice.

Mama had been so thrilled when everyone in town started referring to me as the "boy who sings." I was equally thrilled to be paid twenty whole dollars a night. For a year, I'd had my heart set on buying Mama a new mattress. The one she had was lumpy and too soft. She didn't complain, but I could see her lower back troubled her by the way she'd press her hands into the area above her tailbone.

Spending time with Teagan and Chris had brought back so many memories of Mama and me. We'd been close, like these two.

"Wyatt," Chris asked, pulling me from my thoughts.

"Yep?"

"What's your favorite ice cream?"

"Cookie dough." Currently, we were eating chocolate chip, which I liked a lot, but cookie dough was what I'd have chosen. "What about you?"

"Any kind except coffee." He made a face as if he were gagging. "My aunt Charlotte likes that kind but I think it's gross."

"I'd have to agree with you on that. Coffee should be hot and had in the morning."

"Mom loves coffee." He scooped the last of the ice cream from his bowl and brought the spoon to his mouth.

"I do too," I said.

"I don't understand why."

"You will, later, when you're all grown."

Chris didn't answer, but a slight raise of his eyebrow told me he was skeptical of this prediction.

Having finished, I set my bowl aside. The sun hovered just above Blue Mountain. This evening, there were no bright colors to paint the cloudless sky as the sun crept behind the mountains.

"Wyatt, did you have a dad?" Chris asked.

Startled by the question, I looked over at him. His brown eyes watched me with such earnestness I almost teared up. This kid was enough to break my heart. "No, I didn't. It was just Mama and me."

"Like us." He rested his chin in the palm of one hand and continued to peer at me. He hadn't yet learned to avoid eye contact, I thought.

"Yep, like you and your mom."

"Did you ever know where he was?"

"My dad, you mean?"

"Yeah. 'Cause I don't know anything about mine. Mom doesn't talk about him."

"I never knew anything much about mine, either," I said. "Mama was all I needed anyway."

"Did your Mama ever have a boyfriend?"

"Nope, not that I knew of."

"Mom never had one either." His forehead wrinkled. "Are you her boyfriend?"

I turned my gaze toward the mountains. A little boy wouldn't understand. "It's complicated between us." Or his mother was complicated and I wasn't, and perhaps that was the problem. A hummingbird flew close and stopped at the sugar feeder to take a drink. Only for a moment, one so quick that after she was gone I questioned whether I'd seen her. Maybe the best way to explain all of it to Chris was to describe his mother like a hummingbird. Breathtakingly beautiful, elusive, easily frightened away.

"Wyatt? Are you?" Chris asked again, this time with more urgency.

"Let me put it to you this way. I'd like to be."

"What's stopping you?" Chris asked.

"It's up to her to decide if she wants me. And remember this, okay? A woman's the one who decides if they want to be your girlfriend. You never force a girl to do what you want. Do you understand?"

"Sure, yeah. There's this girl at school I like but I'm not allowed to just go up and kiss her even if I wanted to."

"That's right." If only some adult men understood this a little better. "You treat women and girls with respect."

"I will." He rested both elbows on the table and yawned.

I fought one off myself and put a hand on top of his head. Teagan had asked him to take a shower when we returned from swimming. Even a foot away, I could smell the pleasant scent of his shampoo. "You ready for bed?"

"I never am, but I have to go to bed at eight thirty anyway. Mom lets me read for a few minutes, but lights-out at nine."

I glanced at my watch. Five more minutes until his bedtime. "Getting about that time."

"Will you tuck me in?" Chris asked.

"If it's okay with your mom."

"She'll want to kiss me on the forehead. She always does. But I don't think she'd mind if you were there too."

Teagan came out to the patio carrying a dish towel. "Chris, time to brush your teeth and get into bed."

"Okay, Mom." Chris hopped up from his chair.

"Take the bowls with you to the kitchen," Teagan said. "Then head upstairs to brush your teeth. I'll be right up to tuck you in."

Chris shot me a conspiratorial look before he gathered the bowls, stacking them one on top of the other and trudging into the kitchen. I stood and tucked the chairs under the table.

"That's a tired boy. We did a good job wearing him out." Teagan faced the setting sun, which cast an orange glow over the patio. "This was a good day."

"Like Chris said—the best day ever." I came to stand next to her.

"What were you two talking about out here?'

"He asked if I could help tuck him in. I told him it was up to you."

"He did? Oh, well, I guess that's okay. I mean, if you want to." She stuffed her hands into the pockets of her shorts.

"I would, sure." I turned toward the sun and shut my eyes for a second, soaking in the last light of the day. "He asked if I was your boyfriend."

"What did you say?"

Her terse tone chilled me. I opened my eyes. "I said I wanted to be, but it was up to you."

She folded her arms over chest. "Why'd you do that?"

My stomach flipped nervously. I'd said the wrong thing. "Because it's true."

"So now I'm the bad guy if I send you away?" Cold and hostile, just like that. A complicated woman.

I took in a deep breath and held it for a moment, hoping the correct thing to say would pop into my head. "I'm sorry. I thought it was best to tell him the truth."

"I can't have you setting him up for heartbreak."

I nodded, figuring it was best to keep my big trap shut.

"What happens when you get spooked or restless and take off on us?"

"What happens if you never give me a chance to prove that I won't?" I asked.

Her mouth opened, then shut. She unfolded her arms from her chest and glared at me.

"Tell me something," I said. "Do you have any feelings for me? Or am I wasting my time and setting both Chris and myself up for heartbreak?" I knew I was pushing too hard. At any moment, she would let me have it, but I had to ask her these questions. At some point, she had to make a decision. Either let me in or tell me to go.

"I like having you here," she said. "What more can I say?"

I let out a dry laugh and shook my head. "You could say a lot more."

"This isn't just you and me. There's a very sweet little boy upstairs brushing his teeth who wants his new hero to tuck him into bed."

I spoke as softly and slowly as I could, given that I wanted to pick her up and toss her on my back and take her upstairs to show her exactly what I felt about her. "I'm going to explain something to you."

"Mansplain, you mean?"

My temper flared, but I pushed it down. Mama always told me you could never take back words said in anger, even if you didn't mean them. "I meant that I'm going to explain something to you about me."

"Fine."

"I was that sweet little boy once upon a time. It was Mama and me against the world. I remember exactly what it was like to be him. I was the kid who learned to cook so that she wouldn't have to come home and do it. Do you think for one second that I would hurt your boy?

"I came here when I was broken. You were who I wanted to be with during the lowest point of my life. You, Teagan. And I knew exactly what was waiting for me here. You and your son. Yeah, I get it. Your job is to protect him. But it's not me who you need to protect him from. I want a relationship. I want a family. This is on you now. You have to choose. All I want is to be the best thing that ever happened to you and Chris."

Through the entirety of my speech, she hadn't moved. If my pleas had gotten to her, not an ounce of it showed on her face. The woman could remain stoic like no one I'd ever met. If she hadn't become a costume designer, she could have worked as a spy. They'd never be able to get anything out of her.

"Tell me to go, Teagan. Or tell me to stay. I'm not playing here." My stomach hurt. Actually, all of me hurt. I wanted to pull her into my arms and kiss her and tell her how much I loved her. But maybe I was wrong. Maybe she didn't feel anything but a physical attraction.

"You can't show up out of the blue and expect me to change my entire life." She spoke through gritted teeth that didn't hide the tremor in her voice. I *had* gotten to her. Finally. "You're going too fast for me."

I deflated, all intensity dissipating. She was right. Simply because I knew what I wanted didn't mean she would change her whole life because I showed up with no warning. "That's fair. I'm way ahead of you." Perhaps I'd always been. From the first night we were together, I'd felt a tugging at my heart. Right away I'd had a sense that this was the woman I wanted and needed. The only difference between now and then? Before, I was willing to let her go. My pride was bigger than my love.

"Teagan," I said softly. "You invited me to spend the day with you guys. If you don't want me around Chris, then why did you do that? Was it a test?"

"I don't know. Maybe." She let her arms fall to her sides.

"Tell me what to do here. Whatever you want, I'll do."

"I didn't ask you to come here." A muscle in her cheek twitched.

"I know." I clenched my stomach, waiting for the blow.

Instead, she ducked her chin and rested her forehead on my chest. "I'm confused. And scared." The warmth of her breath came through my thin T-shirt.

Instinctively, I put my arms around her.

"I'm sorry I'm such a bitch," she said.

"You're not. I threw too much at you all at once. It's this damn thing that happened. I'm suddenly unwilling to leave anything unsaid. I'll go now and give you some peace. Tell Chris I had to leave before I could say good night." My big dumb heart. I wanted to cry like a baby.

She wrapped her arms around my neck. "Don't go. I don't want you to go. I'm not sure I ever want you to go, and I don't know what to do about it. Falling in love with a rock star is How to Get Your Heart Broken 101."

She had feelings for me. She'd admitted them to me. I wanted to shout it out to Blue Mountain—*she just might love me.* I held her tighter and rested my chin on the top of her head. "I'm not a rock star. This here is a country boy. We care about our trucks, our dogs, and our families. This one cares about you and Chris."

She raised her gaze to mine. Her shoulders rose and fell as she took in a deep breath. "I've never thought much about what my life was missing. Things have been fine. Chris and my family have been enough. But now...now you came here and you're so nice to my boy and you took a nap by the creek and made potato salad and I'm about to fall into a hole I can't get out of. I'll die down there, looking up at the light and wishing someone would pull me out."

"Why would you be in a hole?" I asked, stifling a laugh.

"I don't know. You're the songwriter, not me. I was trying to think of a metaphor."

"I'm not a hole. I'm not going to leave you in a hole. Unless I'm in there with you." I cupped her face in my hands. "What do you want?"

"Chris has fallen hard for you." There was a slight tremor in her voice.

"What about you?" I traced my finger down to the hollow of her throat, then tapped just above her breast. "What's in your heart?"

"I plead the Fifth."

"I'll just keep praying to the good Lord that someday you'll love me."

"Maybe I do, but I can't say it," she said softly. "The words don't just flow out of my mouth like they do yours."

"That's good enough for now."

Her phone buzzed from inside her shorts pocket and startled us both. She drew it out and looked at the screen. "Crap. It's Cryer."

"Answer it." My stomach hollowed. The lyrics from "Bad Moon Rising" played in my head.

"Yes, hello." Teagan flinched. She grabbed hold of my forearm. "When?" She nodded. "Okay, yes, I will. All right. Thank you."

"What is it?" I asked.

"There's been another murder. Ryan Chambers was found dead in his home."

"What? How?"

"A gunshot wound." She sagged against me. "What's happening, Wyatt? Do you think we're in danger? What about Chris?"

I wrapped her in my tight embrace. "It's all right. You're safe here with me." I may have sounded calm on the surface. However, inside I was reeling. Was the murderer targeting certain people? Why did he kill again? Or she? Were we in danger?

"I want you to stay here at the house," Teagan said. "Move your stuff from the inn. I don't want to be alone."

"Whatever you want." Thank God she'd asked, because there was no way in hell I was letting her or Chris stay alone. What about the gate? Who had the code? "Did you change the code on the gate?"

"Yes. Only the detective has it now."

"Okay, good." I sighed with relief. "I don't know how I didn't think about it until now." If I was going to look after these two, I had to step up my game. There was a killer on the loose.

14

TEAGAN

The next morning, I woke early and crept out of bed as quietly as I could so as not to wake Wyatt. After tucking Chris in the night before, he'd gone into town to collect his things and check out of the inn. We'd been too tired to unpack, so his suitcase was open on the floor. He'd packed light from what I could tell. Men. If I'd come across the country, I would have had a suitcase for just my shoes.

Downstairs, I made coffee. While I waited, I flipped through the latest *Vanity Fair* but couldn't get interested in any of the articles. I had murder on my mind. And love, too.

When the coffee had finished, I poured a cup and added cream. I wandered into the living room and curled up on one end of the couch. Even during summer, Idaho mornings were crisp and cool. I covered my bare legs with a blanket and looked out to Blue Mountain. This time of morning and during twilight, the old girl did indeed look blue.

A friend had once told me I had a mind more like a man because I was only able to focus on one thing at a time. Today, however, I had two things to ponder. Why had another murder occurred? What did the two victims have in common? Were they connected? They had to be. It was too much of a coincidence that two of the people we'd hired for the party had been murdered only days apart.

The detective had said Ryan Chambers was found dead in his one-room apartment in Hailey. I wasn't sure but I thought Jodi had mentioned she'd never met him before the night of the party. His references were good, she'd said, and there weren't many choices. I'd agreed to him, not worried about the quality of his skills. It was really only a family birthday party. I didn't think twice about him.

I didn't know Jodi well. As much as I hated to admit it, I didn't know her well enough to decide if she was capable of murder. Was she involved in something illegal and Paula and Ryan had discovered her secret? Had she killed them to keep them from talking?

What kind of secret was worth killing over?

My mind skipped to Wyatt. Our conversation the night before echoed through my mind.

I'd admitted my feelings to him and to myself. Now I had to live with the consequences.

I sipped my coffee and let myself daydream for a moment. If Wyatt wanted to marry me, would I say yes? For years my mantra, to anyone who would listen, had been that I had no use for a man other than sex. I didn't need a life partner. I had Chris, my family and an occasional fling. It kept everything nice and simple and safe. Yes, that was the key word. Safe. No more broken heart for me.

Now, however, everything was different. I had cracked open the door to my heart. No, not just a crack but as wide open as it would go. The man could do things to me that no one had ever done before. Not even Chris's dad, whom I'd been utterly in love with, had ignited the kind of passion Wyatt evoked.

Was it possible I loved him? This man I'd dismissed as a frivolous affair? That was before I'd seen him in this place I loved so much. He seemed to belong here. A country boy in *my* country. Holy hell. I was in love with him.

But love and passion were not the same thing as living with a person. Could I imagine him as a permanent part of our lives? What kind of partner would I be long term? I'd never had to negotiate with anyone. What would it be like to have to work through issues of parenting, work schedules, chores? As a single mother, I decided what I wanted for Chris, how to discipline him, where he went to school. What happened when it wasn't just up to me? Was I a family type of woman? I mean, sure, my brothers and their wives and even my mother were the reasons I moved back here. I wanted that for Chris and for myself. But a man? A husband? That was a whole different type of commitment. Did I even have it in me?

I'd brought my phone down with me and now it buzzed from the table. I picked it up, expecting a call from one of my family. Moonstone had probably spilled the details of my liaison and someone wanted more details. To my surprise, it wasn't a family member. The name that came up was Andi Quinn, the assistant to film director Ned Broadstone. A few years back, I'd worked on the design team for one of his films. I'd learned a lot from the head designer, Marsha Phillips. She'd shown me how to lead a team and negotiate the tricky egos of artistic people, including crew, cast, and director. She'd believed in my talent and leadership enough that she'd then recommended me to another director, which led to my first job as a head designer. When I told her I was taking an extended sabbatical to be with my son, she'd shaken her head sadly and said it was such a waste of talent. "Women with children," she'd said. "We can't have it all, even after we've fought for the right to sit at the table all this time. Still, we must choose, it seems."

Single mothers in particular had to choose. But I'd made my peace. Chris came first. "I'll be back someday," I'd said to her.

Was that true? I didn't know. All I knew was that I would only get one chance with Chris. He would be gone and on his own before I knew it. My career could wait. If there was a career to go back to, that is. After more than ten years off, would anyone even remember me? The promising designer who chose family over career?

I answered the phone. "Hello, this is Teagan."

"Teagan, I don't know if you remember me, but this is Andi Quinn, Ned Broadstone's assistant."

"Yes, yes, of course I remember you." Andi was one of my favorite people to work with. Funny, down-to-earth, and extremely competent. "What's going on?"

"I'm calling to see if you'd take a meeting with Ned about heading up the design team for his newest project."

My stomach fluttered. Ned Broadstone was such a talent.

"Me? Really?" I asked, squeaking like a child.

"Yes, he's a big fan, as you know. This is a historical piece. Right in your sweet spot."

"What's the film?" I asked. My favorite costuming jobs were historical projects. I could put my love of fashion history and knowledge to their best use on films like that. They usually tended to have large budgets as well, making it that much more fun.

"It's set in the Gilded Age in New York City. Murder and socialites. That kind of thing."

"Sounds fun." I hesitated. Did they know I'd walked away from the film Wyatt had starred in? I was sure they did. Hollywood gossip traveled fast.

"He understands you're semiretired," Andi said. "But he's hoping you'll reconsider."

"I don't know. My little boy goes back to school in the fall. Shooting in New York is impossible for me. And I can't really leave right now to fly to LA for a meeting."

"Ned thought you might feel that way. But listen, he's

spending the summer in Idaho. Working on the script and fly-fishing in Sun Valley. He said he'd meet you anywhere you want. Your house. His place. A restaurant. You know how he is. When he wants something, he doesn't hesitate to pull out all the stops to get it."

What harm could a meeting do? If he was in Idaho, why shouldn't I at least entertain the idea?

"As long as he knows it probably can't happen, then sure," I said.

"He understands your loyalty to your son," Andi said. "He's a softy that way."

We agreed on a restaurant in Hailey for lunch next week. I thanked her and hung up. By this time, my stomach was growling. I got up from my spot on the couch and went into the kitchen to make some toast and eggs. Knowing Chris, he'd be up in a few minutes. As my brothers had been growing up, he was always starving in the morning.

I was cracking eggs into a bowl when Wyatt came into the kitchen dressed in gym shorts and a workout shirt. His hair was uncombed, and he needed a shave. Maybe he shaved after his workout? These were all details of his life that I didn't yet know. *See*, I told myself. *You have no idea what you're getting yourself into.*

"Good morning, Pretty Girl." He came to stand behind me and wrapped his arms around me waist, then kissed my neck. I caught the scent of toothpaste on his breath.

"You want some breakfast?" I asked.

"Absolutely. And some coffee too. Afterward, I thought I'd get a workout in before it gets too hot." He pressed against me. "I like this outfit you have on."

"These are pajamas, not an outfit." I wore cotton shorts and a sweatshirt over my spaghetti-strap tank.

"Right. I should learn the proper names of clothes, shouldn't I? Now that I'm with an expert." He reached under the sweatshirt and caressed the curve of my waist with his wicked fingers. "Unless you have time for a quickie."

"Stop it." I giggled. If only Charlotte could see me this way. She'd never believe how her hard-boiled sister-in-law reacted to the touch of Wyatt Black. "Chris will be up any minute."

"I'll take a rain check." He nibbled on my ear.

"Don't be so sure of yourself." I smiled as he worked his fingers under my panties.

He jumped away from me when Chris arrived in the kitchen. "Good morning, buddy," Wyatt said.

Chris wore his favorite pajamas decorated with soccer balls and clutched his stuffed monkey, Mickey, to his chest. One side of his thick hair stood up like a wing in flight. "You're still here?" He rubbed his eyes and blinked as if he couldn't believe his luck.

"I sure am."

Chris tossed Mickey aside and ran to Wyatt and threw his arms around his legs.

Wyatt picked Chris up and set him on one of the island stools. "Are you ready for some grub?"

"Grub?" Chris's expression changed from happy to disgusted.

"He just means breakfast." I laughed as I opened a drawer and pulled out the whisk. "He's going to stay with us instead of at the inn from now on."

"Killer." Chris made a fist pump in the air. Where did he learn these things? Ciaran, most likely.

"Don't forget Mickey." Wyatt picked up Mickey from the counter and set him next to Chris on one of the stools as though he would be having breakfast, too. When Chris outgrew Mickey, I might cry.

Chris chattered away, asking questions one after the other. "Can we go swimming again today? What's for breakfast? What room did Wyatt sleep in? Can we get a dog?"

I dropped the whisk into the bowl of eggs. Dog? Where had

that come from? "That's a lot of questions, young man. Let's start with breakfast. We're having toast, eggs, and strawberries."

"I love toast," Chris said to Wyatt. "Do you?"

"Toast is one of life's best inventions. I like mine with butter and blackberry jam."

"I like mine with just butter," Chris said. "Mom says I'm a purist when it comes to toast."

Wyatt laughed. "Nothing wrong with keeping it simple, little man."

Chris beamed as he rested his chin in his hands and looked back and forth between Wyatt and me. The pure joy in his eyes made my chest ache. Wyatt was special. Any boy would want him for their father. Look at him, I thought. Bigger than life with his muscular frame and strong jawline. He was a man's man, yet humble and kind. So talented, too. Who wouldn't love him?

Not me.

"What can we do to help?" Wyatt asked.

"Mom lets me do the toast, right?" Chris hopped from the stool and headed toward the stainless steel toaster on the counter.

"Yes, the bread's in there." I pointed toward the pantry, as if Chris didn't know its location. Wyatt flustered me, especially when Chris was around. I took a plate from the cabinet and set it near the toaster.

"I got a call from Cryer just now," Wyatt said quietly. "He heard I checked out of the inn and wanted to make sure I hadn't left town. I told him I was here with you. He wants to come by later to ask us some more questions."

"Great," I said. "Like we know anything."

"I told him that." Wyatt shut up when Chris came out of the pantry with a loaf of wheat bread.

"There are some strawberries in the refrigerator," I said to Wyatt. "Do you mind getting them out?"

"Yes ma'am." Wyatt went around the island to the refrigerator and opened the doors. He stood in front of it for a moment, obviously searching.

"They're in the bottom drawer," I said.

"Found them." Wyatt held up the carton of strawberries with a triumphant flourish. "Do you want me to hull them?"

I nodded, distracted, as I used the whisk to further blend the whites and yolks. My mother often said I didn't mix them well enough. I poured the egg mixture into a hot frying pan and waited for a moment before using a spatula to stir them. The scent of toasted bread and strawberries filled the kitchen. By the time the eggs were done, both the boys were finished with their tasks. Chris had piled six pieces of toast onto a plate.

"Do you want to eat at the table?" Chris asked. "That's what families do. At Aunt Blythe's house and Aunt Bliss's houses, anyway. They all sit together and eat. Even for breakfast."

"I think eating together sounds like a fine idea," Wyatt said. "Where do you normally eat?"

Chris gestured toward the island. "Me and Mickey sit there. Mom usually stands up when she eats. At night, we watch TV and eat." I inwardly cringed. We mostly ate our meals at the island. Most of the time I didn't sit. Now that Chris had been exposed to my brothers' wives, he was getting all these ideas about how people should live. I couldn't keep up, frankly. I was a bad mom.

"Mama and I used to eat our dinner on trays in front of the television," Wyatt said. "I loved it."

"You did?" Chris's eyes narrowed. "How come?"

"It was a special time just for my mom and me." Wyatt went to the cabinet and pulled out three plates. "She worked so hard at the diner that she was always really tired and just wanted to watch her shows. That's what she called her soap operas." He set the plates at three spots at the table, then opened the silverware drawer and grabbed three forks and knives. How had he known where they were? For a moment, it seemed as if he'd always been here.

Chris carefully carried the toast to the table. I poured Wyatt a cup of coffee and joined the boys at the table.

My boys.

That phrase had come out of nowhere.

We sat and I was about to tell Chris to dig in when Wyatt asked, "Who wants to say grace?"

Chris looked over at me, clearly puzzled. We said grace whenever the whole family was together, but never when it was just the two of us.

"How about you do the honors," I said to Wyatt.

"I'd be happy to." Wyatt grinned at me before bowing his head. I gestured for Chris to do the same.

"Dear Lord, thank you for this food we're about to enjoy. Thank you for keeping us safe and for this beautiful house and land and for allowing us to be together on this fine morning. Amen."

"Amen," I said.

"Amen," Chris said.

They dug into their food while discussing the best way to butter toast. How much and should the crusts be included? Chris was in favor of crusts and both sides of the bread. Wyatt laughed and said toast was only meant to have one buttered side. "Otherwise, how would you eat it without getting your hands greasy?"

I smiled at the way he replaced the *s* sound with *z* in the word greasy. The longer he was here, the more of his roots showed. Maybe it was Idaho. Here, with the clear, dry air, it was impossible to be anything but yourself. That's why I wanted Chris here. What I wanted most for him was to be comfortable with himself. To enjoy his own company and be at peace.

"But think about how much more buttery every bite would be," Chris said.

139

"You've got a point there," Wyatt said. "But what about our tickers?"

"Tickers?"

Wyatt thumped his chest. "Our hearts, buddy. Your mom worries about that kind of thing."

"She's a health nut, like my aunts." Chris said this matter-of-factly. "Uncle Ciaran says they're a buzzkill."

"Chris," I said, chastising him. "When did you hear him say that?"

"Last family dinner," Chris said to me before turning back to Wyatt. "We have family dinner on Sundays. Do you want to come next time we have one?"

Wyatt shrugged as he looked over at me. "If it's all right with your mom. She's in charge."

I shrugged and glanced away, evasive. The question made me nervous. Bringing a man to dinner was a statement. "We'll see." Yesterday, I'd begged off to spend time alone with Wyatt and Chris. Plus, I hadn't wanted to spend the whole night talking about a dead girl and all the theories of what had happened. I loved my family, but all of us together overwhelmed me. Too many smart, opinionated people in the same room, all of whom were related, had a way of making my head swim. The Lanigans were better outside on horses or hiking, with our land as the buffer. Since the boys all married, however, Sunday dinners had become a thing. My sisters-in-law were obsessed with eating together as a family. Bliss and Blythe had been raised by a single mother, isolated in the country. They craved family life. Charlotte was an only child who loved the big messiness of our extended family, especially because we included her parents.

I, on the other hand, the youngest of five, craved solitude and quiet. When I'd learned to sew, I'd finally found an activity that I liked to do indoors. I could ignore the world when I was hunched over the sewing machine. Later, after design school, when I'd branched into pattern designs and costumes, I could spend hours working without realizing how long it had been since I'd taken a break. I loved the release of that creative zone when all time and place disappeared and it was only me and my creation. I didn't have to answer to anyone or figure out how to talk and engage, which exhausted me. I'd have loved to be like Bliss or Charlotte, able to talk to anyone. If I was correct in my assumption, I think they actually liked talking to other people. I was a loner. Different from the beginning, being the only girl after four boys.

Now the conversation had veered into jam. Wyatt listed all the different kinds of jam there were: strawberry, orange marmalade, blackberry, huckleberry, and a few others. By then, I was only half listening, enjoying the tone and cadence of the conversation without too much interest in the content. These two could entertain each other without any need for me.

"Mama made her own jam," Wyatt said.

"How?" Chris asked before taking a large bite from his toast.

"She put all the blackberries in this big pot and cooked them up like soup."

Chris giggled. "Jam soup?" He slapped his knee. "That's a knee-slapper, right, Wyatt?"

"Sure is."

"Do you think we could go fishing sometime?" Chris asked. "My best friend goes fishing with his dad all the time."

"I've never really fished before," Wyatt said. "But I'm game."

"Awesome. Mom, can we?"

"You'd have to get poles and supplies in town," I said. "But I don't see why not." A thought occurred to me. Without me along, they would have an opportunity to bond. "You know, it would probably be best if just the two of you went. I have a few things to take care of today." Curious to see how Wyatt would respond, I watched him covertly from under my lashes.

Wyatt grinned. "A boys' day. That sounds mighty fine."

"Yeah. A boys' day." Chris patted my shoulder. "Sorry, Mom."

"No problem. Just behave yourself for Wyatt, okay?"

"I will."

They spent the next few minutes deciding what kind of supplies they needed.

I remained quiet, taking in this sweet scene as the morning sun crept up over the side of the house and splashed light across the patio. This was how meals had been when I was a child, only there had been five of us kids, all talking at once, and my mother complaining that we should focus on our food, not on chattering away about nonsense. Did she really hate it as much as she said she did? All that noise and bickering and laughter? Now that I was a mother, I suspected she didn't.

A home isn't really a home without a family, I thought now. Chris and I had been a family of two, but was there room for Wyatt at our table? The house felt brighter and livelier with him here. Or was that me, not the house?

I felt a hand on my shoulder. The scent of cigar filled my nose. My father's cigar. I looked up, expecting him to be there, but he wasn't. Nothing but thin air.

Then I heard his voice in my head. *The time is now.*

For what? I asked silently.

To make a home.

WYATT

A little before eleven, Chris and I stopped first at the sporting goods store.

"What say we get some fishing poles?" I asked Chris.

His face lit up. "I'm ready."

"But listen, this is going to be the old-fashioned kind of fishing. Not fly-fishing like your uncle Ardan. I don't know how to do that." Where I was from, we stuck a worm on a hook and put our line in, then opened a beer. From what I'd observed, westerners were always making relaxing activities work. A walk was called a hike out here, making it seem way worse than it really was. "Like I said, I've never been fishing before."

"Is it because you didn't have a dad?" Chris asked.

"I guess so. I never really thought about it before."

We hopped out of the truck and headed into the store together. The place smelled like old wood, leather, and rubber boots.

We headed toward the back where fishing equipment hung on the wall. There was fancy stuff like wading boots and a display case of fly-making materials as well as old-fashioned rods and reels. I picked out a small pole for him and normal-sized for me. There was a kid-sized reel, so I grabbed it and an adult version for me. I gathered up hooks, a few flies, and a tackle box and headed to the counter.

The man at the register wore overalls and a plastic name tag that read "Bill." Rotund, red-cheeked, and quick with a smile, he appeared to be in his mid-fifties.

"Welcome to town," Bill said. "People treating you right?"

"Yes, sir," I said.

"We don't make a fuss if we can help it, Mr. Black." He squinted as he read the price tag on one of the rods. "But it's a real honor to meet you. Around here most everyone loves your music."

"Call me Wyatt." I'd known this type of man growing up back home. They were the first to come to the aid of their neighbor during a storm or make sure no kid at Christmas went without a toy.

"You guys going fishing today?" Bill asked Chris as he rung up my purchases on a cash register from the 1950s. I reckoned it had come with the building.

"Yes, sir," Chris said, imitating me. "A boys' day out. Like dads and sons do."

Chris stared up at me and damned if I couldn't read it in his eyes as sure as I knew the chords to my favorite country songs. This boy wanted to be mine. I swallowed a lump in my throat.

"Any advice for us?" I asked Bill.

"Sure, head up to the lake on Cutter's Road. They stock it every spring with trout. You'll need a net, though." He came out from behind the counter and grabbed a net from one of the shelves. "You're buying out the store. I best give you a discount."

"No, don't do that," I said. "I'm happy to support local businesses."

Chris had picked up a baseball glove. He ran a finger over the stitching.

Bill slipped back behind the register. He chuckled and spoke quietly, obviously aware of Chris overhearing. "Teagan Lanigan is quite a woman."

"Yes, sir."

"Wasn't a boy in town wasn't in love with her back in the day. My son was one of them."

"Is he still here?" I didn't need any local competition.

"Nah, he moved to Boise after college." Bill's chest swelled in obvious pride as he spoke about his son. "Got one of them computer programming degrees and makes more money in a year than I saw in ten. Met a woman there and married her. They come out for a few weeks in the summer. City folks now." He chuckled as he wrapped his thumbs around the straps of his overalls. "Listen to me, talking on about my son. The wife says I'll brag to whoever will listen. You plan on sticking around?"

"As long as she'll let me."

"Good." He nodded with a distinct look of approval in his eyes. "I'm not trying to sell you anything else, but you might consider buying a few baseball gloves and a ball." He gestured toward Chris, who now had his hand in the glove and pretended to pitch a ball. "And maybe a bat."

"You're right." I called out to Chris, "You want that glove?"

He lifted his shoulders in a shrug. "I don't have anyone to play with since all my friends live in Hailey."

I joined him by the row of gloves. "You and I could play. I used to play on my high school team."

"Do you have a glove?" Chris asked.

"I do back home, but I think it's about time for a new one. Then you and I can throw around a ball in the yard if you'd like."

"That'd be cool." He picked up the adult size. "I saw this one and thought it might fit you."

I hid a smile as I picked up a small wooden bat. "You're way ahead of me, kid. Let's get this too."

We took our gloves, ball, and bat up to the counter. "We'd like these too."

"You got it." Bill punched a few more numbers into the register.

"Can you tell me how to get to the lake?" I asked.

"Yeah, it's real easy to find. Turn right at the twenty-two-mile marker. Drive for about five minutes and you'll see a parking area where you can unload your stuff. Day like today, there will be others but most likely you can find a private spot. You need chairs? Nothing much to sit on." He gestured toward a display of folding chairs.

"Nope. Got those in the truck," I said.

"Are we allowed to take what we catch home?" I asked. "Are they safe to eat?"

He nodded. "Around here anyways. In Peregrine the land and water aren't ruined by chemicals. Anything you catch is fit to eat. If those flies don't work, you can try worms. I find old-school night crawlers are best for fish in the lake. I'll throw those in for free." Bill walked over to the small refrigerator with a glass door. There were various sodas lined up on the shelves, along with some saggy-looking sandwiches. On the bottom were shallow Styrofoam cups with lids. Bill picked one out and brought it back to the counter. "These suckers are fat and juicy. They should make the fish bite."

A few minutes later, Bill had us rung up and insisted he help us out to the car. He stood in the doorway of his store and waved to us as I drove away.

WE SAT IN THE PORTABLE CHAIRS AT THE EDGE OF THE LAKE. Chris's feet didn't reach the ground, but he didn't care. He devoured the turkey-and-cheddar sandwich his mother had made for him and washed it down with an apple juice I'd sneaked into the backpack. I was sure to catch hell from Teagan for the juice, but I figured it wasn't as bad as the soda I'd have gotten if it were up to me.

The clear lake water served as a mirror to the blue sky. We'd found a shady spot under a birch tree. Its leaves fluttered in the slight breeze like a soft percussion instrument. I'd brought Mabel with us, hoping for inspiration in between bites. Maybe the birch tree would give me some of her music.

"Is it time to fish now?" Chris asked.

I tossed the plastic that had held my sandwich into the bag. "Yes, let's do it."

We set up our reels and attached flies to hooks. "I'm not sure these work if you don't skim them just above the water so the fish think it's a real bug."

What happened next amazed me. "You mean like this?" Chris, with a flick of his wrist, sent the line in a zigzag across the water, then pulled it back and repeated the motion, fluid and easy, as though he'd been born with a fly-fishing pole in his hand.

"How'd you learn that?" I asked.

"Uncle Ardan taught me."

"I feel inadequate now," I said, only half teasing. "I thought we were going to let them hang in the water while we sat in our chairs."

"We can do it your way too," Chris said. "It sounds a lot more relaxing."

I was saved from comment when Chris sent the line sailing once more through the air. As the fly hovered just above the surface of the water, a shiny silver head of a fish surfaced and bit.

"Oh, I got one. I got one," Chris said, shouting.

"Can you reel it in or do you need help?"

"I need help." He thrust the pole toward me. "Uncle Ardan

always does this part." The fish tugged on the line, bending the tip of the pole.

"I don't know anything about catching fish, so don't be mad if I lose him." I took it from him. "Get the net. Once he gets close, we'll catch him in it."

Chris grabbed the net as I continued to slowly reel in the fish. He was small but hadn't given up the fight. When I had him near the shore, Chris squealed and plunged the net under the water. He once again amazed me when he pulled the net out of the water with the fish. I took hold of the handle of the net and inspected our catch. He wasn't big, not much larger than the length of my hand. The silver beauty flopped, struggling, his mouth opening and closing. My chest tightened. "I don't like it. Seeing him this way. All trapped and everything. Gasping for water."

Chris looked up at me. "That's kind of what they do when they're dying."

Dying? Oh God. This was awful. "It makes me sad." I couldn't take the life of this poor creature. Not when he'd been so happy swimming in the crystal-clear water. "I don't even like to eat fish." This wasn't technically true. I'd enjoyed a lot of fish-and-chips in my lifetime.

"Me either. Should we put him back?"

"Yes, please." I felt light-headed. "Can you take the hook out?"

Chris nodded. "I'll take care of it. You have to take the hook out really carefully. At least that's what Ardan told me."

Carefully, he wrapped his fingers around the trout and slipped the hook from his mouth. I swear that fish looked at me with one eye in a way that made me feel even more ashamed. Chris set him back in the water. I took in a deep breath and watched him swim away.

"That was rough," I said. "Maybe fishing isn't for me. I didn't know it would be so awful to see him flopping around like that.

It's too sad." I leaned down to rinse my hands in the lake. I'd had a romantic notion that was now gone. "Can I live in Idaho and not fish? Will you still want to hang out with me?"

"Sure. There's lots of other things we can do together." Chris crouched to pick up a stone. "My grandma says fish don't have souls."

"Maybe I should become a vegetarian." Right then, I meant it absolutely. How could I be responsible for the death of a living creature? Especially one with shiny scales. "Because I can't kill anything."

"Is it because of the shooting?" Chris asked.

"What?" I straightened, alarmed by his question. "How do you know about that?"

"I overheard some grown-ups talking about it at Mom's party. They said you saw people being shot."

I sank back into my chair. "I'm sorry you had to hear about that."

"It's okay. I'm around grown-ups all the time. I know stuff other kids don't."

I didn't like hearing that. Not at all. I'd been that way as a kid. The curse of a boy raised by a single mother.

"Is that why you came here?" Chris asked. "To recuperate?" He elongated the word, making it sound like *re-coop-are-rate*. "That's what Aunt Charlotte said, anyway. She and Uncle Ardan were talking when they didn't think I could hear."

"It's true that I was having a hard time before I came here. But mostly I came to Idaho because I wanted to see your mom and get to know you."

He sat back in his own chair, quiet for a few minutes. "Are you better at baseball than fishing?"

"A lot better. When I was growing up we didn't have lakes or creeks like the ones here. Plus I never had anyone to take me."

"Because your mom worked all the time?"

"That's right."

"If you ever want to come again, I'll come too. We don't have to keep any of the fish."

I shuddered, remembering the way the fish had gasped for air. "Maybe I should stick with playing catch with you?"

He grinned and patted my shoulder. "And swimming. You're good at that too."

"Thanks, kid. I appreciate the kind words."

Chris looked out over the water. A fish jumped, just a glimpse of its silver splendor rising from the water. "I don't care what we do as long as we do it together. I hope Mom lets you stay forever."

I swear to God, I almost started bawling. "Mama used to tell me that when you wanted something really badly to ask God for it. If he wants you to have it, then he'll give it to you."

"How do we know what God wants?"

"I'm not sure exactly. All I know is what I want. And that's to stay here with you and your mom. I know that's not something I should probably say to you."

"Why not?"

"Because if it doesn't come true I'm afraid you'll be disappointed."

He wrinkled his nose. "Mom says to try my best and never give up. So I'm not giving up what I hope for. I'm going to pray every single night until it comes true."

"What is it that you want?"

"I want you to be my dad," he said, as if it were the most obvious thing in the world.

I lost my battle and teared up and had to bite the inside of my lip to keep from blubbering like a child. This kid. He just did me in. All the way in.

"I want that too. But it's more important that your mom's happy. Whatever she wants is what I want."

"Because we're not supposed to push ourselves on girls."

"That's correct."

"I'm not worried. I already know she loves you. It's like Aunt Charlotte said. Mom is stubborn and proud. She takes longer to figure things out that would be obvious to other people."

I chuckled and wiped my eyes. "I hope Aunt Charlotte's correct."

"She is. She always is when it comes to love stuff. You'll see."

16

TEAGAN

"You let Chris go with Wyatt for the entire afternoon?" Mother's blank, unseeing eyes stared in my general direction. She did remarkably well tracking where we were by the direction of our voices.

I sat across from Mother in the front room of Charlotte and Ardan's house. "I did. Do you disapprove?"

"Not at all." Mother's lips twitched into one of her half smiles. "I'm simply surprised. I thought he was leaving after the party."

"Don't be coy, Mother."

Charlotte came in with a tray of iced tea and cookies, put together by the efficient Effie. "What's our favorite cranky lady being coy about?" She set the tray on the coffee table.

"I'm not being coy," Mother said. "I'm merely trying to get to the bottom of Teagan's strange behavior. She told us this Wyatt person meant nothing to her and that he was leaving right after the party, and yet here he is. In town. And according to Moonstone, he's checked out of the inn."

Perspiration dribbled down the small of my back. Mother

was an expert at triggering my flight response. If only I could talk to Charlotte alone. No such luck. Mother had been with Effie in the kitchen when I arrived and invited herself into the conversation. There was no way to get rid of her. She was as sticky as a piece of gum stuck under a desk.

I shifted in the soft armchair, crossing one leg over the other.

"Is it true that he's living with you?" Charlotte poured Mother a glass of tea and set it in her hands. "I've put a coaster to your left. At three o'clock."

"Thank you, Charlotte." Mother took a dainty sip of her tea, then winced. "Why isn't there sweetener in this? It's awful. Too strong. Effie and her English tea."

"I thought you hated sugar in your tea," Charlotte said without a hint of impatience. I don't know how she did it. Mother was enough to try the saintliest of the saints' patience.

"I've changed my mind, thanks to you." Mother sounded accusatory with a hint of humor. She loved torturing us with her whims. "You're the one who's always putting that fake sweetener in everything. Now I'm used to it. I'm at your mercy, after all."

"Riona Lanigan, you're impossible." Charlotte laughed. "I'll pour a packet into your glass if you'd like."

A twinge of envy came over me. Charlotte and Mother were so close. I didn't think it was possible for Mother and me to ever have that kind of relationship. Since I'd been home, the tension between us had lessened, but there was still this barrier. I thought of it as like the lining of a wool jacket. There was this layer that kept us from truly reaching each other on a deeper level. I worried that Mother wouldn't be with us for much longer. If I didn't repair it now, I might never have the chance. I didn't want it to be like Father and me.

"No, Charlotte, don't go to any trouble on my account."

Mother flashed an innocent smile. "I'm happy to drink whatever you give me."

"Suit yourself." Charlotte looked over at me and winked.

Mother sniffed but didn't say anything further. She enjoyed baiting Charlotte but only to a point. No one, even Mother, would mess with Charlotte for long. It was no fun to argue with someone who never burst into a temper. I swear, seeing the humor in every situation was Charlotte's superpower. When one could laugh, nothing was ever as bad as it seemed.

"Anyway, back to you, Teagan," Charlotte said. "How are things going at your house?"

"You mean, how is it with Wyatt staying with us?" I gave her my best smirk to let her know I was onto her.

Charlotte pushed her dark brown curls off her forehead. "Sure, I mean, if you want to talk about it. I don't want to be nosy."

"Nosy is your middle name," Mother said.

Charlotte laughed again. "I'm a writer. I get a pass."

"Can we stay focused on me?" I asked.

"Yes, yes. Tell us everything." Charlotte, having skipped the iced tea for a cookie, curled into one corner of a couch, as if she were about to watch a movie.

"Fine. Having him at the house has been nice. He's really good with Chris." I told them how he'd suggested a boys' day. "They've gone fishing."

"How cute," Charlotte said.

"Unless he runs off," Mother said. "And then it's heartbreaking."

"That's exactly what I'm worried about."

"Don't be," Charlotte said. "Just be in the moment. If it's meant to be, then everything will work out as it should."

"You sound like one of Wyatt's songs," I said.

Charlotte grinned. "Maybe I should ask him if I can collaborate on some lyrics."

"Anyway," I said. "Wyatt's trying to convince me that he's a family guy and wants to be around for the long term."

"Really? He said that?" Charlotte sat up straighter and looked as if she were about to run for her office to grab a pad of paper for initial wedding plans.

"Don't start planning the wedding," Mother said. "Teagan will surely find a way to run him off."

"Mother," I said, hurt that she would say such a thing out loud.

"Riona," Charlotte said.

"I'm sorry. I didn't mean it to sound like an insult," Mother said. "It's just that you've said yourself you don't believe in love or marriage."

"You do, though, don't you?" Charlotte asked me. "Wyatt's breaking you down."

"Maybe," I said under my breath.

"Interesting," Mother said.

"Don't sound so pleased with yourself, Mother. It's not a personal triumph of yours if I happen to be softening toward Wyatt."

"I didn't say it was." Mother folded her hands on her lap. "But I'd be terribly pleased to see you happy before I die."

"You're not dying," Charlotte said.

"Charlotte thinks only the good die young," Mother said drily. "Which means I'll live to a hundred and two."

"I hope so," Charlotte said.

"Thank you, dear."

Another twinge of jealousy tickled my throat. I wanted to say something sweet and kind. Something to tell Mother I loved her. But as always, I couldn't quite get the words out.

"Do you think you could fall in love with Wyatt?" Charlotte asked. "Or have you already?"

I thought for a moment about how to answer honestly. "I didn't think so."

"But now?" Charlotte asked.

"I can't resist him. He's impossible not to love. Kind of like you, Charlotte."

"What's the problem then?" Mother asked.

"Maybe there isn't one," I said. "He's a man who loved his mama. Today, he's taken my son fishing."

"And you know what they say about that," Charlotte said. "If a man's good to his mother, then he'll make a great husband."

"Your father said actions always spoke louder than words," Mother said. "He drove a thousand miles to come find you."

"And poured out his heart," Charlotte added. "Now he's with your precious boy, trying to win him over too."

I hadn't come here to talk about Wyatt. I'd wanted to talk about the murders that had happened in our small town. I needn't have worried long, because as I was about to broach the subject, Moonstone swept into the room like a debutante into a ball. She was the kind to sweep, bigger than life and unapologetically herself. Bliss had given her a makeover a few years back, ostensibly to capture Sam's heart. The transformation had toned down the purple eye shadow and bright lipstick. Her hair was no longer various shades of the rainbow but a mainstream honey blond. Even so, Moonstone wasn't the type to blend into a crowd. If I were designing her costumes, they would be in lavenders and purples in materials that draped just so and showed off her generous cleavage. Honestly, her new look made me a little sad. I'd liked her outrageous hair and clothes. Even her makeup had made me smile. But that's the way of the world, isn't it? We have to conform at some point or risk too much. In her case, she'd gotten Sam to notice her. Now they were happy together. That's all that mattered.

"I've come to tell you about my vision," Moonstone said without the usual polite transition. "It's about the murders."

"Murders? Plural?" Charlotte asked.

"Yes. Haven't you heard? The DJ was killed. Murdered. It has

something to do with the first one, if my vision is correct."
Moonstone sank into the empty chair and fanned herself. "My
God, it's unbearably hot. Menopause is kicking my large ass."

"Moonstone," Mother said. "Language."

"Sorry, Mrs. L.," Moonstone said.

"You poor thing. I'll turn up the air-conditioning," Charlotte
said.

"What about your vision?" I asked. "Please tell me it wasn't
about Wyatt."

Moonstone frowned. "About Wyatt? Why would it be about
him? He has nothing to do with any of this."

I let out a sigh of relief. I knew he didn't. I mean, deep down,
I did. Still, there was a tiny part of me that worried.

Don't be an idiot, I told myself. *That's just your fear talking.*

Charlotte returned from adjusting the temperature. "What
happened to the DJ?"

"He was shot in his apartment," I said. "That's all I know."

"I don't know what this means," Moonstone said. "But I had
a vision of a street sign with one of those slashes across the
middle. You know, the ones that mean 'no' or 'wrong.'"

Charlotte nodded. "Sure, like unauthorized personnel not
allowed inside. Sometimes they have a symbol of whatever they
want to keep out, like a dog."

"Yes, exactly," Moonstone said. "The one in my vision had a
picture of a woman with a long ponytail, then that slash over it."

"What does that mean?" I asked.

"That the wrong girl was killed." Moonstone twisted one of
her rings round and round her finger.

"That makes no sense," I said.

"Unless it was premeditated," Charlotte said. "And the
murderer killed the wrong person."

"If it was premeditated, why would that happen?" Mother
asked. "The nature of a planned killing means they knew who
they wanted dead."

"Unless it was a murder for hire," Charlotte said.

"And the killer was a complete idiot," Mother said.

"Also, it doesn't explain the second killing," Charlotte said. "Could it be possible your vision had the wrong gender?"

"Maybe," Moonstone said. "That would explain the second death, wouldn't it? The killer came back for the right person."

"Which would mean that Paula Neal's death was random," I said. "Should we call the detective?" I had a feeling Cryer wouldn't be too keen on listening to Moonstone. He struck me as more of an old-school type.

"Yes, we should," Charlotte said. "Moonstone can tell him what she told us."

I'd already dug my phone from my bag. "He might want us to come into the station. Isn't that what they do on television?"

"I can't," Moonstone said. "I need to get back to the inn. I left Sam in charge, and he's not the greatest with the customers."

"I'll see if he can meet you at the inn," I said as I punched in his number.

Cryer answered on the third ring, sounding breathless, as though he was walking up a steep hill. "It's Teagan Lanigan. I was wondering if you would meet with our family friend. The one I told you about. The psychic."

To my surprise, he agreed. "Hell, I've got nothing else to go on. I might as well give it a try."

He asked if we'd meet him in an hour at the inn. "Do you want me there?" I asked him. "Since I'm a suspect?"

"I can meet with her alone." He paused. "Listen, you be careful snooping around. Whoever did this has killed two people already."

My stomach tightened. "Do you think it's connected to me or the party?"

"I don't know. But two of the staff that worked your party are dead. There's a connection there somehow. I just have to figure out what it is."

"Does this mean you've ruled out Wyatt and me?" I asked.

"Don't be ridiculous."

I stifled a snarky response.

"Tell your psychic I'll meet her at the inn. For now, try to stay out of trouble."

I hung up and conveyed the conversation to the ladies.

"I don't think he really believes you and Wyatt are suspects," Charlotte said.

"He doesn't have that many suspects to look at," I said. "One of us did it. That said, the force of the injury to Paula Neal had to have been done by a man. Don't you think?"

"Hope weighs no more than a sparrow," Mother said. "And we know you didn't do it. What about Jodi? Does she seem strong?"

"Not really," I said.

"With the right angle and weapon, a woman might be able to do it," Charlotte said.

"I find it strange that the second victim was killed with a gunshot. If it's the same murderer, don't they usually use the same type of weapon?"

"Not necessarily," Charlotte said. "If it's a serial killer, then yes. They usually have a signature way of killing. If we're right and this murder is because of something personal, like revenge or a secret, then they would use whatever was the most convenient. For example, they couldn't use a gun unless they had a silencer to kill Paula, or everyone would have heard."

Moonstone had risen from her chair. "The problem is motive. None of these people seem connected in any way."

"Agree. For example, what would Ashton or Hope have to do with either of the victims?" Charlotte asked.

"Unless they knew them from the past," I said. "But it seems strange they would suddenly murder someone who happened to be catering a party."

"I think we should talk to Hope," Moonstone said. "See if she'll give anything away."

"She's an actress," I said. "A damn good one. I'm not sure we'll be able to tell."

"You're right," Moonstone said. "Let's have a girls' night out at the bar. Get a few cocktails in her and see if she blabs."

"What about Ashton?" I asked. "How do we get to know more about him?"

"I already did a little online snooping," Charlotte said. "As far as I can tell the guy's clean as a whistle. Almost monk-like. No famous girlfriends or boyfriends. He gives a ton of money to troubled kids. That's how Ardan knows him."

"Maybe he's too good to be true," Mother said. "The choirboy thing could be an act."

"I really hope he's not a murderer," Charlotte said, sounding mournful. "I thought he and Hope might be a love match. They talked all night."

"Hope's always been wild," Mother said. "I caught her and Ciaran smoking weed in the backyard when they were both in high school."

"Smoking weed doesn't make you a killer," I said.

"True," Charlotte said. "But I already know it's not Hope."

"How?" I asked.

Charlotte wiped the side of her iced tea glass with a cocktail napkin. "Your family has known her forever. There's no way one of you wouldn't have picked up on her tendency toward violence."

"I don't know," I said. "The girl has a dark side. I've seen her temper flare when she doesn't get what she wants." There was the time when we were teenagers and a boy had done something to her—we never knew what—and she'd slashed his tires like the woman in the country song.

"Maybe Hope has a secret she needed kept hidden enough to murder someone."

"Still doesn't make sense, though, if the wrong woman was murdered," Moonstone said.

"And we're positive that's what your vision meant?" I asked. Could someone have wanted me dead? Or Hope?

"I could be wrong," Moonstone said. "Sometimes my wires get crossed or I interpret a vision the wrong way. If I am mistaken, we need to figure out the connection between the two victims. There has to be something that ties them together." She smoothed the front of her dress. "I'll see what I can get out of the detective. Let's all meet for drinks at seven and compare notes. I'll tell Hope to come at seven thirty to give us time to talk first. Don't be late." She turned to me. "Do you know anything about Jodi Sapp?"

"Other than from book club, no," I said. "She's quiet. Hardly says a word during discussion. Although I can tell she always reads the book, unlike some of the others."

"What about you?" Charlotte asked Moonstone. "She's been staying at the inn for months. Has she ever done anything strange?"

Moonstone shook her head. "The only thing strange is that she paid for three months all at once and in cash."

"That's definitely weird," Charlotte said. "Maybe someone on the run? Because she's a serial killer?"

"Makes more sense than Hope or Ashton," I said.

"I think we should have Ardan and Wyatt talk with Ashton like we're talking with Hope," Charlotte said. "Maybe he'll give something away."

"Good idea," I said. "Wyatt's discerning. He might notice something."

Moonstone clapped her hands. "Groovy. We have a plan."

"Why do I suddenly feel like Scooby-Doo is going to bound into the house and ask for a sandwich?" Mother asked.

We all laughed, despite the seriousness of the situation. "I want to be Shaggy," I said.

"I call Velma. She's the smartest," Charlotte said. "And kind of short and plump like me."

"You're not plump," Moonstone said. "But if we're deciding who is who, then I'm definitely Daphne."

"That means I'm Fred," Mother said. "I always wondered what it felt like to be a frat boy."

17

WYATT

On the way home from our failed fishing expedition, Chris fell asleep using his new glove for a pillow. When I pulled up to Teagan's house, he woke, rubbed his eyes, and asked what was for dinner.

"Not fish," I said.

He grinned and slapped his knee. "That's a knee-slapper."

"Hopefully your mother has something in the freezer. Not catching fish makes a guy hungry."

We hopped out of the truck and gathered the gear from the back. Chris said there was a lot of room in the garage, and that's where his mom would want our fishing paraphernalia.

After a few loads, we had it all put away on the empty shelves. Her car wasn't in the garage either, which meant she'd gone out somewhere. "Let's get inside and cleaned up before she gets back," I said to Chris. "I'm pretty sure we stink."

He sniffed his arm. "Smells fine to me."

"Women have sensitive noses," I said. "We better not take our chances."

"Okay."

We took off our shoes and left them in the mudroom off the garage.

"You good on your own?" I asked him.

"Yeah, I don't need help with that. Mom inspects me when I'm done, though, to make sure I washed my hair and behind my ears."

At the top of the stairs, we agreed to meet back in the kitchen after we showered and changed clothes.

Minutes later, I scrubbed away the day from my skin. After we'd decided fishing wasn't for us, we'd spent the rest of the afternoon swimming. There was a dock just around the corner from where we'd been fishing. When Chris saw kids jumping into the water, he asked if we could join them. Who was I to deny him that, since I'd failed him as a fisherman?

After I had toweled dry, I went to the closet where Teagan had asked me to put my suitcase. The closet was as large as the bathroom and organized with built-in cupboards and drawers. To my surprise, she'd hung up my clothes. A Post-it note on one of the drawers said, "Wyatt, unmentionables in here."

I dressed in khaki shorts and a T-shirt and was about to step out of the closet when I heard the bedroom door open and Teagan's voice call out, "Wyatt?"

"Yeah, here." I came out to find her perched on the side of the bed. Her shoulders curved inward and her eyes seemed dull and tired. "Everything all right?"

She gave me a smile. "Yes, fine. Just tired. Moonstone had a vision." She proceeded to describe what our local psychic had seen. "Which makes me wonder if the first victim was a mistake. They meant to kill someone else. Or she's wrong about the vision and somehow the victims are connected. None of it makes any sense."

I crossed the room to sit next to her. Her comforter made a sighing sound as I settled next to her. "You hungry? I can make us some dinner."

"Moonstone wants to meet at the bar and grill. She has this idea that Hope might spill something after a few drinks."

"If she has anything to spill," I said.

"Right." She rested her cheek on my shoulder. "They want you to get to know Ashton better. Ardan's going to ask you both over tonight for burgers and beer. He's sure Ashton's clean but you're observant of people. Maybe you can pick up on something."

"Okay, sure. I can do that. But what about Jodi Sapp and Ralph Jones? How do we learn about them?" I rested my hand on her knee. She wore shorts, and her skin was soft but cold.

"Moonstone's going to dig around and see if she can find anything on Jodi."

"You ladies are like a detective agency." I shifted to kiss her forehead.

"Cryer told me to be careful and not snoop around too much."

"Cryer's right. I don't want you in any danger. Ryan Chambers could have been killed because he figured out who the killer was."

"Exactly," Teagan said. "Which means one of us could be next if we get too close to the truth."

"Whatever we find out, if anything, we need to tell Cryer right away."

"Agreed," Teagan said. "But enough of our amateur sleuthing for now. How was fishing?"

"Yeah, about that." I grimaced and scratched the back of my neck. "Turns out I don't have the heart to kill a living creature. I had no idea what a hypocrite I am—eating meat that other people killed is not the same as killing it myself." I groaned. "I had such a romantic idea about how the whole day would go. We'd bring a mess of fish back here and grill them for supper. You'd think I was totally cool and manly. But the minute we caught one and the poor silver bastard flopped around in the net, I lost my mind. You should have seen him. He made these horrible moves with his mouth, looking for water that wasn't there." I imitated the fish by opening and closing my mouth.

"You let it go?"

"I made Chris do it."

She doubled over, laughing so hard her shoulders shook.

"It's not funny."

She straightened, wiping the corners of her eyes. "Did you give the fish a kiss before you tossed it back?"

"No kissing of fish happened on my watch."

"What did Chris do?"

"Unlike you, he was very kind. I promised to play catch with him instead. He had his eye on a glove at the store, so I got it and one for myself. And a baseball."

She blinked, as if she hadn't heard me correctly. Had I messed up again?

"I'm much better at sports that include a ball. But if you don't want him to play, we can take the stuff back." My heart sank at the thought. Taking back that mitt would disappoint my new buddy. That's the last thing I wanted after I'd seen the excitement in his eyes.

"No, it's fine." She smiled and grazed her knuckles against my cheekbone. "Actually, it's truly sweet. Thank you."

"I was worried for a minute I may have overstepped again."

She looked down at her lap and spoke quietly. "The way he looks at you breaks my heart a little."

"No, don't think that way."

"A boy wants a father."

"You've been more than enough. He's a great kid. That's all because of you."

"I've had help." She got up from the bed and went to the window that overlooked Blue Mountain.

I stood as well but stayed where I was, wrapping a hand around one of the bedposts. "Talk to me."

She turned slowly, then crossed over to sit in the easy chair and clasped her hands together. "I got a call for a head design job on Ned Broadstone's new film. It films in New York this fall. Set during the Gilded Age. It's a dream job. A few years ago, I would've jumped at it, but now my life's different. It has to be about Chris."

A dream job. This was what it was a like to be a single parent. She couldn't take what she wanted without hurting her son.

"The whole reason I brought him here was so he could have a normal life," she said. "A tutor on a film set for Chris would be hell. You see what he's like here."

"I do, yeah." However, I'd also seen how her eyes had brightened when she talked about the job. "How long would you have to be gone?"

"A couple of months."

"Could you fly back and forth?" I asked.

"Yes, but I can't leave him for that amount of time. He's only six. I'm his only parent."

"What if I were here?" I asked.

"You?" She cocked her head to the side with an incredulous expression, as if I were incapable of taking care of a child.

I might as well say it. I was all the way in now. Even if she mocked me, I had to make the offer. "I could stay with him. Take him to school. Cook his meals."

"Won't you have your own work to take care of this fall?"

The fall? Everything I'd planned was now different. I'd thought the fall would include recording new songs for a new album. I had no songs. Without them I had no album. No work for my band. No new tour to plan. Not to mention the dates I'd canceled for the last one. "I'm free, as it turns out."

She crossed her legs. "You're not going to be stuck in writer's block forever. At some point, the muses will return."

"I can write songs here just as well as any other place." The next steps in my career were elusive at the moment. I was adrift, maybe like that poor fish. "I'm not ready to return to work. I want to be here where it's quiet. Where I can think."

She rose to her feet and joined me by the bed. "You're going to be fine. Hiding away here is not the answer, though."

"I'm not hiding. I'm choosing. You and Chris. Time to write and reflect."

She placed her hands palms-down on my chest. "I don't want you choosing us because you can't face your life. Eventually you'll feel better. What if you look around and see that you're living someone else's life instead of your own?"

I covered her hands with mine but kept them against my chest. "Being with Chris today…" How could I describe how he touched my soul without sounding like the biggest sap on the planet? *I want you to be my dad.* "This time with you and Chris has reminded me of what's most important. Family. I haven't had one since Mama died. I have to tell you, it feels damn good to be needed and wanted. Let me give you this."

She withdrew from me and stepped back a few feet. "I don't know. What would be the difference between having him stay with Charlotte and Ardan or you? I'm sure you'd all do a great job taking care of him. However, I'm still bailing on him."

"Would you feel like this if you were married to his father? Guilty to work? Refusing to leave him to take a job?"

Her eyelids fluttered. "I think so."

"So what you're saying is that mothers shouldn't get to do anything other than raise their children? Even when the job of a lifetime comes along? Even when they have family or partners to help?"

She raised one eyebrow. "When you say it like that, the answer seems obvious. But you don't know what it's like to be a mother. Every choice we make means we have to leave something else behind. No one can have it all. Women, anyway."

"You're right that I don't know how it feels to be a mother.

However, I had one who never had the chance to make any dreams come true. Because of me, she had to work low-paying jobs just to keep us from starving." My voice cracked. "That haunts me. Chris will not want to think that he held you back. You're a talented artist. Creativity feeds you. I admire you for putting Chris first, but you also have to pay attention to your own needs in order to be the best mother you can be." I paused, calibrating what to say next. What would convince her? "Go to the meeting. Hear what he has to say. Lay out what you like as far as a schedule goes."

"I guess it wouldn't hurt to hear him out."

"Give it a shot." I pulled her to me and wrapped my arms around her waist. "Give me a shot."

"Isn't that what I'm doing?"

"I guess it is." I smiled as I held her close and breathed in the scent of her hair. "I haven't felt this good in a long time. Thank you for letting me stay."

"Good enough to start writing again?" Teagan lifted her gaze upward to look into my eyes.

"Maybe. And maybe they'll all be love songs about you."

She laughed. "Whatever, cowboy."

"I'm serious. I love you. Always will."

She rested her cheek against my shoulder. "Fine. If you want to know, you've worn me down. I love you too."

My spirits soared. She loved me.

I want you to be my dad.

I lifted her off the ground and tossed her onto the bed, then lay on my side, propping my head up with one hand to gaze down at her. "I want to marry you. I want to adopt Chris."

"Wyatt," she whispered. "It's all too fast."

"I can be patient. But I want you to understand my intentions."

"Duly noted." Her green eyes looked into mine. "I'm glad you came here."

"Me too, Pretty Girl. Me too."

―――――――

LATER THAT EVENING, I WAS SITTING OUTSIDE ON ARDAN'S PATIO drinking a beer. Ashton was also there, looking more relaxed than a murder suspect should.

"Did the detective call you in again?" I asked.

"No, but he stopped by my house." Ashton took off his glasses and wiped the lenses with the corner of his cotton shirt. "To tell me about the second murder."

"Are you worried he thinks it's you?" Ardan asked.

"No. Unless someone tries to frame me like in the movies, I'll be fine." Ashton put his glasses back on. "I have no connection to the victims. And I didn't do it. No matter how much dirt he digs up on me, I'm innocent."

"Dirt?" I asked, remembering my instructions to get him to talk. "Do you have any of that?"

"Let's see," Ashton said. "I've had a few stalkers. Not anyone I knew in real life but who followed me online. One of them managed to break into my offices back in California to proposition me. Fortunately, security got to me before anything happened."

"That's super scary," Ardan said.

"That was one of the reasons I moved to such a remote place. I got tired of all the hassle."

"Is there anything else that he could possibly misconstrue?" Ardan asked. "Something that would make you seem capable of murder?"

"There are a few ex-girlfriends who won't have anything kind to say. But nothing like abuse or anything close. They could cause some trouble, I suppose."

Again, for a man on the suspect list, he was remarkably lackadaisical. His slow cadence, as if he had all the time in the world to choose every word carefully, was not that of a guilty man. I didn't think, anyway. Not that I was an expert. Still, my gut told me this guy was not guilty of anything. Other than being at the wrong place at the wrong time.

"What's going on with you and Hope?" Ardan asked.

Ashton got up from his chair to get another beer from a silver bucket filled with ice that Effie had brought out for us. "Nothing. Why do you ask?" He returned to his chair and crossed one jean-clad leg over the other.

"Charlotte wondered," Ardan said. "She noticed you talked a long time at the party."

Good point. Was Ashton lying?

"We were talking business. She has an idea for an app," Ashton said. "Smart idea, actually. She came out for dinner last night to talk through some of the details. Trust me, she's not into me either."

I wasn't sure I liked this guy. He was a little too holier-than-thou and smug for me.

"Hope's totally interesting," Ashton said. "And obviously, gorgeous. That said, I think she could be the murderer."

"You're kidding, right?" Ardan asked.

"She's troubled," Ashton said. "Impulsive. Emotional. Headstrong."

"She had no motive," Ardan said, with a slight edge to his voice. Hope was a longtime friend. Hearing her disparaged by someone who didn't know her well would stick in my craw too. If it had been one of my band members, I could easily imagine getting defensive on his behalf. Still, if Hope were troubled, perhaps she was capable of murder? I'd known a few mentally fragile actresses in my time. And by "known," I mean slept with. There were several where I'd misjudged their characters by a gross margin. Once we were alone, I understood they were nothing like their onscreen personas.

"People have darkness inside them," Ashton said.

"What about you, Ashton?" Ardan asked with the same edge to his voice. "Do you have any secrets we should know about? Ones that will connect *you* back to the victims?"

"If I told you them, they would no longer be secrets," Ashton said gently. "But no, I have no connection to the poor souls who were murdered."

Effie appeared in the shadow between the house lights and patio lamps. "Ardan, the detective's here," she said in her clipped English accent. "He's asking to speak to you. Do you want to meet him inside?"

"No, bring him out here," Ardan said.

We all exchanged worried glances. Why would Cryer be showing up now? At Ardan's, who had no connection to the murders.

A second later, Cryer came out to the patio. Ardan stood up to greet him and offered him a beer.

"No thanks," Cryer said as he took the remaining chair from around the firepit. "Sorry to barge in on you like this, but I wanted to ask you a few questions about Ms. Manning, if I might."

Ardan had settled back in his chair. "Sure." His voice sounded tight and defensive.

"Alone would be best," Cryer said. "If you boys wouldn't mind excusing us for a moment."

Both Ashton and I stood. "You got it," I said. "We'll be in the kitchen."

Effie was at the stove when we ambled into the bright kitchen that smelled of garlic and fresh tomatoes. She looked up from whatever she was stirring in a pan. "Hello there. Can I get you anything?"

"Will we bother you if we hang out here for a few minutes?" I asked. "The detective kicked us off the patio."

"Not at all. Have a seat."

The two of us climbed onto the stools at the island. "What're you making?" I asked.

"Fresh sauce and spaghetti. Would you like a bowl now or later?"

"Now, please. I'm starving. Chris and I played hard today." I glanced at Ashton to see if he was as excited as I was.

He was staring at Effie as though he'd rather have her for dinner. She was adorable, I had to give him that, with her cap of dark brown hair and large eyes framed with thick lashes. Small and darting, like a graceful bird. Teagan had told me she'd just celebrated her twenty-second birthday. Ashton, I knew, because I'd googled him, was a good ten years older. Age aside, this man had eyes for Miss Effie. She seemed oblivious, which made me like her even more.

"Mr. Carter?" Effie put her hands to her flushed cheeks. "Do I have something on my face?"

"What? No." Ashton looked down, suddenly interested in the nail of his left thumb. "I'm sorry for staring. You're so pretty. It's hard to look away."

He was honest. That was something.

Effie flushed a deeper pink. Very becoming, given her fair skin. "Thank you, Mr. Carter."

"I'm sorry again. Inappropriate of me to say so." Ashton was as pink as she was. "Do you have a boyfriend?"

For a split second I thought about leaving them alone. However, I quickly set that idea aside. I didn't think the women in my life, namely Teagan and Charlotte, would approve of me leaving sweet Effie with a murder suspect. What if under that nerdy exterior lay the heart of a serial killer? I shivered as an image from the night of the murder flashed before my eyes. Contrary to that thought—if young women were his thing, then why had the DJ gotten it next?

If the wrong woman was murdered, then who was the intended? Hope? Jodi? Teagan?

None of this made sense. Moonstone had not impressed me with her so-called psychic abilities.

I focused on the present, which frankly was a heck of a lot more entertaining than trying to figure out a murder case. How did the detective do this for a living?

"No, sir," Effie said. "I've no interest in men. Even if there were any around here to speak of. Which there aren't. One of the best things about Peregrine, if you ask me."

There was one right here in front of her.

"Oh, that's too bad," Ashton said, not sounding at all sad.

"Would you boys care for Parmesan on your pasta?" Effie efficiently moved around the kitchen.

"Yes, please," Ashton said. "The sauce smells great."

"It's my mum's recipe. Only better because Charlotte's mum, Mrs. Wilde, brings me the tomatoes from her garden. We can grow so many decadent vegetables here in Idaho. It's the sun, you know, that makes the difference. At home we can't get enough sun to ripen a bloody tomato."

"Where's home?" Ashton asked.

"Just outside of London," Effie said.

For the next few minutes, I listened as Effie answered Ashton's questions about her family and what brought her to America. "A man. A terrible man." She slid two generous bowls of pasta across the island. "He left me high and dry in San Francisco. Thank God for Ardan, or who knows where I'd be. He hired me out of pity, I suspect. I'd had no experience as a housekeeper, other than taking care of my brothers and sisters and helping Mum as much as I could while keeping up with my studies. I was a terrible student, so university wasn't a possibility. I suppose that's why I fell in love with a cad and followed him to America."

"Cad," I said. "Haven't heard that word in a while." Mama had used that word occasionally, passed down to her from her grandmother.

We were interrupted when Cryer and Ardan came into the kitchen. Ardan looked visibly shaken, pale and clammy. While Ardan walked the detective to the door, the three of us were quiet. The foreboding of bad news hung in the air.

"What did he want?" Effie asked when Ardan reappeared.

"He had a bunch of questions about Hope," Ardan said. "They've found a link between her and the first victim. Paula Neal had been sending harassing emails to Hope. Kind of stalking her, I guess you'd say. First, just asking to meet for coffee. But as the days passed, they became more and more hostile and threatening. The last one was written the day before the party. She said she would meet Hope one way or another and to be watching for her."

"Did Hope answer her back?" Effie asked.

"No, not to any of the emails." Ardan leaned his elbows on the island. "But the detective says they were opened."

My mind was torpedoing ahead to what this meant. Had the woman been harassing Hope? Maybe she confronted Hope at the party and things got ugly. Hope might have killed her out of anger and fear. But how did that fit with the DJ? Had he seen her and come after her for money in exchange for his silence? Where was the murder weapon? Did Hope know how to shoot a gun?

"Opened by Hope?" Effie asked. "Or an assistant? She might not have even seen them. She doesn't strike me as the detail-oriented sort."

"That's what I thought, too," Ardan said. "I told Cryer that very thing. He said he'd look into it. I just don't see how she could have done this. Why would she risk everything?"

"A moment of rage?" Ashton said. "Like road rage. Ordinary people sometimes lose it."

"Maybe," Ardan said. "But I don't think so."

I could tell by the tremor in his voice that his faith in Hope was wavering.

"He isn't going to arrest her, is he?" Effie asked.

"No. He doesn't have anything else but the emails," Ardan said. "So far, she's the only connection to the victims that he can find."

"Still, that doesn't mean she did it," Effie said. "She's too pretty to be a murderer."

"I don't know about that," I said. "A lot of beautiful women have killed. I just don't buy the strength, though. How did that tiny woman sneak up from behind her and have enough strength to…" I trailed off, not wanting to describe what I saw.

"I agree," Ardan said.

"If she did do this, she's a cool cucumber," Ashton said. "When she came back from the bathroom to continue our chat, she showed no signs of stress. In fact, she was pretty drunk."

Drunk. Which meant her judgment was further impaired. Could it be true? One of the most beautiful actresses in the world had murdered an obsessed fan out of a drunken rage?

"How long was she away from you?" I asked.

"Fifteen minutes," Ashton said. "The reason I know is because my mother had called on the phone just as Hope excused herself for the bathroom. Not wanting to be rude, I hung up with Mom when Hope returned. The call times were on my phone."

Fifteen minutes? Was that enough time to find a weapon and kill?

The weapon. Had the killer brought it with them or had they found it in Teagan's garage?

"Does Teagan golf?" I asked.

"No, she hates it," Ardan said. "Why?"

"They said the injury was caused by something like a golf club or baseball bat," I said. "Unless it was premeditated, the weapon would have been spontaneously taken from Teagan's house or garage."

"Which indicates to me it had to be planned," Ardan said. "I can guarantee you, Hope Manning didn't plan to kill a crazed fan before Teagan's birthday party. Plus, Teagan doesn't have a set of clubs."

"Or a baseball bat," I said. Until today, anyway.

"Eat your supper," Effie said. "Before it gets cold."

I dug in, thinking through everything I knew about the murders and coming up blank. I hoped Cryer was a better detective than the rest of us.

18

TEAGAN

The Peregrine Bar and Grill was in its usual state of haggard familiarity that evening. For as long as I could remember, the place had looked and smelled the same. Even blindfolded, I'd have known exactly where I was. Kitchen grease and spilled beer combined with old wood and peanut shells was the grill's special scent.

Hope had accepted our invitation to dinner and drinks without hesitation. The four of us, Moonstone, Charlotte, Hope, and me, shared a booth in the restaurant section. Along with some locals I recognized, a tired-seeming family of four most likely passing through to somewhere else was tucked into one of the booths. Given their dirty clothing and hair, I assumed they'd been camping for a few days without showers. If they recognized Hope, they were too polite to stare.

"All right, spill it," Hope said quietly. "I know you didn't call this little meeting for no reason."

I matched her low volume, conscious of our surroundings. Maybe I should have had everyone out to the house instead. "No agenda. I just thought it would be nice to get out for a few hours."

I'd left Chris with Bliss and Ciaran, who'd promised him a movie and popcorn after they got their two small daughters tucked in for the night.

Hope let out a long breath as she gripped the side of the table. Her nails were bitten to the quick. She wore no makeup, which made her look years younger than her forty years. Dewy skin and perfect teeth required little enhancement. She'd hardly touched the salad she'd ordered.

Next to her, Moonstone, dressed in a tie-dyed dress of her own design, nibbled on a plate of french fries. She caught my eye before dipping another fry into ketchup.

Charlotte, having ordered a salad and a ginger ale, seemed off tonight. Her usual dark complexion looked a bit green, and she'd asked me to smell her chicken to see if I thought it was rancid. To me, the rubbery piece of chicken smelled the same as usual. For a moment, I'd wondered if she had a touch of the flu. In the next second, it occurred to me she might be pregnant. I put that happy thought aside to think about later.

"That detective came by to see me earlier," Hope said as she picked up her vodka martini. "I'm pretty sure he thinks I did it."

I almost choked on a bite of my veggie burger. "Why do you think that?"

Hope downed her drink and motioned to the waitress to bring another martini. She'd consumed the first so quickly I hadn't even noticed her drinking. "Do you think they'll have Grey Goose vodka in prison?"

"You're not going to prison," Charlotte said.

"I didn't do it, if that's what you're all wondering." Hope pushed the tips of her fingers against her cheekbones. To my shock, her eyes filled with tears. Except for onscreen, I'd never seen her cry. She was this beautiful feminine package that appeared fragile on the outside. But I knew better. Hope Manning was tough and often cold. Only those of us who knew her understood there was more inside her than she showed the world.

I went back to my unanswered question. "What did the detective say that makes you think he's suspicious of you?"

"He found a link between Paula Neal and me." Hope quieted as the waitress approached with her drink. She waited for her to leave before continuing. "The woman was sending me emails. Like stalker-type stuff. Before tonight, I hadn't read any of them. My assistant, Sue, handles all that for me. It's not the first time I've gotten mail from obsessed fans, so she didn't think anything of it. I read them after the detective left, and by the end, she'd turned threatening. Again, that's happened before. Sue always moves them to a saved folder in case we ever need them. Like, if someone tries to kill me." She paused to sip her drink. "Anyway, he got all bad cop on me and basically accused me of losing my temper and killing her with a blunt object. Or something like that."

"But why would you do that?" Charlotte asked. "Wouldn't it be the other way around?"

"Thank you. That's what I said." Hope lifted her hands from the table in a gesture of frustration. "I was the one threatened."

"What was his response?" Charlotte asked.

I looked closely at my sister-in-law. She wrote mysteries and talked to cops on a regular basis. Did she have a motive for asking such simple questions? Was she as clueless as she sounded? Charlotte always saw the best in people. Maybe that quality blinded her to Hope's dark side? Or did my natural suspicion of others make me assume she was more sinister than she really was?

Hope took another drink from her glass. "He said she might have come at me and my response was a knee-jerk reaction." She made a disgusted growl in the back of her throat. "As if I could just suddenly hit her from behind."

"It makes no sense," Charlotte said. "The way she was killed could not have come from a fight response. This was a premeditated murder. I think by someone who knew what they were doing."

"I agree," Moonstone said.

She'd been unusually quiet. For all I knew, she could be in the middle of one of her visions and not really here with us.

"I hope he finds something on someone else," Hope said. "All I need is a murder accusation to further sink my career."

"What's wrong with your career?" I asked.

"Don't act like you don't know." She said this as if she were weary, not hostile. Yet her words stung. Did she see me as a Hollywood insider and not her childhood friend?

"I don't know," Charlotte said in her sweet voice. "Tell me."

"This movie that I'm now late on was supposed to be a comeback. The last three have tanked at the box office. I'm getting old. Pretty soon no one will want me except for a B-list reality show."

"That's not true," I said. "You're a huge star. Those movies flopping had nothing to do with you."

"Did you see them?" Hope asked.

"I see everything you're in," I said. "You know that."

"Everything I thought I knew, I don't anymore." Hope snatched the two green olives stuck into a toothpick from her drink and popped one in her mouth. "Do you know how hungry I've been for twenty years? Just to stay thin enough for the camera?"

"That's awful," Charlotte said. "I hate being hungry."

"Maybe you're done with Hollywood," Moonstone said. "You have enough money, don't you?"

"Yes. It's not the money. You'd be surprised how little I've spent. I built this house out here when I sold the Beverly Hills house." Hope sighed, then popped the second olive into her mouth. "But admitting defeat is not something that comes easily to me. I want this film. Even if it's the last one. The role is one

I've been waiting for. Now I'm stuck here and this Cryer bastard thinks I killed two people."

"What did the director say when you told him you couldn't leave?" Charlotte asked.

"He said he'd wait a few weeks. He's going to film some other scenes without me first. Robert's an old friend of mine from back in college. Loyal, even though he would have probably been smarter to pick someone else. Someone younger. Someone cheaper." Several tears leaked from her eyes. She wiped her face with a cocktail napkin. "I'm scared. Like really scared. I might be accused of this murder...murders...that I didn't commit. You guys believe me, right?"

We were all quiet a second too long.

"Oh my God. You guys think I'm guilty too?" Hope pressed the napkin to the side of her left eye and looked at each of us in turn.

I looked down at my hands, then reached for my glass of wine.

Moonstone was the first to speak. "I don't think you're guilty. Actually, I know you're not."

"How?" Hope asked.

She told Hope about her vision. "This has nothing to do with any of us. The more I think about it, the more I believe that to be true."

Charlotte nodded. "There's a connection somehow between the two victims. I just don't know what it is."

"What about Ashton or the caterer person, Jodi?" Hope asked. "Could it be either of them?"

"Ardan knows Ashton well," Charlotte said. "He doesn't think it could be him. As far as Jodi goes, I asked my cop friend to see if he could dig up anything on her. He couldn't find any trace of her before she opened her catering business here in Peregrine. Another thing I find strange, she doesn't have a photo on her website. It's an avatar instead of her photo. Don't you think an attractive woman like her would want her photo on her site?"

"I do, yes," Moonstone said. "And there's the paying in cash thing, too." She explained to Hope that Jodi had paid in advance for her room at the inn.

"What if she's murdered before?" Moonstone asked. "And she's running from the law?"

"Like she's a serial killer?" Hope asked, sounding frightened. "What if she comes after one of us?"

"Have you seen her since the party?" I asked Moonstone.

"She's been in her room," Moonstone said. "She told me she's come down with the flu and doesn't want to give it to me or the other guests. She asked if I'd get her a few groceries for her mini fridge. Cryer's come by a few times to talk to her but she's been gone from her room. She must slip out when I'm not around, because I never see her come or go."

"He must not think it's her now that he's found the connection between the victim and me." Hope laughed through her tears. "I'm too pretty for jail."

"You're not going to jail," Charlotte said. "The truth will come out soon. Just hang tight."

"Your assistant will vouch for you not reading the emails," I said. "Once she does that, Cryer will see how wrong he is."

"I hope you're right," Hope said.

"What happened with Ashton the other night?" I asked, curious to see if he was lying about whether they'd had a thing.

"Ashton? Nothing," Hope said. "Other than I told him about an idea I have for an app. He was interested to talk more about it so we got together for dinner."

Charlotte's shoulders sagged. "Darn. I thought maybe you two hit it off."

"He's not my type," Hope said. "Too geeky and smart for me. You know I like the party boys."

"That's your problem," Charlotte said. "You're not looking at the right men."

"You need the right man," Moonstone said. "Not the one in the closest proximity."

"If only I wanted one for something other than sex," Hope said. "But what else are they good for?"

"When you meet your soul mate, you'll see," Charlotte said. "It's not even about the sex when you're with the right one. You just have to have your eyes open to see him when he comes."

Hope gave Charlotte a tight smile. "You're made for love, Charlotte. God made me for something else entirely. Don't look so disappointed."

"I really wanted you to like Ashton," Charlotte said.

"First of all, he might be a murderer. Secondly, he likes Effie," Hope said.

"How do you know?" Charlotte asked.

"He told me." Hope drank more of her martini. For someone so small, she could drink like a crusty Irishman. "This was before the murder."

"What is it with men?" I asked. "She's at least ten years younger than him."

"Love is love, no matter how mismatched a pair might seem," Moonstone said. "Look at Sam and me, for example."

"What about you, Teagan?" Hope asked. "Have you gone to the dark side with these ladies and fallen in love?"

I hesitated, planting my hands on my thighs under the table. Could I say it out loud? Why not? These women were my friends. They wouldn't judge me. "Yes, I'm in love with Wyatt Black. He wants to marry me." I blurted that last part out before thinking it all the way through.

"Oh my God," Charlotte said. "Did you say yes?"

"Not yet," I said.

"But you will?" Charlotte asked.

"I told him to slow down, but yes, I'm a goner. I didn't think it was possible."

Hope was looking at me as if I'd betrayed her to the devil. "I can't believe it. My only ally."

I smiled. "I tried, but he broke me."

Charlotte bounced in the booth she shared with Moonstone. "I'm thinking a spring wedding. Or Christmas. I love Christmas weddings."

"Hopefully I'll be able to attend," Hope said. "If I'm not in the pokey."

I patted Hope's hand. "It's going to be all right. Stay strong."

CHARLOTTE AND I HAD COME TO TOWN TOGETHER. ON THE WAY home in my SUV, Charlotte asked if she could open her window to let in the fresh air. "My stomach feels funky tonight."

"I noticed you ordered a ginger ale."

"Wine sounded bad, which is strange. *I* feel strange."

"Strange how?"

"Nauseous and really tired. I couldn't focus today during my morning writing. It was like the words just wouldn't come. I took a nap after you left. I'm not sure I'll make my deadline, which has never happened before."

"Are you late?" I kept my eyes on the road, even though I wanted to look at her to see if my suspicion had occurred to her yet.

"Yes, that's what I just said." Her already high-pitched voice rose a few notes. For Charlotte, she sounded cross. Most people's pleasant tone sounded like Charlotte's irritated one. "The book's probably going to be late."

That answered that question. She had no clue. "No, I mean, is your period late?"

"What? Oh, you mean…I don't know. I never keep track of that kind of thing. I'm irregular."

"Are you on the pill?"

"No, not exactly."

"How is one 'not exactly' on the pill? Either you are or you aren't."

"I'm not. I don't like them because they make my boobs even bigger than they already are."

If I could be so lucky. I was an A-cup on a good day. "What are you using?"

"Condoms." She let out an exasperated sigh. "Why are you asking me all this? I hate talking about this kind of stuff with my husband's sister."

"In addition to being Ardan's wife, you're also my best friend, so you have to." I patted her knee. "Now, come on. Think. When was the last time you had your period?"

No answer. I slowed and then turned down the driveway to our property. The tires made a pleasant crunch in the gravel.

Finally, a small voice came from the other seat. "I don't think I've had it since I started the new book. Which was about eight weeks ago. Oh my God, I must be pregnant."

I tried to stifle a laugh, but it came out anyway. "Charlotte, how could you not know?"

"I'm irregular. Like I said already." Again, the annoyed voice of Charlotte. "And you know how I get when I'm working on a new book. Time evaporates."

"Take a test tomorrow. Then you'll know for sure."

"I might need to take one tonight, or I won't sleep a wink."

"Do you want me to take you back to town to buy one?" I asked.

"No. God no. Everyone in town will know if I buy one from our store. I'll have to go into Hailey." Charlotte gasped, as if it had just occurred to her. "What am I going to tell Ardan?"

"Won't he be happy?" I asked.

"I don't know. We've talked about how we weren't ready yet. I wanted to get a few more books out, and he's so busy with his new foundation."

"No offense, but you're not getting any younger."

"I'm only thirty-six," she said.

"Practically geriatric in pregnancy age."

"I don't like you right now."

I laughed again. "If you *are* pregnant, it's going to be wonderful. You and Ardan will be great parents. I mean, look how attached you are to Chris."

"But he's perfect. Plus, he knows how to use the potty and sleeps through the night. I'll probably have pregnancy brain and won't be able to finish my book and then my career will be over before it's even started." Her voice had risen to a frantic pitch.

"I think you're being a little dramatic. I had Chris on my own and he didn't ruin my career." Or had he?

"You came here because of him. You're probably going to give up the movie offer. What if I resent my own child?"

I sobered as I turned into Ardan's driveway. She was truly struggling with the idea of becoming a mother. "It's not easy to do everything well or even everything at all. Motherhood has a way of shaping and molding our lives and our hearts. Everything changes inside you the moment you hold your baby in your arms. He or she will become your world. There won't be a thing you won't do for him or her. And I promise you, Charlotte, you're not going to care. Believe it or not, your work will become secondary to your family."

"It took me so long to get where I am."

"You'll still write books," I said. "You can write anywhere, for one thing. As an artist myself, I have no doubt that becoming a mother will enrich your work." I patted her knee. "And I'll get to be an auntie again. I'll be here every step of the way. We're sisters now."

Charlotte sniffed. "Thanks."

"Our mothers will be over the moon. And how sweet will your dad be with a grandchild?"

"Another baby cousin for poor Chris."

I laughed. "He'll pray for a boy cousin." We didn't have one yet besides Chris. Ironic, since it had been me growing up with four boys.

"What happened with Wyatt and Chris today?" Charlotte asked. "Did they have a good time fishing?"

"Yes, although Wyatt couldn't stand killing a fish. He had to throw it back."

"That's exactly what happened when I went with Ardan. Their scales are so pretty."

I seemed to have a pattern when it came to my favorite people.

"Wyatt got them both gloves and a baseball. They played catch earlier." When I'd gone upstairs to dress for the evening, I'd looked out the window to see the two of them tossing the ball back and forth on the grass just off the patio. Tears had stung my eyes.

"That is the cutest thing I've ever heard," Charlotte said. "What if I have a boy? I won't know what to do with him."

"You're with Chris all the time, and he adores you," I said.

"True. But Teagan, this could change everything."

"It will. You'll love every minute of it, too." We were at the house now. "Here we are. Get some rest, okay?"

"I will." Charlotte leaned over to kiss me on the cheek. "I'll see you tomorrow."

"Will you tell Ardan tonight?"

"Yes. We tell each other everything." She opened the door and slipped to the ground, then leaned back inside to say one last thing. "You know, it's okay to rely on Wyatt. He wants to be there for you. Maybe take the job. Let him be the partner you need."

"We'll see." I waved her off, then waited until she was inside before pulling out of the driveway and heading to Ciaran's to pick up Chris. Then we would go home to Wyatt. He'd be waiting for us, ready to tuck my son into bed and to hold my hand on the patio as we watched the stars.

A new baby Lanigan. Life was sweet sometimes. This was one of them.

19

WYATT

Without Teagan or Chris home, the house seemed too quiet. While I waited for them to arrive, Mabel caught my eye. I'd laid her upright against the stone fireplace instead of in her case. She didn't like to be stashed away in the dark like that, even though it was good for her to rest.

I wandered over and picked her up, ashamed by the way she glinted under the soft lighting, untouched and abandoned. She was slightly out of tune, so I spent a few minutes taking care of that, messing with the strings until they were back where they should be. Driving home from Ardan's, I'd had the beginning of a line. I wasn't sure if it would lead to anything, but it was better than I'd had for a long time.

When I work on songs, I usually scratch down lines as they come to me in the notebook I keep in Mabel's case. Since I had this little nugget, I took out the notebook and jotted down the line. Maybe this was the beginning of the end of my dry spell. I didn't want to jinx myself, so I didn't think too much more about what this meant.

I settled on the couch and strummed a few chords, then

picked out a melody. I was an organic songwriter, letting the words and music come to me as I worked.

I'd managed to come up with a decent first verse by the time Teagan and Chris returned. My little buddy was up way past his bedtime, but it didn't seem to have affected his bounce. I set aside Mabel and stood to greet them.

"Wyatt, guess what? Aunt Bliss made homemade ice cream, and I got to pick the flavor."

"Awesome," I said. "What did you choose?"

"She didn't have the stuff for cookie dough or mint chocolate chip." He turned to his mother. "Those are Wyatt's and my favorites." He whipped back toward me. "So we had to use strawberries and chocolate chunks and they were delicious."

"Bliss sent some home for us," Teagan said. "I put it in the freezer."

"That was nice of her," I said.

"Were you writing a song?" Chris asked. "With Mabel?"

I shrugged. "Nothing special. But yeah, a little something came to me."

"Is it about us?" Chris asked.

I chuckled and grabbed him close, then tousled his hair. "I can't tell you until it's finished."

"It *is* about us. I knew it."

"Christopher, don't mess with his artistic process," Teagan said. "And I'm sure his song was *not* about us."

It was, of course. But I kept that to myself.

"Time for bed, little man," I said, and threw him over my shoulder. He giggled, hanging over my back as I marched up the stairs. When we got to his room, I tossed him on his bed and pretended to be worn out by hunching over my knees and taking in deep breaths. "What did you eat today beside ice cream? You're heavier than yesterday."

He giggled again and jumped from the bed. "I had a

hamburger at Aunt Bliss's. She said I must have a hollow leg. Whatever that means."

Teagan had arrived in the doorway by then. She crossed her arms over her chest and pointed toward the bathroom with her chin. "Time to wash some of that Idaho dirt off you, and then it's off to sleep town. It's an hour and a half past your bedtime."

"But Mom, it's summer so I can sleep in." He tugged his shirt over his head as he trudged toward his bathroom.

"Wash behind your ears," Teagan said.

"I know, Mom." The bathroom door shut.

I yawned and rubbed my eyes. "I'm beat. How was your night?"

"Interesting," she said. "Let's compare notes before bed."

"You got it. I'm going to shower, too, if you don't mind."

"Just be back in time to say good night to Chris. You've set a precedent now."

"You got it, Pretty Girl." I kissed her on the cheek and passed through the doorway. Another line for the song struck me, so I ran downstairs to get Mabel and my notebook. I wanted them both close in case I thought of another.

AFTER WE TUCKED CHRIS IN, THE TWO OF US HEADED FOR HER bedroom. My hair was still damp from my shower and I had that clean, physically worn-out feeling I loved. All proof of a full day. I'd wasted too many before I came here.

I'd already brushed my teeth, so I slid between the sheets and turned on the television while Teagan got ready for bed. I wanted to check the baseball scores. My team was terrible this year, so I hadn't minded missing a few of the games. I'd rather have spent the time with Teagan and Chris anyway. Although maybe he'd like to watch a game with me. I'd have to ask him about that tomorrow.

I yawned again and settled back into the pillows. I'd almost drifted off by the time Teagan came out of the bathroom. I loved how she looked before bed, scrubbed clean of makeup and her hair falling down her back. As long as I lived, I'd never tire of her shiny copper hair.

"You look cozy." She smiled as she reached for the hand lotion she kept by the side of the bed. Every night she did the same thing. I liked knowing her rituals and seeing what her real life was like. Not the Hollywood one where we met, but this one where she was truly herself. "Does this mean we're not fooling around?"

I chuckled and rolled over to look at her as she got into bed. Tonight she had on a white cotton nightgown that fell just above her knees.

"*You* look pretty," I said.

She shifted to her side and rested her head against the pillow to gaze back at me. "When I was younger, I never wanted to show a guy what I looked like without makeup."

"Why? You're beautiful with or without it."

"All these freckles, for one." She touched the tip of her nose with her finger. "And I don't have thick eyelashes like Charlotte. Have you ever noticed how one of my nostrils is thinner than the other?" She tilted her head back to show me.

"They *are* different," I said. "But no one would see them that way or even notice if you didn't point it out." That wasn't totally true. I'd noticed before that they weren't totally symmetrical. Not that I cared. To me, she was just right.

"My mother was a beauty. Blonde and petite." She fiddled with the collar of my T-shirt as she spoke, not meeting my eyes. "Growing up I always wished I looked like her. Instead I grew into a giraffe. And this hair."

"I'm sorry you felt that way." I picked up a strand of her hair and twirled it around my finger. "I couldn't love your hair more.

Or your freckles and your nose, too. Don't get me started on those long legs of yours."

"I always wondered why I was the only one who looked like this. Two of my brothers took after my father and two after my mother. How did I happen?"

"There are a lot of redheads in Ireland. I'm glad you came out just as you are."

She lifted her gaze to mine. "Do you mean all the things you say, Wyatt Black?"

"Every one of them. You're just going to have to accept that my feelings are true."

She stroked the side of my face with her thumb. "None of this feels completely real. I keep thinking I'll wake up and you won't really have been here."

"I'm here until you make me go," I said.

"You were working on a song." She smiled, a little like a satisfied cat.

"A few lines came to me. I'm not sure I'm totally cured."

"But Idaho agrees with you," she said.

"You and Chris agree with me."

She looked at me with those pools of green. "What about you? Was there ever anything when you were small or even now that you didn't like about yourself?"

"Like what? I mean, look at me." I grinned at her.

She laughed and playfully shoved her hand into my chest. "So you are in love with yourself. I thought so."

I shrugged one shoulder, still smiling. Making her laugh was better than a stadium full of fans shouting my name. "I've had my share of insecurities. I still do, actually."

"Tell me what they are."

"I hated being poor. Growing up, I had a chip on my shoulder about a mile high. I pushed myself in sports and at school to prove I was just as good as anyone else. Even now that I've done so well, I don't feel like I belong in certain groups. Tonight was a perfect example." I told her how Ashton had bothered me. "He's one of those Ivy League types. Already rich and now even richer. They bug me. Even though I'm sure he's a perfectly nice guy."

"I wouldn't have known that had you not told me." Her eyes had softened.

"Your family's intimidating, too. Rich and smart and such good talkers."

"You're the one who puts poetry to music." She tapped my bottom lip. "Don't ever let my family intimidate you. We're rich, true. But that's just what we have in our bank accounts, not who we are."

"Thanks, Pretty Girl." I brushed her lips with mine.

"Did you learn anything tonight from Ashton?"

"Not really. Other than Cryer came by to talk with Ardan about Hope." I told her what we'd learned of her connection with the first victim.

"Hope told us the same thing. But she also said her assistant handles all her email correspondence. She hadn't read any of them prior to the party."

"You believe her?"

"I've known her a long time. She has some demons, but I don't see her killing someone, especially a weird fan. She's dealt with that for a long time."

"Ashton seems to think that Hope's the killer. Or maybe he's trying hard to steer us all in that direction."

"Because he did it," she said.

"Right."

"I want all this to be over. I'm so creeped out all the time."

"I know. It will be soon. Cryer's no dummy. He'll get to the bottom of this." I rolled onto my back and pulled her close. "Best thing to do is get some rest. We have our own lives to focus on right now."

She snuggled into the crook of my arm. "Have we reached the skipping sex part of our relationship?"

"I think a night off for recovery might be necessary." I closed my eyes. "Your son wore me out today."

"He does that."

"Every day here is the best day yet."

"You're such a big softy." She sounded drowsy, so I kept quiet. "Oh, Charlotte's pregnant."

"That's great," I said.

"Won't she be a great mom?"

"Absolutely. Just like you." I drifted off to sleep with the scent of her hair in my nose.

20

TEAGAN

The next morning, I drove into town determined to have a chat with Jodi Sapp. The longer I thought about her, the more certain I was that she or her employee, Ralph Jones, had murdered the two victims. My plan was just to swing by as if I were merely checking on her. If I could, I'd get her to talk about her past, maybe open up to me. Like the tiniest thread in a garment, I was hoping something would unravel enough to give me a clue to pass on to Cryer. My mother had told me more than once to keep my nose out of situations that had nothing to do with me, but fat chance that was going to happen. Hope needed to go make her movie. Wyatt and I needed to focus on our relationship instead of playing amateur sleuths.

I'd left the boys at home together to swim in the pool, using the excuse that I needed groceries. I'd lied, because I knew Wyatt would insist on coming with me or beg me not to go. This way he had of trying to keep me safe and sheltered was completely foreign to me. I wasn't sure I liked it. After all, I'd taken care of myself all these years without a man. Anyway, the point was, someone had to solve these murders. Cryer didn't seem to have a clue.

Since admitting to Wyatt how I felt, I was now consumed with an urgency to get on with our lives. I wanted to find the daily rhythm to our routine as a couple. Until all this was behind us, I wasn't sure that would happen.

Moonstone was not at her desk in the lobby. The faint scent of snickerdoodle cookies and coffee came from the kitchen. No Moonstone there, either. I knew Jodi was in a room on the third floor. Should I just go up and knock? Moonstone had said Jodi hadn't been feeling well. I highly doubted she was sick. Jodi was most likely faking it to keep a low profile. What if she'd already left town and there was no one in her room? If she were gone, wasn't that a sure sign of her guilt?

The stairs let out a tired croak as I made my way up to the third floor. It would be difficult to get up or down without Moonstone hearing the creaks. In every nook and cranny of the winding stairwell, she had displayed antiques: a vintage typewriter and telephone, a phonograph, stacks of old books. Dust tickled my nose, and I sneezed. My orderly sensibilities didn't react well to clutter.

When I reached the top, there were two rooms. Jodi had mentioned to me that her room faced the street, which would be 3B. I knocked on the door, careful not to pound for fear of startling her. Should I say I was housekeeping? No, that would just set us up for an awkward conversation once she knew it was me. No answer. I'm not sure why, but I knocked again. For several seconds I heard nothing. Then, a slight groan of floorboards, followed by what sounded like a kitten's muffled mew. Pinpricks of alarm ran up my spine as the hair on my arms stiffened. Something wasn't right. Obviously.

Someone was inside the room. Was it Jodi and a captor? Or was she the captor with her next victim? Could it be that she'd tied up someone and left?

Too many questions to answer without breaking down the door. I thought of myself as a badass country girl, but I didn't think my skinny legs could crash down a door. I should call Cryer. Right. He was the best choice. But if I called him and it took a while for him to get here, would it be too late for whoever was on the other side of the door?

I made a decision, knowing that I had to make a move one way or the other. To give the impression that I thought the room had merely been empty, I moved away from the door the same way I'd approached. My sandals made a slight click on the floorboards as I strolled over to the top of the stairwell. I held my breath and willed myself to stay calm. What I really wanted was to take the stairs two at a time. I held on to the railing as I descended. The old boards did their job and creaked as they had on my way upstairs. When I got to the lobby, I broke into a sprint, through the kitchen and out to the parking lot.

My hands were shaking as I called Cryer.

"This is Cryer."

"It's Teagan Lanigan. I think something's wrong. I'm at the inn." As quickly as possible I told him what I'd heard.

"I'm at the precinct in Hailey," Cryer said. "I'll get there as soon as I can. But I'll alert your deputy and send him over."

"Tell him to walk around to the back. Her room faces the street."

"Will do. And Teagan, don't do anything dangerous. Wait for the deputy."

"Okay, yes. Please hurry."

"Stay safe. I'll see you soon."

After I hung up, I called Wyatt. He picked up right away. "What's up, Pretty Girl?"

I told him what I'd told Cryer.

"I'll be right there," Wyatt said.

"No, stay with Chris."

"I'm dropping him with Charlotte," he said.

He sounded so resolute, I didn't argue. "I'm fine. Don't worry."

"I'll be there as fast as I can."

I was slouched by my car when Moonstone came around the corner carrying a bag of groceries.

"Teagan, what's wrong?"

For the third time, I told her what I'd heard. "The deputy's supposedly on his way."

"Good." Moonstone hugged the groceries to her chest. "I don't know why I'm not getting anything on this. My powers are all off."

The deputy arrived next. I knew him from around town. His name was Kevin Brown, and he had been assigned to Peregrine right out of the police academy. He had wiry brown hair and skin so smooth he didn't look much older than sixteen. I approached him and introduced myself. "I don't know exactly what's going on, but I know what I heard."

"You two stay down here. I'm going upstairs." He drew his gun from his holster. "Not to dismiss you, Ms. Lanigan, but most of the time these things are false alarms or misunderstandings. You might have just heard the television."

I sure hoped that's all it was. In this case, I was happy to be wrong.

Moonstone set the groceries on the back steps and joined me in the shade of the old cherry tree at the far end of the gravel parking lot. Too nervous to sit, we leaned against the trunk of the tree and held tight to each other's arms.

Minutes passed. "What's taking so long?" I asked, as if Moonstone would know. And then the sound of a gunshot echoed through the quiet summer morning. Another and one more.

We looked at each other, frozen with fear. Out of the corner of my eye, I saw movement at the back door. I turned to see a man with his arm in a chokehold around Jodi Sapp's neck stumble out of the inn and head for the rented minivan parked next to mine. She was handcuffed. Her face was bruised and bloodied.

He had a gun pointed at her head.

A guttural scream came from deep inside me.

The man's head spun around, and he spotted us standing like idiots under that cherry tree. Even in my terrified state, I took him in. Nice-looking with an air about him of money and power. Expensive haircut and shoes. A designer shirt and jeans, both splotched with blood.

"Run," Jodi screamed. "Run."

He had the gun pointed right at her head. "You run and I shoot her dead right here." He pushed the barrel of the gun into her temple so hard that Jodi cried out in pain. "Come here. Both of you."

We inched toward him. Could we take him? All three of us were a lot to handle. Even if he had a gun. When we reached them, he gestured toward me. "Open the van door or she's dead."

Jodi continued to sob.

I did as was asked, pulling on the handle of the sliding door. Once it was open, he shoved Jodi inside, then turned the gun on us. "Hand me your cell phones."

We both reached into our pockets and handed them to him.

Jump him, I silently begged Jodi. *Kick him. Anything.*

"Get in the van," he said.

I knew then with total clarity that whoever this man was had shot the deputy and that he planned to kill us, too. He'd take us somewhere in the wilderness where no one would find our bodies for years. My son would never know what happened to me.

"Get in, now. I won't hesitate to shoot both of you interfering bitches."

I went first, taking the seat next to Jodi. The bruises that marred her pretty face were in various shades of purple. Bruises doled out over multiple days. Her bare arms were also black and blue. Blood stained her white shorts and blouse. What had he done? Had he kept her captive all these days? But if he was the murderer, how did he kill someone on my fenced and gated property?

Moonstone sat next to me on the bench seat. Jodi had stopped crying and was now slumped against the window of the van. All fight had gone out of her.

The man closed the door. Moonstone jerked forward in an attempt to grab the handle, but the child safety locks were on. There was no way out unless we had the key.

He jumped into the driver's seat and pressed the engine button and backed out of the driveway so fast that gravel spewed into the air.

"He's going to kill us," Jodi whispered. "He can't leave any witnesses, and now you've seen his face."

"Shut up, bitch." The man slammed his hand against the steering wheel. "Haven't you learned by now to keep your stupid mouth shut?" He accelerated and we barreled down the street toward the south. The opposite direction of my family's land.

"This is Conrad Jenkins," she whispered. "My husband."

Her husband. I hadn't known she was married. Was that why there was no trace of her? She'd left an abusive husband and changed her name? No wonder she'd acted so elusive about her past. Now he'd found her. How had he kept her inside her room at the inn and no one heard her screams?

Moonstone, whose psychic abilities had apparently kicked in, answered my question. "They weren't there. He must have wanted something from her room."

"My wedding ring," Jodi murmured as her head rolled back against the top of the seat cushion. "He wanted me to have it on when he killed me."

My heart stopped beating for a split second. Fear as black as ink swallowed me whole. I wrapped my arms around my middle and rocked back and forth. We were all going to die at the hands of this crazy man. Had he murdered the others, or was this separate from all that? It had to be connected, but my terror was too great just then to reason through it all. We were going to be dead within hours. Unless I could think of something. But what could I do? We were trapped in a van headed God knew where.

Except I knew where. The place where my grave would be. A spot no one would know to look for three missing women.

I started to talk to everyone and say all those words I'd never been able to say. *Mother, I'm sorry I wasn't more willing to talk to you, to let you in. Wyatt, I'm so sorry it took me so long to tell you how I felt and that I didn't agree to marry you when you asked. I'm such a selfish, stupid person, but I love you so much.*

And my sweet Chris. I'd never see him grow up and graduate from college and see him pick a profession and a wife. I'd never be a grandmother. *My sweet boy. You'll be fine without me. You'll have your uncles and Charlotte.*

I wouldn't get to meet Charlotte and Ardan's baby. *Charlotte, you're the sister I always wanted. I would have chosen you if I could.*

Wyatt, I'll never be able to give you a baby.

Despite my desire to stay strong, tears streamed down my face. Moonstone took my hand in hers. We sped out of town and onto the highway.

I knew then exactly what had happened.

A hired killer.

The wrong girl.

Jodi and Paula had looked the same that night, especially from the back.

WYATT

I knew the minute I arrived at the inn that something was wrong. The back door was wide open. A brown bag of groceries had spilled onto the bottom step. A skid mark in the gravel indicated a car or truck had left in a hurry.

Shouting Teagan's name and delirious with fear, I charged into the kitchen. Empty. I went to the lobby. No one. The front desk where Moonstone sometimes sat held only her computer.

I shouted for Teagan and then Moonstone as I leaped up the stairs. When I reached the second floor, a door opened only an inch. A female voice said, "There were gunshots from upstairs. I think someone shot a policeman."

My legs weakened. I thought I might fall over, but I had to keep it together. "How do you know a policeman was shot?"

"Because I heard him announce himself, and then the door came down. Three gunshots came after that."

"Did you hear anything else?" I asked.

"Two sets of footsteps coming down the stairs." Only her mouth and one eye showed through the crack in the door. "A woman was screaming and crying. I hid in the closet until I heard a car start. I ran to the window and I saw a white minivan tear out of the alley and onto the street."

"Could you see who it was?"

The answer made my blood run cold. "I caught a glimpse through the window of the backseat. I think it was Moonstone and a lady with red hair, plus the lady upstairs."

"What direction did they go?"

"South on the main street. Toward the highway, I think."

"Stay here in your room. Lock the door until the cops get here."

"Yes, okay."

I didn't wait around to hear anything else. There was no time to waste. Cryer, by my calculations, should be arriving at any moment. I felt sure the deputy hadn't survived three gunshots, and I was levelheaded enough to know I shouldn't mess with a crime scene. Still, if he were only hurt, I couldn't leave him up there. I bolted up the stairs three at a time. At the top of the stairs, I stopped, my heart in my throat. A young deputy was sprawled in the doorway in a pool of blood. I knelt to take his pulse. As I feared, there was none. "I'm sorry, buddy." Everything in me wanted to start screaming for help.

Keep it together.

I sprinted back downstairs and out to the parking lot just as Cryer was getting out of his car.

"It's bad," I said. "Real bad. The deputy's dead." I reported everything the woman told me. "She's upstairs scared out of her mind but she knew exactly what went down. We have to go after them."

Cryer put up a hand. "Get in my car. We'll go together."

We both jumped in the car and Cryer backed up and out of the parking lot. The moment we were on the street, he called his backup and told them to skip the inn and head south on the highway. "A witness saw a white minivan speed that direction. Yes, we're about five minutes ahead of you."

Cryer didn't speak as he turned onto the two-lane highway leading south. I sat frozen in the seat, silently praying. *Please, God, shield them from harm.*

"Who is this guy?" I asked. "What does he want with Jodi and her staff?"

"I was developing a theory. Like your friend Moonstone said, I think the murder was a case of mistaken identity. The women looked the same from the back. They were the same build and wore long brown hair in ponytails. They were dressed in the same catering outfit. Jodi was the intended victim all along."

"Then why the murder the DJ?"

"I haven't been able to track down who he really is, but my guess is that wasn't his real name. I think he was a hired killer."

"He killed the wrong girl, then whoever hired him killed him? Like for revenge?"

"That's what I think, yes. I figured out that Jodi Sapp isn't her real name. She's Mrs. Conrad Jenkins. First name is Jennifer. She'd reported several instances of spousal abuse. The last time put her in the hospital. She disappeared from there and was never seen or heard from again. My guess is Jenkins found her and put a hit out on her. When it didn't work, he came to finish the job himself. If he's the type of man I think he is, then he wouldn't have been able to tolerate the hired gun's incompetence."

I thought I might be sick. He had my girl. Could we get to them in time? I pressed my foot against the floor of the car as if that would get us there faster.

Cryer continued to talk through his theory. "When the deputy showed up at the inn, he must have panicked, killed him, and decided to take all of them captive. No witnesses."

"He'll kill all three if we don't get there first." The fear and panic I'd felt that night of the shooting and in the nightmares since enveloped me. I couldn't stop shaking. The sight of the poor deputy flashed before my eyes again and again. Was it me? Did death follow me?

If anything happened to Teagan, I might not survive. The thought of never seeing her alive again made me more afraid than I'd ever been in my life. More so than the night of the shooting. *Not my Teagan, God, please.* Chris's trusting eyes looking at me over his cereal bowl this morning danced before my eyes. I almost started bawling like a baby. What about him? How would he go on without his mother? She was his world.

God, please, give me a chance to make us a family. Don't take her from me. I'm begging you.

"Wait, look. What is that?" I pointed to car tracks in the long grass by the side of the road. "Those look fresh."

"You're right. But they could be from anyone."

A voice as clear as that of Cryer's came to me. Moonstone. *That's right. Follow the tracks.*

"Crap, Cryer, this is going to sound crazy but I just heard Moonstone's voice. She said to follow the tracks."

"I thought she was the psychic one, not you."

"I swear to God, I heard her."

"I hope you're not crazy and this is real." Cryer jerked his car to the right and followed the tracks.

We bounced along, the dry grass almost like a cushion under the tires. I tasted blood in my mouth and realized I'd been biting the inside of my lip. Squinting into the sun, I searched for any signs of them but saw nothing but dry grass swaying in the breeze and a bank of trees. The creek. Those trees were the kind that grew beside the swimming spot we'd gone to the other day.

The tracks made an abrupt turn. Cryer followed them for another minute. As we got closer, the landscape turned downward. And there it was, slightly hidden behind a tall bank of blackberry bushes. The white van.

Cryer cursed under his breath and reached for his phone.

"Yeah. We found them. Turn into the meadow where you see tracks. Just after mile marker fifty-six."

How in the world had he known that?

"What do we do?" I asked.

"I'm sure he's already spotted us by now. Unless he took them somewhere."

He pulled up beside the van. "Stay here. I don't want a civilian getting shot."

Like hell I was staying in the car. "Will do." I let him get a few feet ahead before opening my door quietly and slipping to the ground. My eyes scanned the landscape for clues. The area was quiet other than a few birds chirping and the rustle of leaves in the maples and birch trees that grew along the side of the creek.

I wanted to shout for Teagan but stayed silent as I'd been asked. He noticed me but must have figured it was useless to try to lose me. He motioned for me to stay behind as he raised his gun and went around the other side of the van. Seconds later, he reappeared. "Passenger door's open. They left in a hurry."

I peered in from behind as he opened the passenger-side front door. Inside was empty, other than a can of Coke in the driver's cup holder and a map of Idaho. Cryer opened it and spread it out on the seat. "He's marked a spot with an X. That has to be where he's planning to kill them and bury them." He pulled out his phone and opened the map app. "Yeah, okay. So this X is about a mile from here."

He squinted, then turned his body in the direction of the creek and pointed. "Head north."

We started to run.

22

TEAGAN

My hands had blistered and were bleeding by the time the hole was only a foot deep and six feet wide. We were near the banks of Owen Creek. The ground was softer here by the water but still hard for three women to shovel. Especially when there was a gun pointed at your head.

We'd been ordered by Conrad Jenkins to dig our own grave. After the four-foot-by-six-foot ditch was finished, he would kill and bury us where no one would ever find the bodies.

Moonstone, never one to succumb to pessimism, was still holding out hope. I could see her mind working, trying to hear the man's thoughts and somehow get to him that way. She was currently telling him about how inept the police were in rural Idaho. "They don't have enough force to find you if you just leave us here alive. We'll keep quiet. No one will ever know you were here."

Conrad sat against a fallen log mere feet from us with his legs spread out long. As though he was on a freaking picnic. Put a beer in his hand instead of a gun and he would have looked like any city slicker. Instead he was a killer. He'd already killed two and probably the deputy as well. Pretty soon it would be six. He gestured toward Jodi, who was doing her best to contribute to the hole but was in such pain from the beatings her husband had given her that she wasn't much help. "If she'd just done as I told her and not run away like a child, this wouldn't have happened. She's to blame, not me."

"It doesn't matter whose fault it is," Moonstone said in a soothing voice. "No one will ever need to know about this. You can just leave us here alive and take off. By the time we were able to get out to the highway, you'd be long gone."

"No, it's too risky. I have a business to go back to. Employees who rely on my leadership."

"What do you do?" Moonstone asked, as if he were a guest at her inn.

"An investment firm," Jenkins said. "I started out with nothing, and now I'm worth a billion dollars. I had everything. Money, the prettiest wife in our circle. Respect. Until this spoiled bitch decided to leave me. And for what, Jodi? Another man?"

"There's no one else," Jodi said. "I had to leave before you finally hurt me bad enough to kill me."

"It's a terrible thing when a marriage breaks up," Moonstone said, continuing using her placating tone. She was trying to appeal to his ego, but it clearly wasn't working. "But there are other fish in the sea. You could leave here and start again with someone new."

"Don't think I won't. As soon as you're all in the ground, I can finally move on from this conniving bitch's betrayal." He gestured toward Jodi with his gun. "Do you know how embarrassing it was to have to explain where you were to all my colleagues and friends?" Then, back to Moonstone. "Not a word to me that she was unhappy. Just up and left. Not so much as a note."

"Shut up," Jodi said, no louder than a frightened child. "Just shut up."

Quick as a rattlesnake striking its victim, Conrad was up. He slapped her face with the back of his hand. She let out an awful sound like a tormented animal and fell in a heap on the ground.

Moonstone went to her and cradled Jodi's bloody head in her lap. "What's wrong with you? She's a defenseless woman."

Conrad smacked Moonstone with the barrel of the gun. Blood ran from her nose. But God bless her, she wouldn't give him the satisfaction of crying out.

"Why are you doing this?" I leaned on my shovel for a second and tried to catch my breath. "Why did you kill Jodi's employees? It makes no sense."

"Get back to work. You're clearly the strongest of the three. I'm looking at you to get this done, or I'll make all of your deaths long and painful."

Moonstone and I exchanged a glance. She was terrified. Her face was already turning purple. He might have broken her nose. Even she couldn't get us out of this one. Not with her psychic abilities or her charming tongue.

"Let them rest, then," I said. "Please."

He liked the pleading tone. "Get on it. I don't have all day." This was a man who craved control more than anything. And respect. His wife's betrayal was something he thought should be punished. He'd probably done everything in his power to find Jodi. Men with his resources could make things happen—pay people off to give him answers.

I dug and dug. My shoulders and core ached, but I kept on. If only I could get him to talk and distract him, then go for his gun. Or hit him over the head with the shovel.

I still had one hope alive in me. Along the way, I'd dropped a clue for Cryer. One that I hoped they'd find if by some miracle they'd come this far. The tennis bracelet my father had given me when I graduated from college.

If the most precious gift my father ever gave me sparkled under the sun, we might be saved. My father had taken care of me my whole life. Would his love come through for me now?

Moonstone and Jodi huddled together. Tears streaked down their muddy and bloody faces. I continued to dig.

I started talking to Father silently. *I'm sorry we fought about Chris. I should never have been so hotheaded and awful. I'd give anything to have had the chance to say I'm sorry. Please forgive me. It's just that I loved you so much and feeling like I let you down made me angry. I had to react in anger or I would not have survived. Please be there with Finn when I get to you. It'll be soon. Your princess is coming back to you.*

A shadow moved over my shovel. I looked up toward the sky. A peregrine falcon, at least two hundred feet above, dived straight for us. They dive for their prey headfirst. He must have spotted a duck or crow. He flapped his wide wings, then brought them close to his sides to give him more speed. Like a rocket falling from the sky, he headed toward us. Or rather, he headed straight toward Conrad Jenkins. And then he was there, so close I could see his talons outstretched. A swish of wind lifted the damp hairs on the back of my neck.

Conrad Jenkins stared at the bird, then stood and raised his gun. But he was no match for the small bird, the fastest of all living creatures. The peregrine, with his talons outstretched, landed on Jenkins's face and knocked him to the ground. He latched onto Jenkins's cheeks as he would a fish in an Idaho stream. With his pointed black beak, he poked into the man's head. All the while Jenkins screamed and tried to disentangle the bird from his head.

Moonstone, obviously thinking quicker than Jodi or me, grabbed the gun. She stood over Jenkins with the weapon aimed at his chest, unafraid of the bird. They almost seemed to speak to each other, the magnificent bird and the remarkable woman.

Had an understanding passed between them? Conspirators, I thought.

"Good man," Moonstone said. "You've done enough now."

The peregrine nodded and hopped from his prey and flew to the branch of a nearby tree. He fixed one of his black eyes upon me. I was powerless to look away as he peered into my soul. Something inside me shifted. My heart was no longer just an organ that pumped blood through my veins, but love as the poets claim. I wept as he continued to stare at me. So familiar. So safe. *My princess, my beautiful girl,* my father's voice whispered. *I'm proud of you. I should have told you that more often.* Then I knew. Father. He'd come one last time to save me.

"You heard me," I whispered.

His wings expanded. He winked at me, then sailed upward, no longer a bullet but a graceful majestic king of the sky until I could no longer see him. "Don't go," I shouted into the breeze he left behind. But he was gone. Then his voice once more.

I'm always here, princess. I've never left. Now go home to your boys.

A rustling in the grasses stole my attention just as Cryer and Wyatt appeared, running toward us. At the look of sheer panic on Wyatt's face, I started to cry all over again and sank into the hole I'd created for my grave. Not today. I'd go home to my boys instead.

213

23

WYATT

I dropped to my knees in the shallow grave and scooped my love into my arms. She sobbed into my chest as I held her tightly. Her hands were bloodied and her clothes damp from sweat. Dirt covered every inch of her. Bile rose from my gut as I took in the scene. Jodi Sapp was curled in a fetal position, her face and body black and blue. Moonstone had a gun pointed on a man. Whatever had attacked him had shredded his face. Had one of the women had a sharp knife? I couldn't imagine how they could possibly have cut him in so many places. Even his head bled. He moaned quietly. From pain or fear, I wasn't sure.

Despite Cryer's appearance, Moonstone kept the gun aimed at the man. At first glance she seemed calm and cool, but upon better inspection I saw that her hands shook. Her nose had been bloodied but didn't look broken. I'd played enough sports to know what a broken nose looked like, and that wasn't it.

"This is Jodi's husband," Moonstone said. "Conrad Jenkins. He's had Jodi locked away and has beaten and raped her. As you can see, he had us digging our own grave. A peregrine falcon swooped down on his face. Knocked the gun from his hands. I snatched it up, and then you guys showed up."

"You're good now," Cryer said to Moonstone. "Set down the gun. We don't want that thing going off." He pulled a set of handcuffs from his pocket and knelt next to Jenkins. "Can you see, Mr. Jenkins?"

"No, you idiot. Everything's blurry. That bird scratched my eyes."

I looked more carefully at Jenkins. His eyes were starting to bruise and watered the way they did when you had something in them, only about four thousand times worse.

Cryer nudged Jenkins onto his side and slipped the handcuffs on him, then started to read him his rights, just like in the movies. When he finished, he picked up Jenkin's gun and turned the safety on. "You know how to use this thing, Moonstone?"

"Are you kidding? I'm a lover, not a fighter," Moonstone said as she sank down next to Jodi and stroked her hair. "I think she needs an ambulance."

Cryer nodded. "Backup's on the way, as are the EMTs."

Teagan had stopped crying and had fixed her gaze on me as if she couldn't really believe I was here. "I thought we were all going to die."

"It's okay now." I smoothed her hair from her damp, dirty cheeks.

"How did you find us?" Teagan asked. "I didn't think there was any way, not when he went off-road."

"I saw the tracks in the grass," I said. "And heard Moonstone's voice in my head telling me to follow them."

"You did?" Moonstone asked. "I wasn't sure if you had the gift, other than your chakras sure seemed to indicate it to be true. Have you had visions or voices before?"

"Some might say the songs that come to me are from a source other than my own mind," I said. I'd long had a theory that creativity was really only whispers from God. "Maybe hearing your voice was from the same source." She could call it anything she wanted, but I knew what had happened. Jesus had been riding along with all of us.

"The falcon just appeared out of nowhere," Teagan said. "Right when I was silently talking to my dad, asking him to come save us."

I didn't have time to ask more questions, because the backup police arrived. They hauled Jenkins out while the EMTs went to work, first on Jodi. Her arm and several ribs were broken. That was the least of it, I thought. She would be tormented for the rest of her life.

The EMTs disinfected Teagan's blistered hands and took a look at Moonstone's nose. As I'd thought, she was bruised and sore, but her nose had not been broken.

"She didn't even cry out," Teagan said. "And he hit her hard with the gun."

"I was crying on the inside," Moonstone said. "But I'd be damned if I let him know he hurt me."

"You're going to heal up fine," the shorter of the two EMTs said to Moonstone. "It's a miracle he didn't break your nose."

"I have a protective shield of love and light around me," Moonstone said, sounding slightly smug, especially given her injury.

"May I use your phone?" she asked me. "I need to text Sam that I'm all right. He won't even know I've been gone since he's at work, but just in case."

I handed her my phone. "What happened to your phones?" I asked Teagan.

"Jenkins tossed them out the window just as we left town. He was probably worried about the tracking devices. If he'd succeeded in killing us, the phones wouldn't have given you much clue as to where we were." She shuddered.

One of the EMTs wrapped a blanket around Teagan's shoulders. "Have her sit in the shade there," he said to me. "And give her some water."

I took the bottle of water and led Teagan to sit on soft grass under a tree. Moonstone handed me my phone and sat next to us.

Jodi had been laid on the ground with a blanket over her. At least half a dozen cops were examining the crime scene, including a photographer who took pictures of everything.

After the EMTs had examined Jodi and wrapped her in a blanket, she was able to sit up against a log. Cryer asked her to tell him exactly what she remembered. Although it hurt to hear her awful tale, I was also curious.

He was right that she'd run away from her abusive husband and hoped to remain anonymous in nowhere, Idaho. "Did you know he'd hired a hit man who got the wrong woman?" Cryer asked.

"No, not at first. It never occurred to me," Jodi said. "Even though it should have. We did look so similar and were wearing the exact same outfit. We both smoked, too, so that was another thing that threw him off. I had no idea that Ryan Chambers wasn't a real DJ. He had a website and everything. But yes, he killed the wrong woman. When Conrad found out, he came here to do it himself. He killed Ryan Chambers, or whatever his real name is, and then came to the inn. He made me leave a message for Moonstone that I had the flu and not to disturb me. Then he took me to this house he rented in Hailey. He wanted to torture me for a few days before he killed me."

"What did he do to you?" Cryer asked.

I winced at her answer.

"He beat me and raped me. For two days it went on, until finally I guess he had his fill."

"Then what happened?" Cryer asked.

"We came back to inn because I made the mistake of telling him that my wedding ring was there. One time when he was punching me I told him where it was. He was obsessed with knowing what I'd done with it. I was keeping it in case I got desperate for money. He wanted me to be buried wearing it."

"He drove you to the inn?"

"Yes, in the middle of the night when all the guests were asleep. He tied me up and gagged me to keep me quiet while he slept for a few hours. I fell asleep, too. The sound of Teagan coming up the stairs and then her knock on the door woke us both. I made a muffled sound to let her know I was in there, hoping she would go for help. But that was a bad idea. That cop." She wiped tears from her dirty face. "He was so young. Conrad shot him three times. Then he dragged me down the stairs. I was praying that Teagan and Moonstone wouldn't be anywhere near, but they were in the parking lot. That's when he made Moonstone and Teagan get into the car, too. He couldn't risk being identified. I'm so very sorry for everything. All of this is my fault." She folded over her knees and began to cry.

"It's all over now," Cryer said, sounding surprisingly gentle for such a large man.

She leaned into him and let him put an arm around her. She needed a man like Cryer, I thought. Someone who could nurse her back to health. Treat her like a precious gift instead of a punching bag.

Rage toward Jenkins rose up from my belly. Before the shooter killed dozens of my fans and now this, I'd never felt violent. But right now I wanted to kill either or both of them with my bare hands.

"I'll have more questions later," Cryer said. "But for now, let the EMTs take you to a hospital."

Jodi nodded. "Okay."

They put her on a stretcher even though she said she could walk. "You've been through enough," Cryer said. "They'll take care of you now."

When we were finally finished, Cryer took us all back to the inn in his car. Sam was sitting on the back steps waiting for us when we arrived. He turned ashen at the sight of Moonstone's bruised face.

"I'm all right, love," Moonstone said. "Let's go inside, and I'll tell you all about it."

I talked Teagan into leaving her car at the inn so I could drive her back to the house. She hadn't stopped shaking even though she kept saying she was fine.

It was nearly five o'clock by the time I got her home and into the shower. Hovering like a mother hen, I paced between the bathroom and bedroom. When she finished, I helped her into her fluffy robe and guided her over to the bed. She'd stopped shaking, but I could sense how weary and exhausted she was.

"I'll have Charlotte bring Chris home," I said as I picked up my phone to text. I'd already sent a message to her earlier that Teagan was fine and not to worry. "I don't want to leave you alone."

She gave a weak smile as she sank onto the bed. "I'm all right. Just sore. My back and arms especially."

I sat next to her. "Show me your hands."

She let me turn them over and examine her blisters. "I'll wrap them for you. Do you have anything I can use?"

"They're fine. I don't want to scare Chris by having giant bandages on my hands. Anyway, I should get dressed."

Even though I wanted her to stay in bed, I knew how unlikely it was she'd agree to my wishes. Nothing came before protecting Chris. "Don't get up. I'll bring you something to wear."

She sighed and relented. "I have a clean pair of shorts and a T-shirt folded on the chair there. Underwear and bras are in the top drawer of my closet."

I grabbed everything and returned to her. Since I'd been gone, she'd collapsed onto her side with her cheek resting on a pillow.

"That's enough," I said. "You're resting now. No dressing or getting up. I'm putting my foot down."

"Fine. I'm too tired to argue with you."

I covered her with the throw blanket and sat next to her. She closed her eyes. "I'm sorry I've tried so hard to drive you away."

"But you didn't."

She smiled as her eyes fluttered open. "You're a stubborn man, Wyatt Black."

"Only when it's something important." I remembered the bracelet. "Oh, wait. I almost forgot. I found this." I tugged it from my pocket. "The minute I saw it glinting in the sun, I knew you'd left it for me to find."

"I'd completely forgotten. I didn't think it would work. The grass was so high."

"Strangely, it was on a tree stump, like someone had placed it there carefully." I tugged the blanket up and around her shoulder, careful not to press too hard.

"How strange. I dropped it as we were walking so he wouldn't see. Maybe Father moved it for me."

"Nothing would surprise me at this point."

She poked her arm out from under the blanket. "Father was the first man to put it around my wrist. I know he'd be pleased to pass the torch to you."

"I'd be honored." I wrapped the delicate bracelet around her wrist and then closed the clasp. "Back where it belongs."

She lifted her gaze from the bracelet. "You're where I belong."

"Does that mean you'll marry me?"

"You say when and I'll be there." She closed her eyes. "The sooner the better."

IN THE END, I MADE THE FIRST DECISION AS CHRIS'S DAD AND asked Charlotte to keep him another night. I didn't want him to come home and have to ask why his mother was in bed before dinner. Teagan slept all through the night and didn't wake until seven the next morning. I made her breakfast and gave her a few over-the-counter painkillers to combat her sore muscles. Other than that, though, she looked remarkably unharmed. By the time Charlotte brought Chris home in the afternoon, she was out on the patio reading. She had braided her hair and wore a loose cotton sundress. After some convincing, she'd allowed me to put discreet bandages on her blistered hands.

Besides the fact that she burst into tears at the sight of her little boy, no one would have guessed how close she'd come to death.

"Come here, my love," Teagan said, holding out her arms.

Chris ran to her. She winced as he launched himself into her arms, but that didn't stop her from hugging him tightly.

"Mom, why are you crying?" Chris asked after escaping from her fierce hug.

"I'm happy to see you, that's all." Teagan grasped both his shoulders and smiled at him. "I missed you."

"Gosh, Mom, you're acting weird. I was only gone for like a day. What are we doing this afternoon?"

"We're going to hang out around the pool today," I said, stepping in, feeling like a father and a husband. This was my job now—to protect them and love them. "Your mom's tired."

Chris shrugged and grinned up at me. "Okay, cool."

"Run upstairs and get your swim trunks on." I tugged on the waistband of my shorts. "I've been waiting for you."

"Awesome." Chris tore across the patio and into the house.

Charlotte, who had stopped in the kitchen before coming out to see Teagan, stepped out to the patio. She teared up as she knelt to embrace Teagan. "Thank God you're all right."

"I didn't know if I'd ever see you again," Teagan said, crying again. "When it got bad and I thought I wasn't coming back, I wished I'd said so many things. To you. To my brothers and Mother."

"No, no, it's not like that. We're your family. We know your heart." Charlotte wrapped her hand around Teagan's wrist.

"I have to do better," Teagan said. "You're the first real friend I've ever had, and I never told you what you mean to me. Or that you're the sister I wanted."

"Teagan Lanigan, you're not going soft on me, are you?" Charlotte tugged on Teagan's long braid that hung over one shoulder.

"Never." Teagan's eyes continued to spill tears. "Except I can't stop crying. Everything's brighter now. More clear." She waved her hand toward the mountain.

Charlotte must have noticed Teagan's bandages for the first time. She asked in a trembling voice, "Did he hurt you?"

"No, that's just from the shovel. From digging the grave."

Charlotte shuddered. "Oh God, Teagan. When I think of what you must have been thinking... It's too awful."

"I'm here, though. We're all together again," Teagan said. "And Wyatt. You know. He's here now, too."

"Yes, I can see that." Charlotte smiled as she rose up to hug me. "Thank you for bringing my best friend back to me."

"My pleasure," I said, choking up.

"Also, I have confirmed your suspicions." Charlotte paused dramatically. "A positive pregnancy test is now on the counter in my kitchen."

"I knew it," Teagan said. "I'm so happy." We'd have to take her word for it because she was now crying again.

"I'm a nervous wreck and Ardan's already ordering parenting books," Charlotte said.

"That baby's a lucky one to have you for his or her mama," I said.

"Oh, Wyatt, you always know just what to say." Charlotte smacked my shoulder. "I love it."

"I'm also a fan of yours, Miss Charlotte."

"For heaven's sake." Teagan sniffed, then rolled her eyes. "You two are enough to make a girl sick to her stomach from all the sweetness."

"I know you don't mean that." Charlotte returned to the chair next to Teagan. "My mom made a mess of enchiladas. And I'm afraid everyone's on their way over. You know how it is. The Lanigans don't know how to give someone space."

"You know what, Charlotte? I guess that makes us pretty lucky," Teagan said.

"I'd have to agree," Charlotte said.

Ardan and Mrs. Lanigan came out from the kitchen. He had her hand on his arm as they walked carefully toward us. Charlotte got up from her chair.

"Teagan?" Mrs. Lanigan asked.

"I'm here, Mother."

Ardan escorted Mrs. Lanigan over to the chair Charlotte had occupied and helped her to sit. Mrs. Lanigan reached toward Teagan, who took her hand between hers.

"Bandages?" Mrs. Lanigan asked.

"Nothing to worry over," Teagan said.

"My girl." Mrs. Lanigan's face crumpled as she started to cry.

"I'm here, Mother. No harm done. Please don't cry."

"I can't lose you. Not when I just got you back."

Teagan rose from her chair to kiss her mother's cheek. "Never. Wyatt made sure of that."

Mrs. Lanigan reached her hands out, searching for me. "Young man, come here so I can hug you."

I obeyed, holding her fragile body gently in my arms. "You're a good boy," she whispered. "Thank you for taking care of my girl."

"I'll spend the rest of my life doing just that," I said before straightening.

"I want to know what happened," Mrs. Lanigan said. "Tell me everything. Charlotte and Ardan won't tell me the details."

"Mother, it's all over. There's no reason for you to know."

"I want to know." Mrs. Lanigan set her mouth in a stubborn line. "I'm not some delicate old lady."

Teagan and Charlotte exchanged a glance.

"There's something I should tell you," Teagan said. "Something amazing."

Ardan turned to me. "Let's get a beer."

I nodded, understanding the women needed privacy to talk.

When we got in the kitchen, Ardan pulled a few beers from the refrigerator. "I don't even know what to say." He handed me one of the bottles. "When I think about what would've happened if you weren't there…"

"Not necessary," I said, embarrassed.

Ardan clinked my bottle with his. "I guess all I can really say is thank you and welcome to the family. You're stuck with us now."

"I couldn't imagine a better one to be stuck with," I said.

"I've seen the falcon," Ardan said. "So has Blythe."

"I'd seen him before yesterday too. When I first got here."

"Father was a force. Like the peregrine."

"I guess he still is."

We clinked bottles again. "To the mysteries of this world," Ardan said.

"And the miracles."

24

TEAGAN

Charlotte excused herself shortly after Ardan and Wyatt, leaving Mother and me alone to talk. I took Mother's hand. Her skin felt so thin under my young fingertips as I told her the facts of what had happened. She listened without moving a muscle.

"As I dug, I started talking to Father, asking for his forgiveness. And then, out of nowhere, this shadow appeared." I proceeded to describe how the peregrine had swooped down on the man and how he'd perched in the tree to look at me. "I heard his voice as he flew away, Mother. Clear as if he were standing next to me."

"Your father was constantly talking about how they were the fastest of all animals," Mother said. "He told me once that if he had to be something besides a human, the peregrine would be his choice."

I sat stunned for a few moments. How strange it all was. Yet the pieces came together.

"And the bracelet? Wyatt found it?" Mother asked.

"He saw it, not in the grass but on the stump. Laid out like it was for sale at a jewelry store."

"Yes, yes, I see." She moved her hand from mine to squeeze my knee. "Your father loved you very much."

"I know."

"Before today, I'm not sure I would've believed you. But I am sure it was him today. He was there. This isn't the first peregrine story in this family. Blythe and Ardan had similar experiences, although not to the extent you did today."

"Really?" I couldn't believe what I was hearing.

"Isn't it remarkable?" Mother asked. "All the things we cannot see, yet are there."

"Yes." An image of Wyatt as he came through the thicket of trees flashed before me. If I'd been unsure of the depth of his love, it was certainly evident in that moment. "Mother, I've been such a fool. So many mistakes."

"You can't expect to get through life without a few of those."

"I tried to push Wyatt away, but he wouldn't give up," I said. "He wants to marry me."

"Honey, that's wonderful."

Surprised at the hitch in her voice, I squeezed her hand. "I'm still not sure why."

"It takes a man completely sure of himself to be with a strong, independent woman." Mother's sightless eyes filled with tears. "Your father understood me better than any other person. He knew my soft underbelly, even though I tried to hide it. Sometimes I wondered how he loved me. But he did. I was blessed with his companionship for longer than I deserved. Enjoy every moment with Wyatt. You never know how many you'll have."

"I'll try, Mother."

"I'm glad you came home."

"I wasn't sure I would. I've never been more certain that I was going to die right then and there."

"No, I meant come home to Idaho." She stared toward the pool as if she were seeing the green tiles. No one would know that her world had become only darkness. Her eyes were still as bright and intelligent as they'd always been. "If Charlotte hadn't been such an interfering thing, we might not be back together."

I laughed. "Yes, for someone who seems so sweet, she's totally sneaky."

LATER THAT DAY, AFTER SWIMMING AND BADMINTON AND A WHOLE lot of noise and laughter and an enchilada dinner, Mother and I sat together on the patio while the rest of the family cleaned up the dishes.

"Charlotte told me about the job offer," Mother said. "I think you should do it. Let Wyatt take some of your burden. That's what partners do."

"I don't know. I don't want to miss anything. Chris will be grown before I know it."

"That's the God's honest truth." She found my knee with her hand. "Motherhood is our most important job, but it's not our only one. Women of my generation fought hard to give you choices. If you can juggle a project every now and then that feeds your soul, then I say do it. Chris will be grown soon and venture out to make his own life. If all you've done is focus on him, there won't be anything left of you. Women always put themselves last—their health, their creative desires, even friend-ships—to take care of their families. It's permissible to have a little something of your own."

I thought about what she'd said, inspired by her advice. Perhaps she was right. Taking the job didn't make me a bad mother. "Did you feel like you gave up too much for us?"

"Never. Your father always made sure I had time to do the things I wanted. They always say that there's a powerful woman behind every successful man. While I'm sure that's true, there are many women supported by their husbands. Wyatt's that type of man. Be thankful."

"I will, Mother." I leaned my head against her shoulder.

"Tell me about the sunset. I can feel the rays still on my face."

Touched and surprised, I took a moment before answering. Usually she asked Charlotte to describe the visual scene. The sun hung just above Blue Mountain, golden and warm. "There are no bright colors tonight, just a yellow ball over the mountain. It'll be one of those nights where the sun will slowly dim as it falls behind the mountain. The patio rock looks almost gold."

"One of those evenings where the warmth remains in the stones of the patio even after the sun goes down," Mother said. "I used to love those kinds of days."

"Take off your sandals," I said. "Let's walk."

She slid out of them and I helped her stand, then stepped out of my flip-flops. "The stones are smooth. So don't worry about hurting a toe."

"All right. Hold on tight to me."

"I will." I linked my arm with hers and we strolled across the patio.

"Does the warmth feel good on the soles of your feet?" Mother asked.

"It does." The bottom edge of the sun had dipped below the mountain.

"The warmth captured in these stones is what remains of the day. Like a memory." Mother halted and turned toward the sun. With her eyes closed, she spoke softly. "A reminder that once we lived under the rays of the sun. Maybe we even danced under them or sang or shouted with glee. And now we can only feel what's been left behind."

I teared up, knowing she was thinking of Father and Finn. We had only our memories of them now. I thought of Finn, the way the sunlight had glinted in the locks of his yellow hair just before he jumped into the swimming hole. "Do you ever think Finn was the best of us?"

"Not the best, but the one who never hid his love. Of us. Of the world. Of music. Do you remember how he loved music?"

"I do, yes."

Mother turned away from the sun, and we ambled farther across the patio. Someone had turned on music that traveled out to the deck from the outdoor speakers. Before he came, they'd allowed me to have a part of Wyatt. Even then, I'd known.

"John Denver," Mother said. "Your father used to love him."

An image of an evening when I was young, maybe five, played before my eyes. The boys had found a frog and were arguing about whether to let him go or keep him in an aquarium. I wore my favorite polka-dot bikini, damp against my skin from running through the sprinkler. Steaks on the grill and sunscreen smelled of summer. My parents danced barefoot in the grass to a John Denver album. She wore a sundress with a pattern of daisies. I'd loved that dress. As they swayed to the music, she rested her cheek against Father's chest. His chin perched on the top of her shiny blond hair.

I'd gone completely still, not something I did often, and watched them, struck by the utter beauty of my parents. Father had seen me and gestured for me to join them. "Come here, Princess. I'll dance with both my girls." He boosted me into his arms and held my cold, damp body against him and put the other arm around Mother. We'd danced in the last sun rays of the day, laughing.

"Mother, do you remember when Father lifted me up and the three of us danced together?"

"More than once," she said. "He was so strong he could dance with you in one arm with the other around me."

"I'd forgotten until just now."

"Those were glorious days. When I think back, it's never the big events I remember. The small ones, like the slam of the screen door in our old house. That was the sound of family. You kids were always running in and out all day long from your adventures. That door open and closed a hundred times a day. I'd think, 'What dirt or animal or stick will they be bringing in now?' Oh, Teagan, I loved those days out here when you guys were still mine to look after. Those plain, ordinary moments all add up to your life. You don't realize it at the time because you're too busy sweeping up dirt and making dinners and running baths. And you're tired a lot, which makes you less appreciative than you should be for all of the messy joy children bring."

"I don't know how you did it, Mother. So many of us."

"Sometimes I thought I wouldn't make it to bedtime. But there was so much laughing. Do you remember how Ciaran used to make us laugh so hard you had to run to the bathroom?"

"Yes, I remember," I said. "Especially the time I didn't make it. I was so mad at him."

"When you're an old lady like me, you remember all of it with such fondness. Like childbirth, the hard parts fade." She was quiet for a moment. "As a grandmother to Chris and the little girls, I get all the joy without all the work. Do you know how good they all smell to me now that I can't see? I'm soaking up every moment."

We strolled past the stone and onto the stretch of grass. "The sun's almost gone now. There's just a golden half circle left. Blue Mountain looks blue."

"It always did this time of day." Once more, she lifted her chin and closed her eyes as if the sun healed them. "Will you think of me when I'm gone?" Mother asked, after a moment.

"Of course I will."

"Charlotte says I'm too mean to die any time soon."

I laughed. "I hope so, Mother, because we have a lot more memories to make."

"A new baby," she said softly. "Won't Charlotte make the most wonderful mother?"

"Yes, she will."

"Will you have a wedding or run off and elope?"

"A small one. Maybe here at the house with Blue Mountain to bless us."

"So many things to look forward to." She let out a happy sigh. "What a fine life I've had."

The sun was gone now, so I steered her back toward the house. Everyone had come outside and gathered around the firepit. As we neared, Ciaran finished telling some story, and then everyone laughed.

They'd turned the stereo off, and Wyatt had his guitar around his neck. Bliss held one baby on her lap. Ciaran had the other. Ardan and Charlotte were squished together in one of the oversize chairs, always touching. Blythe and Kevan had pulled a love seat over and sat slightly behind everyone else. Lola, looking too grown-up in her cutoff jeans and tank top, was scooping ice cream into bowls while Clementine and Chris passed them around to the adults.

Only Kevan's Rori was missing. She and her boyfriend were still studying overseas and having more fun than I wanted to think about too carefully.

"Grandma, we saved you the best seat," Chris shouted. "Right between me and Clemmie. And we have ice cream." Clementine wore the jean overalls I'd made her with the daisy on the front. She loved daisies. Like Mother, I realized. Or maybe it was I who loved them? Perhaps I'd been emulating my mother's pretty dress and the way she'd looked on that night so long ago.

I escorted Mother over to her chair and helped her get settled.

"I saved a seat for you." Wyatt winked at me as he patted the chair next to him.

"He's going to play his new song that's about us." Chris, too short for the chair, swung his legs back and forth.

I settled next to Wyatt. "A song about us?"

"Yes, ma'am." Wyatt plucked one of Mabel's strings in a final tuning adjustment.

"How come you don't write me a song?" Bliss asked Ciaran as she kicked him playfully with her bare foot.

"Because, baby, you get all this." Ciaran gestured toward himself. "A song would be overkill."

Bliss rolled her eyes. Isabel clapped her hands and shouted, "Dada."

"See, she agrees with me," Ciaran said.

"I love Mama," Felicity said in the same enthusiastic tone.

Bliss kissed her cheek. "That's my girl."

"I'd write Blythe a song if I weren't tone-deaf and completely unmusical," Kevan said.

"You make up for it in other ways, honey," Blythe said.

"Oh for God's sake, get a room," Ciaran said.

Blythe blushed four shades of pink in quick succession. "Ciaran, I wasn't talking about *that*."

"Not in front of the children," Ardan said, only half teasing.

This is my family, I thought. *My big messy family: Kevan and Blythe's blended family; Bliss raising Ciaran's baby he'd had with another woman as her own; my Chris without a father. Until the biggest-hearted man on the planet came into our lives. We might not all be blood, but it didn't matter. Love made a family. We'd chosen one another. Maybe that made it even better.*

Wyatt strummed the first chord of his song, then sang.

You didn't ask for me to come.

Nor for the setting sun.

We're here just the same.

You're mine to claim.

25

TEAGAN

Ned's assistant, Andi Quinn, was waiting for me at a bistro in Hailey. About thirty minutes from home, the small ski town with its quaint shops and restaurants seemed like a metropolis compared to Peregrine. This time of year, vacationers came for the hiking, fishing, and swimming rather than to ski. Still, they were similar. Rich people from the cities of Seattle, Portland, and Boise. I missed the quieter days of my youth, but progress continues on, whether we want it to or not.

Andi rose to greet me, holding out her hand for me to shake. I'd met her before and liked her, even if she made me feel like a giraffe. Small in stature, with round blue eyes and a heart-shaped face. Ridiculously cute. She wore her hair in one of those tousled bobs that looked effortless, but I suspected took longer than I had the patience for.

"Ned should be here any minute." Andi had on a pair of skinny jeans paired with pumps. How could she walk in those? "He's running late. As always. Please, sit. We can order something cool to drink while we wait."

"Sounds great." I sank into one of the chairs at the round

table. Hot and flustered, I thought a glass of iced tea sounded like heaven. I'd dressed in white muslin pants and a light green sleeveless blouse. The weather and my nervousness had made me damp and overly warm.

"How have you been?" Andi asked. "You're looking well. The country life suits you."

"I'm doing all right, thank you." I wondered if she or Ned knew about the murders and that one of them had happened at my house. The Idaho papers and news channels had covered the entire drama at length. I'd already decided not to bring them up unless asked. "Are you staying with Ned out here?"

"Yes, he has an office for us at his house in Ketchum. After the horrid divorce from Prisilla, he wanted to disappear for a while and regain his sanity. The woman did a number on him."

"That's too bad. Although they struck me as unsuited."

"You think?" Andi asked with a slight edge to her tone. "He deserves so much better."

Interesting. I picked up more emotion than an employee usually felt for their boss. Was she in love with him?

"Have you enjoyed Idaho?" I asked. "Or has it been boring?" She and I were about the same age. I wondered if she hated it here and wished she could be back in LA.

"I love it here. If it weren't that I miss my friends, I'd probably stay forever. Not that I have time for a social life anyway. Ned's obsessed with this new project, so I haven't had much time to explore. No love life to speak of, either." Andi smiled at the waitress, who arrived with two glasses of ice water. "Thank you. Could you bring an iced tea when you have a moment?"

"For me too, please," I said.

The server nodded and scurried off to another table. The bistro was crowded and noisy, and I wondered why we hadn't met at Ned's home.

"If you have time, you'll have to come stay at my house," I

said. "We have a bunch of acres about thirty minutes from here. I've got more than enough guest rooms and a pool."

"That sounds lovely. Ned's promised me a few days off before we start filming, so I might take you up on that."

"I thought you had a boyfriend," I said, remembering a man with her when I'd met her at Gennie and Stefan's party last summer.

"I had one. But he couldn't handle my travel and schedule. He wanted a more traditional wife, I guess."

The hurt in her eyes made my chest ache for her. I could have kicked myself for asking. "I'm sorry. It's hard to find a man who understands this kind of work."

"Is that why you've quit the business?" she asked.

"Not for a man but for my son. He's school-age now and I wanted him to have a more stable life. Plus, my family's all here."

"Well, be prepared. Ned's decided he wants you, and he's used to getting his way."

"I'd love to work with him," I said. "That said, I'm struggling reconciling my personal and professional desires."

"Welcome to being a woman," Andi said.

"Amen." We exchanged a smile.

Ned arrived at the same time as the iced teas. He greeted me warmly but without a hug. Hollywood men had changed drastically in the last few years. Physical contact was not thrust upon us now as it was just a short time ago. I'd never minded a hug from most of the men I'd worked with. Most were friendly and innocent. However, like everything, a few bad people ruined it for everyone else.

"Iced tea for me too," Ned said as he took the chair next to Andi. In his early forties, Ned was tall and slender with salt-and-pepper hair and eyes the color of strong tea. Today, he wore trendy glasses and an elegant pair of summer trousers paired with a short-sleeved linen shirt. There was a reason he attracted so many women, I thought. He had a casual, easy charm. I'd heard he was impossible to ruffle on set, which was the opposite of many of the directors I'd worked with in the past. "Teagan, it's nice to see you. I couldn't remember for the life of me when I'd seen you last."

"At Gennie Banks's party last summer," I said.

"Oh yes. Of course. Horrible night. Prisilla and I had the worst fight. She shoved me into the pool."

"I missed that," I said. "I didn't stay long because I had to get home to Chris."

"Quite the spectacle. I'd never been more embarrassed in my life." Ned covered his eyes with his hands for a brief moment before glancing back at me. "Then she left in my car, leaving me at the mercy of Gennie and Stefan. They took pity on me and let me stay the night, which turned into several weeks because Prisilla had changed the locks. Such a mess."

"It wasn't your fault," Andi said. "No one blamed you."

"Prisilla filed for divorce soon thereafter," Ned said to me. "Fortunately, I'd learned from my first wife to prepare for the inevitable. A prenup is a good thing when you have questionable taste in women."

I wanted to ask details about his first wife, but I held my tongue. Maybe Andi would give me the scoop if I ended up taking the job. My recollection of Prisilla was of a skinny neurotic who wanted all the attention all the time. She sucked all the air out of the room.

"I've terrible luck with women," he said. "Other than Andi here, who puts up with me no matter what."

They exchanged a smile. "You're not so bad," Andi said.

The two of them were obviously close, but platonic. I wondered why he didn't see what was right in front of him. Business came first. Boundaries and all that.

The server took our orders. All three of us ordered a salad with chicken.

"Tell me, Ms. Lanigan, what will it take to get you on board with this project?" Ned smiled across the table at me.

"I'll be perfectly honest, I'd love to take the job. This film is completely in my sweet spot."

"But?" Ned asked.

"But I have a son. He's almost seven, and he needs me home with him."

"You can do your designs here and hire union staff to carry out your vision," Ned said.

I took a sip of my tea. Delegating and trusting weren't exactly my best attributes. "I like to be on set to make sure it's exactly how I want."

Ned laughed. "We could fly you out for a day or two a week."

"Or you could trust your staff," Andi said. "Which I know is hard. From one detail-oriented person to another, I get it. That said, I'm sure you know great people to hire. Ones you've worked with before?"

"I do, yes." I had a half dozen people who were my favorites. I knew they'd do good work. "I have a boyfriend," I blurted out. "He's offered to stay with Chris if I wanted to fly out for a day or two a week."

"But you're hesitating because you're worried it makes you a bad mother," Andi said.

"Something like that," I said. "Even though he's great with Chris and has made it clear he'd put his own career on hold for me."

Ned looked down at his hands, which were folded on the tabletop in front of him. "I'm not one to give relationship advice, but he sounds like a man you should marry."

"You definitely should not give marriage advice," Andi said. "However, I agree with you on this one."

I smiled. "I'm very lucky."

"I'd say," Andi said, somewhat wistfully.

"Why me, though?" I asked.

"For me, a film crew becomes my family. I like to work with people who are as decent as they are talented. Plus, I love your aesthetic. Your subtle details are not lost on me."

"Thank you. I'm flattered." I set my glass more squarely on its coaster. Wyatt would help me with Chris. I might be able to do this if I managed my time well. "It would be good to get back to work. I love it out here, but I miss the excitement of creating something with other people."

"Family comes first," Ned said. "Still, an artist needs to feed her muse every so often."

"I'd like to, yes." A shiver of excitement crept up my spine. "I have so many ideas already." I grabbed my portfolio I'd stored next to my chair. I slid a few drawings out to show them. "What do you think of these for Abigail?"

"Yes, wonderful," Ned said. "This bright purple is so eye-catching."

"Inspiration from a good friend of mine," I said.

"I can see Pepper Griffin in it right now," Andi said.

"Pepper Griffin's playing Abigail?" I asked. My excitement grew. "She's perfect."

"Agreed," Ned said. "And Stefan's on board to play Geoff."

"That's an epic pair," I said. Already my mind was flooding with ideas for his costumes. Elegant material that draped just so.

"See there," Ned said to Andi. "I told you she'd agree to join us."

Andi rolled her eyes. "He's insufferable when he's right."

I grinned. "Let's talk details."

DURING LUNCH WE'D TALKED THROUGH NED'S VISION. I HAD enough to get started. Andi and Ned had agreed to come out to the house next week to take a first look at my designs. I was itching to get started, but for now I wanted to spend the rest of the day focused on my boys.

I found them at a sweet shop tucked into a booth finishing up bowls of ice cream. These two were obsessed with ice cream. There were worse vices, I supposed.

"Mom, hi. Did you get the job?" Chris asked.

I slipped into the booth beside him, kissed the top of his head before turning to Wyatt. "I hope you had lunch before this."

"We did. Vegetables and everything." Wyatt smiled. "But afterward we had a fierce hankering for something cold and sweet. Enough about that. How did it go?"

I told them about our agreement that I'd work from here but fly in occasionally to oversee the costuming. "If my name's on it, I want to make sure it's done right."

"That sounds like a good compromise," Wyatt said.

"Who will take me to school?" Chris asked. "Aunt Charlotte?"

"No," I said slowly. "Wyatt's offered to take you when I'm not here."

"Wait, does this mean you're staying forever?" Chris asked.

I looked at Wyatt and gave him a slight nod. He grinned and smacked the table. "Your mom and I want to get married. What do you say?"

"I say yes. You'll be my dad just like I prayed for." Chris's eyes shone with happiness.

"That's right, buddy. That's exactly right."

I could hardly breathe from the lump in my throat.

"How come you didn't tell me before now?" Chris's voice squeaked with excitement. Without waiting for an answer, he continued. "Wyatt, I told you. I told you Aunt Charlotte was right." He turned to me. "Mom, you were so much faster than I thought you'd be. Aunt Charlotte said it might take a long time for you to get a clue."

I laughed. "Aunt Charlotte has a big mouth." I darted a glance toward Wyatt. His eyes were glassy with tears.

"I'd like to adopt you," Wyatt said. "If you'd be willing."

"Totally," Chris said. "Will I change my last name?"

"Yep," Wyatt said. "You'd become Christopher Lanigan Black."

"Has a nice ring to it," I said.

"Speaking of rings," Wyatt said as he reached into the pocket of his cargo shorts and pulled out a black box. "I have a little something." He lifted the lid. A solitaire diamond sparkled under the lights. "Will you accept this ring as a token of my undying love and marry me?"

I laughed and covered my mouth with my hand as if that would stop another maniacal giggle from escaping.

"Why are you laughing?" Wyatt asked as a grin spread over his face.

"Mom, you're not supposed to laugh when a man proposes," Chris said, sounding horrified. "Right, Wyatt?"

"Well, your mom isn't like anyone else in the world." Wyatt took the ring from the box. "A guy just never knows what she's going to do."

"I'm sorry." I took my napkin and dabbed at the corners of my eyes. "I just got nervous, I guess. Ask again."

"Teagan Lanigan, will you be my wife?"

"Yes, yes." I thrust my hand out. "I want nothing more than to be your wife."

He slipped the ring over my knuckle and into its rightful place.

"It's beautiful," I said, unable to stop staring at the princess-cut diamond.

"As is the hand," Wyatt said.

Chris looked from one of us to the other. "Is this really happening? Are we getting married today?"

Wyatt smiled as he wiped under his eyes. "Not today, but

soon. Your mother deserves a wedding and a beautiful dress and a cake. And anything else she wants."

"I love cake," Chris said. "We had cake at Uncle Ardan's wedding and it was awesome."

"I love cake too." Wyatt grinned as he scooped up more ice cream. "Can we have ice cream too?"

"Maybe an ice cream cake?" Chris asked. "I went to a birthday party with one of those."

"And adoption paperwork takes a while," I said as if they hadn't derailed the conversation back to their favorite subject.

"But you can start calling me Dad any time you want." Wyatt shrugged. He might think he sounded casual, but the husky timbre of his voice told me differently. "I mean, if you even want to. Whatever you want to call me is fine."

"Dad." Chris looked up at the ceiling, obviously mulling it over. "Not Daddy. That's babyish."

"I called my father, Father," I said. "But that doesn't seem right for Wyatt."

"Dad sounds good." Chris dug into his ice cream. "This is the best day of my life."

"Mine too, buddy." Wyatt's foot touched mine under the table. "But every day with you two is the best."

I remembered what my mother had said about the sound of the screen door slamming. What would our family sound be? Wyatt tuning his guitar? Water splashing over rocks? A baseball landing in a leather glove?

Whatever it was, the sound would be ours. Someday maybe more voices would be added to our family. Siblings for Chris. Maybe a daughter my husband could name after his mother.

The invisible strings of family, of love. Strings that tie us forever to one another.

MORE BLUE MOUNTAIN

Preorder Book 5 in the Blue Mountain Series Blue Twilight from your favorite retailer! Releases March 23, 2021

BLUE MOUNTAIN SERIES:

Blue Mountain Bundle, Books 1,2,3

Blue Midnight

Blue Moon

Blue Ink

ALSO BY TESS THOMPSON

OTHER BOOKS BY TESS THOMPSON

CLIFFSIDE BAY

Traded: Brody and Kara

Deleted: Jackson and Maggie

Jaded: Zane and Honor

Marred: Kyle and Violet

Tainted: Lance and Mary

Cliffside Bay Christmas, The Season of Cats and Babies (Cliffside Bay Novella to be read after Tainted)

Missed: Rafael and Lisa

Cliffside Bay Christmas Wedding (Cliffside Bay Novella to be read after Missed)

Healed: Stone and Pepper

Chateau Wedding (Cliffside Bay Novella to be read after Healed)

Scarred: Trey and Autumn

STANDALONES

The Santa Trial
Duet for Three Hands
Miller's Secret

ABOUT THE AUTHOR

Tess Thompson Romance...hometowns and heartstrings.

USA Today Bestselling author Tess Thompson writes small-town romances and historical fiction. She started her writing career in fourth grade when she wrote a story about an orphan who opened a pizza restaurant. Oddly enough, her first novel, "Riversong" is about an adult orphan who opens a restaurant. Clearly, she's been obsessed with food and words for a long time now.

With a degree from the University of Southern California in theatre, she's spent her adult life studying story, word craft, and character. Since 2011, she's published 20 novels and 3 novellas. Most days she spends at her desk chasing her daily word count or rewriting a terrible first draft.

She currently lives in a suburb of Seattle, Washington with her husband, the hero of her own love story, and their Brady Bunch clan of two sons, two daughters and five cats. Yes, that's four kids and five cats.

Tess loves to hear from you. Drop her a line at tess@tthompsonwrites.com or visit her website at https://tesswrites.com/ and sign up for my newsletter to get a FREE copy of my holiday novella: The Santa Trial.